DEBBIE MACOMBER

DEBBIE MACOMBER

Rainy Day Kisses

MILLS & BOON

Mills & Boon is a registered trademark of Harlequin Enterprises Limited, used under licence.

RAINY DAY KISSES © 2017 Harlequin Books S.A.

First Published in Great Britain 2017
By Mills & Boon, an imprint of HarperCollinsPublishers
1 London Bridge Street, London, SE1 9GF

Rainy Day Kisses © 1990 Debbie Macomber
The First Man You Meet © 1992 Debbie Macomber

ISBN 978-1-84845-710-2
eBook: 978-1-4740-6904-5

Our policy is to use papers that are natural, renewable and recyclable products and made from wood grown in sustainable forests. The logging and manufacturing processes conform to the legal environmental regulations of the country of origin.

Printed and bound by
CPI Group (UK) Ltd, Croydon, CR0 4YY

Rainy Day Kisses

One

"Is it true, Michelle?" Jolyn Johnson rolled her chair from her cubicle across the aisle and nearly caught the wheel on a drooping length of plastic holly. The Marketing Department had won the Christmas decoration contest for the third year in a row.

Michelle Davidson glanced away from her computer screen and immediately noticed her neighbor's inquisitive expression. It certainly hadn't taken long for the rumors to start. She realized, of course, that it was unusual for a high school senior to be accepted as an intern at a major company like Windy Day Toys, one of the most prestigious toy manufacturers in the country. She'd be working here during the Christmas and summer breaks—and she'd actually be getting paid!

Michelle had connections—*good* connections. She'd been a bit naive, perhaps, to assume she could keep her relationship to Uncle Nate under wraps. Still, she'd hoped that with the Christmas season in full swing, her fellow workers would be too preoccupied with the holidays to pay any attention to her. Apparently that wasn't the case.

"Whatever you heard is probably true," she answered, doing her best to look busy.

"Then you *are* related to Mr. Townsend?" Jolyn's eyes grew large.

"I'm his niece."

"Really?" the other girl said in awe. "Wow."

"I'm the one who introduced my aunt Susannah to my uncle Nate." If the fact that Michelle was related to the company owner and CEO impressed Jolyn, then this piece of information should send her over the moon.

"You've got to be kidding! When was that? I thought the Townsends have been married for years and years. I heard they have three children!"

"Tessa, Junior and Emma Jane." When she left the office this afternoon, Michelle would be heading over to her aunt and uncle's home on Lake Washington to babysit. She didn't think it would be good form to mention that, however. She figured interns for Windy Day Toys didn't usually babysit on the side.

"*You* were responsible for introducing your aunt and

uncle?" Jolyn repeated, sounding even more incredulous. "When?" she asked again.

"I was young at the time," Michelle answered evasively.

"You must have been."

Michelle grinned and gave in to Jolyn's obvious curiosity. Might as well tell the truth, which was bound to emerge anyway. "I think that might be why Uncle Nate agreed to let me intern here." He loved to tease her about her—admittedly inadvertent—role as matchmaker, but Michelle knew he was grateful. So was her aunt Susannah.

Michelle planned to major in marketing when she enrolled in college next September, and doing an internship this winter and during the summer holidays was the perfect opportunity to find out whether she liked the job. It was only her second day, but already Michelle could see that she was going to love it.

A couple of the other workers had apparently been listening in on the conversation and rolled their chairs toward her cubicle, as well. "You can't stop the story there," Karen said.

Originally Michelle had hoped to avoid this kind of attention, but she accepted that it was inevitable. "When my aunt was almost thirty, she was absolutely sure she'd never marry or have a family."

"Susannah Townsend?"

This news astonished the small gathering, as Michelle had guessed it would. Besides working with Nate, her mother and aunt had started their own company, Motherhood, Inc., about ten years ago and they'd done incredibly well. It seemed that everything the Townsend name touched turned to gold.

"I know it sounds crazy, considering everything that's happened since."

"Exactly," Jolyn murmured.

"Aunt Susannah's a great mother. But," Michelle added, "at one time, she couldn't even figure out how to change a diaper." Little did the others know that the diaper Susannah had such difficulty changing had been Michelle's.

"This is a joke, right?"

"I swear it's true. Hardly anyone knows the whole story."

"What really happened?" the third woman, whom Michelle didn't know, asked.

Michelle shrugged. "Actually, I happened."

"What do you mean?"

"My mother was desperate for a babysitter and asked her sister, my aunt Susannah, to look after me."

"How old were you?"

"About nine months," she admitted.

"So how did everything turn out the way it did?" Jolyn asked.

"I'd love to hear, too," Karen said, and the third woman nodded vigorously.

Michelle leaned back in her chair. "Make yourselves comfortable, my friends, because I have a story to tell," she began dramatically. "A story in which I play a crucial part."

The three women scooted their chairs closer.

"It all started seventeen years ago…"

Two

Susannah Simmons blamed her sister, Emily, for this. As far as she was concerned, her weekend was going to be the nightmare on Western Avenue. Emily, a nineties version of the "earth mother," had asked Susannah, the dedicated career woman, to babysit nine-month-old Michelle.

"Emily, I don't think so." Susannah had balked when her sister first phoned. What did she, a twenty-eight-year-old business executive, know about babies? The answer was simple—not much.

"I'm desperate."

Her sister must have been to ask her. Everyone knew what Susannah was like around babies—not only Michelle, but infants in general. She just wasn't the motherly type. Interest rates, negotiations, troubleshooting, staff motivation, these were her strong points. Not formula, teething and diapers.

It was nothing short of astonishing that the same two parents could have produced such completely different daughters. Emily baked her own oat-bran muffins, subscribed to *Organic Gardening* and hung her wash to dry on a clothesline—even in winter.

Susannah, on the other hand, wasn't the least bit domestic and had no intention of ever cultivating the trait. She was too busy with her career to let such tedious tasks disrupt her corporate lifestyle. She was currently a director in charge of marketing for H&J Lima, the nation's largest sporting goods company. The position occupied almost every minute of her time.

Susannah Simmons was a woman on the rise. Her name appeared regularly in trade journals as an up-and-coming achiever. None of that mattered to Emily, however, who needed a babysitter.

"You know I wouldn't ask you if it wasn't an emergency," Emily had pleaded.

Susannah felt herself weakening. Emily was, after all, her younger sister. "Surely, there's got to be someone better qualified."

Emily had hesitated, then tearfully blurted, "I don't know what I'll do if you won't take Michelle." She began to sob pitifully. "Robert's left me."

"What?" If Emily hadn't gained her full attention earlier, she did now. If her sister was an earth mother, then her brother-in-law, Robert Davidson, was Abra-

ham Lincoln, as solid and upright as a thirty-foot oak.
"I don't believe it."

"It's true," Emily wailed. "He…he claims I give Michelle all my attention and that I never have enough energy left to be a decent wife." She paused to draw in a quavery breath. "I know he's right…but being a good mother demands so much time and effort."

"I thought Robert wanted six children."

"He does…or did." Emily's sobbing began anew.

"Oh, Emily, it can't be that bad," Susannah had murmured in a soothing voice, thinking as fast as she could. "I'm sure you misunderstood Robert. He loves you and Michelle, and I'm positive he has no intention of leaving you."

"He does," Emily went on to explain between hiccuping sobs. "He asked me to find someone to look after Michelle for a while. He says we have to have some time to ourselves, or our marriage is dead."

That sounded pretty drastic to Susannah.

"I swear to you, Susannah, I've called everyone who's ever babysat Michelle before, but no one's available. No one—not even for one night. When I told Robert I hadn't found a sitter, he got so angry…and that's not like Robert."

Susannah agreed. The man was the salt of the earth. Not once in the five years she'd known him could she recall him even raising his voice.

"He told me that if I didn't take this weekend trip to San Francisco with him he was going alone. I *tried* to find someone to watch Michelle," Emily said. "I honestly tried, but there's no one else, and now Robert's home and he's loading up the car and, Susannah, he's serious. He's going to leave without me and from the amount of luggage he's taking, I don't think he plans to come back."

The tale of woe barely skimmed the surface of Susannah's mind. The key word that planted itself in fertile ground was *weekend*. "I thought you said you only needed me for one night?" she asked.

At that point, Susannah should've realized she wasn't much brighter than a brainless mouse, innocently nibbling away at the cheese in a steel trap.

Emily sniffled once more, probably for effect, Susannah mused darkly.

"We'll be flying back to Seattle early Sunday afternoon. Robert's got some business in San Francisco Saturday morning, but the rest of the weekend is free… and it's been such a long time since we've been alone."

"Two days and two nights," Susannah said slowly, mentally tabulating the hours.

"Oh, please, Susannah, my whole marriage is at stake. You've always been such a good big sister. I know I don't deserve anyone as good as you."

Silently Susannah agreed.

"Somehow I'll find a way to repay you," Emily continued.

Susannah closed her eyes. Her sister's idea of repaying her was usually freshly baked zucchini bread shortly after Susannah announced she was watching her weight.

"Susannah, please!"

It was then that Susannah had caved in to the pressure. "All right. Go ahead and bring Michelle over."

Somewhere in the distance, she could've sworn she heard the echo of a mousetrap slamming shut.

By the time Emily and Robert had deposited their offspring at Susannah's condominium, her head was swimming with instructions. After planting a kiss on her daughter's rosy cheek, Emily handed the clinging Michelle to a reluctant Susannah.

That was when the nightmare began in earnest.

As soon as her sister left, Susannah could feel herself tense up. Even as a teenager, she hadn't done a lot of babysitting; it wasn't that she didn't like children, but kids didn't seem to take to her.

Holding the squalling infant on her hip, Susannah paced while her mind buzzed with everything she was supposed to remember. She knew what to do in case of diaper rash, colic and several other minor emergencies, but Emily hadn't said one word about how to keep Michelle from crying.

"Shhh," Susannah cooed, jiggling her niece against her hip. She swore the child had a cry that could've been heard a block away.

After the first five minutes, her calm cool composure began to crack under the pressure. She could be in real trouble here. The tenant agreement she'd signed specifically stated "no children."

"Hello, Michelle, remember me?" Susannah asked, doing everything she could think of to quiet the baby. Didn't the kid need to breathe? "I'm your auntie Susannah, the business executive."

Her niece wasn't impressed. Pausing only a few seconds to gulp for air, Michelle increased her volume and glared at the door as if she expected her mother to miraculously appear if she cried long and hard enough.

"Trust me, kid, if I knew a magic trick that'd bring your mother back, I'd use it now."

Ten minutes. Emily had been gone a total of ten minutes. Susannah was seriously considering giving the state Children's Protective Services a call and claiming that a stranger had abandoned a baby on her doorstep.

"Mommy will be home soon," Susannah murmured wistfully.

Michelle screamed louder. Susannah started to worry about her stemware. The kid's voice could shatter glass.

More tortured minutes passed, each one an eternity. Susannah was desperate enough to sing. Not knowing any appropriate lullabies, she began with a couple of ditties from her childhood, but quickly exhausted those. Michelle didn't seem to appreciate them anyway. Since Susannah didn't keep up with the current top twenty, the best she could do was an old Christmas favorite. Somehow singing "Jingle Bells" in the middle of September didn't feel right.

"Michelle," Susannah pleaded, willing to stand on her head if it would keep the baby from wailing, "your mommy will be back, I assure you."

Michelle apparently didn't believe her.

"How about if I buy municipal bonds and put them in your name?" Susannah tried next. "Tax-free bonds, Michelle! This is an offer you shouldn't refuse. All you need to do is stop crying. Oh, please stop crying."

Michelle wasn't interested.

"All right," Susannah cried, growing desperate. "I'll sign over my Microsoft stock. That's my final offer, so you'd better grab it while I'm in a generous mood."

Michelle answered by gripping Susannah's collar with both of her chubby fists and burying her wet face in a once spotless white silk blouse.

"You're a tough nut to crack, Michelle Margaret Davidson," Susannah muttered, gently patting her niece's back as she paced. "You want blood, don't you, kid? You aren't going to be satisfied with anything less."

A half hour after Emily had left, Susannah was ready to resort to tears herself. She'd started singing again, returning to her repertoire of Christmas songs. "You'd better watch out,/ you'd better not cry,/ Aunt Susannah's here telling you why…."

She was just getting into the lyrics when someone knocked heavily on her door.

Like a thief caught in the act, Susannah whirled around, fully expecting the caller to be the building superintendent. No doubt there'd been complaints and he'd come to confront her.

Expelling a weary sigh, Susannah realized she was defenseless. The only option she had was to throw herself on his mercy. She squared her shoulders and walked across the lush carpet, prepared to do exactly that.

Only it wasn't necessary. The building superintendent wasn't the person standing on the other side of her door. It was her new neighbor, wearing a baseball cap and a faded T-shirt, and looking more than a little disgruntled.

"The crying and the baby I can take," he said, crossing his arms and relaxing against the doorframe, "but your singing has got to go."

"Very funny," she grumbled.

"The kid's obviously distressed."

Susannah glared at him. "Nothing gets past you, does it?"

"Do something."

"I'm trying." Apparently Michelle didn't like this stranger any more than Susannah did because she buried her face in Susannah's collar and rubbed it vigorously back and forth. That at least helped muffle her cries, but there was no telling what it would do to white silk. "I offered her my Microsoft stock and it didn't do any good," Susannah explained. "I was even willing to throw in my municipal bonds."

"You offered her stocks and bonds, but did you suggest dinner?"

"Dinner?" Susannah echoed. She hadn't thought of

that. Emily claimed she'd fed Michelle, but Susannah vaguely remembered something about a bottle.

"The poor thing's probably starving."

"I think she's supposed to have a bottle," Susannah said. She turned and glanced at the assorted bags Emily and Robert had deposited in her condominium, along with the necessary baby furniture. From the number of things stacked on the floor, it must seem as if she'd been granted permanent guardianship. "There's got to be one in all this paraphernalia."

"I'll find it—you keep the kid quiet."

Susannah nearly laughed out loud. If she was able to keep Michelle quiet, he wouldn't be here in the first place. She imagined she could convince CIA agents to hand over top-secret documents more easily than she could silence one distressed nine-month-old infant.

Without waiting for an invitation, her neighbor moved into the living room. He picked up one of the three overnight bags and rooted through that. He hesitated when he pulled out a stack of freshly laundered diapers, and glanced at Susannah. "I didn't know anyone used cloth diapers anymore."

"My sister doesn't believe in anything disposable."

"Smart woman."

Susannah made no comment, and within a few seconds noted that he'd come across a plastic bottle. He removed the protective cap and handed the bottle to Susannah, who looked at it and blinked. "Shouldn't the milk be heated?"

"It's room temperature, and frankly, at this point I don't think the kid's going to care."

He was right. The instant Susannah placed the rubber nipple in her niece's mouth, Michelle grasped the bottle with both hands and sucked at it greedily.

For the first time since her mother had left, Michelle stopped crying. The silence was pure bliss. Susannah's tension eased, and she released a sigh that went all the way through her body.

"You might want to sit down," he suggested next.

Susannah did, and with Michelle cradled awkwardly in her arms, leaned against the back of the sofa, trying not to jostle her charge.

"That's better, isn't it?" Her neighbor pushed the baseball cap farther back on his head, looking pleased with himself.

"Much better." Susannah smiled shyly up at him. They hadn't actually met, but she'd certainly noticed her new neighbor. As far as looks went, he was downright handsome. She supposed most women would find his mischievous blue eyes and dark good looks appealing. He was tanned, but she'd have wagered a month's pay that his bronzed features weren't the result of any machine. He obviously spent a great deal of time outdoors, which led her to the conclusion that he didn't work. At least not in an office. And frankly, she doubted he was employed outside of one, either. The clothes he wore and the sporadic hours he kept had led her to speculate about him earlier. If he had money, which apparently he did or else he wouldn't be living in this complex, then he'd inherited it.

"I think it's time I introduced myself," he said conversationally, sitting on the ottoman across from her. "I'm Nate Townsend."

"Susannah Simmons," she said. "I apologize for all the racket. My niece and I are just getting acquainted and—oh, boy—it's going to be a long weekend, so bear with us."

"You're babysitting for the weekend?"

"Two days and two nights." It sounded like a whole lifetime to Susannah. "My sister and her husband are off on a second honeymoon. Normally my parents would watch Michelle and love doing it, but they're visiting friends in Florida."

"It was kind of you to offer."

Susannah thought it best to correct this impression. "Trust me, I didn't volunteer. In case you hadn't noticed, I'm not very maternal."

"You've got to support her back a little more," he said, watching Michelle.

Susannah tried, but it felt awkward to hold on to her niece *and* the bottle.

"You're doing fine."

"Sure," Susannah muttered. She felt like someone with two left feet who'd been unexpectedly ushered onto center stage and told to perform the lead in *Swan Lake*.

"Relax, will you?" Nate encouraged.

"I told you already I'm not into this motherhood business," she snapped. "If you think you can do better, you feed her."

"You're doing great. Don't worry about it."

She wasn't doing great at all, and she knew it, but this was as good as she got.

"When's the last time you had anything to eat?" he asked.

"I beg your pardon?"

"You sound hungry to me."

"Well, I'm not," Susannah said irritably.

"I think you are, but don't worry, I'll take care of that." He walked boldly into her kitchen and paused in front of the refrigerator. "Your mood will improve once you have something in your stomach."

Shifting Michelle higher, Susannah stood and followed him. "You can't just walk in here and—"

"I'll say I can't," he murmured, his head inside her fridge. "Do you realize there's nothing in here except an open box of baking soda and a jar full of pickle juice?"

"I eat out a lot," Susannah said defensively.

"I can see that."

Michelle had finished the bottle and made a slurping sound that prompted Susannah to remove the nipple from her mouth. The baby's eyes were closed. Little wonder, Susannah thought. She was probably exhausted. Certainly Susannah was, and it was barely seven on Friday evening. The weekend was just beginning.

Setting the empty bottle on the kitchen counter, Susannah awkwardly lifted Michelle onto her shoulder and patted her back until she produced a tiny burp. Feeling a real sense of accomplishment, Susannah smiled proudly.

Nate chuckled and when Susannah glanced in his direction, she discovered him watching her, his grin warm and appraising. "You're going to be fine."

Flustered, Susannah lowered her gaze. She always disliked it when a man looked at her that way, examining her features and forming a judgment about her by the size of her nose, or the direction in which her eyebrows grew. Most men seemed to believe they'd been granted a rare gift of insight and could determine a woman's entire character just by looking at her face. Unfortunately, Susannah's was too austere by conventional standards to be classified as beautiful. Her eyes were deep-set and dark, her cheekbones high. Her nose came almost straight from her forehead and together with her full mouth made her look like a classic Greek sculpture. Not pretty, she thought. Interesting perhaps.

It was during Susannah's beleaguered self-evaluation that Michelle stirred and started jabbering cheerfully, reaching one hand toward a strand of Susannah's dark hair.

Without her realizing it, her chignon had come undone. Michelle had somehow managed to loosen the pins and now the long dark tresses fell haphazardly over Susannah's shoulder. If there was one thing Susannah was meticulous about, and actually there were several, it was her appearance. She must look a rare sight, in an expensive business suit with a stained white blouse and her hair tumbling over her shoulder.

"Actually I've been waiting for an opportunity to introduce myself," Nate said, leaning against the counter. "But after the first couple of times we saw each other, our paths didn't seem to cross again."

"I've been working a lot of overtime lately." If the truth be known, Susannah almost always put in extra hours. Often she brought work home with her. She was dedicated, committed and hardworking. Her neighbor, however, didn't seem to possess any of those qualities. She strongly suspected that everything in life had come much too easily for Nate Townsend. She'd never seen him without his baseball cap or his T-shirt. Somehow she doubted he even owned a suit. And if he did, it probably wouldn't look right on him. Nate Townsend was definitely a football-jersey type of guy.

He seemed likable—friendly and outgoing—but from what she'd seen, he lacked ambition. Apparently there'd never been anything he'd wanted badly enough to really strive for.

"I'm glad we had the chance to introduce ourselves," Susannah added, walking back into the living room and toward her front door. "I appreciate the help, but as you said, Michelle and I are going to be fine."

"It didn't sound that way when I arrived."

"I was just getting my feet wet," she returned, defending herself, "and why are you arguing with me? You're the one who said I was doing all right."

"I lied."

"Why would you do that?"

Nate shrugged nonchalantly. "I thought a little self-confidence would do you good, so I offered it."

Susannah glared at him, resenting his attitude. So much for the nice-guy-who-lives-next-door image she'd had of him. "I don't need any favors from you."

"You may not," he agreed, "but unfortunately Michelle does. The poor kid was starving and you didn't so much as suspect."

"I would've figured it out."

Nate gave her a look that seemed to cast doubt on her intelligence, and Susannah frowned right back. She opened the door with far more force than necessary and flipped her hair over her shoulder with flair a Paris model would have envied. "Thanks for stopping in," she said stiffly, "but as you can see everything's under control."

"If you say so." He grinned at her and without another word was gone.

Susannah banged the door shut with her hip, feeling a rush of satisfaction as she did so. She knew this was petty, but her neighbor had annoyed her in more ways than one.

Soon afterward Susannah heard the soft strains of an Italian opera drifting from Nate's condominium. At least she thought it was Italian, which was unfortunate because that made her think of spaghetti and how hungry she actually was.

"Okay, Michelle," she said, smiling down on her niece. "It's time to feed your auntie." Without too much trouble, Susannah assembled the high chair and set her niece in that while she scanned the contents of her freezer.

The best she could come up with was a frozen Mexican entrée. She gazed at the picture on the front of the package, shook her head and tossed it back inside the freezer.

Michelle seemed to approve and vigorously slapped the tray on her high chair.

Crossing her arms and leaning against the freezer door, Susannah paused. "Did you hear what he said?" she asked, still irate. "I guess he was right, but he didn't have to be so superior about it."

Michelle slapped her hands in approval once again. The music was muted by the thick walls, and wanting to hear a little more, Susannah cracked open the sliding glass door to her balcony, which was separated from Nate's by a concrete partition. It bestowed privacy, but didn't muffle the beautiful voices raised in triumphant song.

Susannah opened the glass door completely and stepped outside. The evening was cool, but pleasantly so. The sun had just started to set and had cast a wash of golden shadows over the picturesque waterfront.

"Michelle," she muttered when she came back in, "he's cooking something that smells like lasagna or spaghetti." Her stomach growled and she returned to the freezer, taking out the same Mexican entrée she'd rejected earlier. It didn't seem any more appetizing than it had the first time.

A faint scent of garlic wafted into her kitchen. Susannah turned her classic Greek nose in that direction, then followed the aroma to the open door like a puppet drawn there by a string. She sniffed loudly and turned eagerly back to her niece. "It's definitely Italian, and it smells divine."

Michelle pounded the tray again.

"It's garlic bread," Susannah announced and whirled around to face her niece, who clearly wasn't impressed. But then, thought Susannah, she wouldn't be. She'd eaten.

Under normal conditions, Susannah would've reached for her jacket and headed to Mama Mataloni's, a fabulous Italian restaurant within easy walking distance. Unfortunately Mama Mataloni's didn't deliver.

Against her better judgment, Susannah stuck the frozen entrée into her microwave and set the timer. When there was another knock on her door, she stiffened and looked at Michelle as if the nine-month-old would sit up and tell Susannah who'd come by *this* time.

It was Nate again, holding a plate of spaghetti and a glass of red wine. "Did you fix yourself something to eat?" he asked.

For the life of her Susannah couldn't tear her gaze away from the oversize plate, heaped high with steaming pasta smothered in a thick red sauce. Nothing had ever looked—or smelled—more appetizing. The fresh Parmesan cheese he'd grated over the top had melted onto the rich sauce. A generous slice of garlic bread was balanced on the side.

"I, ah, was just heating up a…microwave dinner." She pointed behind her toward the kitchen as if that would explain what she was trying to say. Her tongue seemed to be stuck to the roof of her mouth.

"I shouldn't have acted like such a know-it-all earlier," he said, pushing the plate toward her. "I'm bringing you a peace offering."

"This…is for me?" She raised her eyes from the plate, wondering if he knew how hungry she felt and was toying with her.

He handed her the meal and the wine. "The sauce has been simmering most of the afternoon. I like to pretend I'm a bit of a gourmet chef. Every once in a while I get creative in the kitchen."

"How…nice." She conjured up a picture of Nate standing in his kitchen stirring sauce while the rest of the world struggled to make a living. Her attitude wasn't at all gracious and she mentally apologized. Without further ado, she marched into her kitchen, reached for a fork and plopped herself down at the table. She might as well eat this feast while it was hot!

One sample told her everything she needed to know. "This is great." She took another bite, pointed her fork in his direction and rolled her eyes. "Marvelous. Wonderful."

Nate pulled a bread stick out of his shirt pocket and gave it to Michelle. "Here's looking at you, kid."

As Michelle chewed contentedly on the bread stick, Nate pulled out a chair and sat across from Susannah, who was too busy enjoying her dinner to notice anything out of the ordinary until Nate's eyes narrowed.

"What's wrong?" Susannah asked. She wiped her mouth with a napkin and sampled the wine.

"I smell something."

Judging by his expression, whatever it was apparently wasn't pleasant. "It might be the microwave dinner," she suggested hopefully, already knowing better.

"I'm afraid not."

Susannah carefully set the fork beside her plate as uneasiness settled over her.

"It seems," Nate said, covering his nose with one hand, "that someone needs to change Michelle's diaper."

Three

Holding a freshly diapered Michelle on her hip, Susannah rushed out of the bathroom into the narrow hallway and gasped for breath.

"Are you all right?" Nate asked, his brow creased with a concerned frown.

She nodded and sagged against the wall, feeling light-headed. Once she'd dragged several clean breaths through her lungs, she straightened and even managed a weak smile.

"That wasn't so bad now, was it?"

Susannah glared at him. "I should've been wearing an oxygen mask."

Nate's responding chuckle did little to improve her mood.

"In light of what I just experienced," she muttered, "I

can't understand why the population continues to grow." To be on the safe side, she opened the hall linen closet and took out a large can of disinfectant spray. Sticking her arm inside the bathroom, she gave a generous squirt.

"While you were busy I assembled the crib," Nate told her, still revealing far too much amusement to suit Susannah. "Where would you like me to put it?"

"The living room will be fine." His action had been thoughtful, but Susannah wasn't accustomed to depending on others, so when she thanked him, the words were forced.

Susannah followed him into the living room and found the bed ready. She laid Michelle down on her stomach and covered her with a handknit blanket. The baby settled down immediately, without fussing.

Nate walked toward the door. "You're sure everything's okay?" he said softly.

"Positive." Susannah wasn't, but Michelle was her niece and their problems weren't his. Nate had done more than enough already. "Thanks for dinner."

"Anytime." He paused at the door and turned back. "I left my phone number on the kitchen counter. Call if you need me."

"Thanks."

He favored her with a grin on his way out the door, and Susannah stood a few moments after he'd left the apartment, thinking about him. Her feelings were decidedly mixed.

She began sorting through the various bags her sister

had brought, depositing the jars of baby food in the cupboard and putting the bottles of formula in the fridge. As Nate had pointed out, there was plenty of room—all she had to do was scoot the empty pickle jar aside.

She supposed she should toss the jar in the garbage, but one of the guys from the office had talked about making pickled eggs. It sounded so simple—all she had to do was peel a few hard-boiled eggs and keep them refrigerated in the jar for a week or so. Susannah had been meaning to try it ever since. But she was afraid that when the mood struck her, she wouldn't have any pickle juice around, so she'd decided to keep it on hand.

Once she'd finished in the kitchen, Susannah soaked in a hot bath, leaving the door ajar in case Michelle woke and needed her. She felt far more relaxed afterward.

Walking back into the living room on the tips of her toes, she brought out her briefcase and removed a file. She glanced down at her sleeping niece and gently patted her back. The little girl looked so angelic, so content.

Suddenly a powerful yearning stirred within Susannah. She felt real affection for Michelle, but the feeling was more than that. This time alone with her niece had evoked a longing buried deep in Susannah's heart, a longing she'd never taken the time to fully examine. And with it came an aching restless sensation that she promptly submerged.

When Susannah had chosen a career in business, she'd realized she was giving up the part of herself that hungered for husband and children. There was nothing that said she couldn't marry, couldn't raise a child, but she knew herself too well. From the time she was in high school it had been painfully apparent that she was completely inadequate in the domestic arena. Especially when she compared herself to Emily, who seemed to have been born with a dust rag in one hand and a cookbook in the other.

Susannah had never regretted the decision she'd made to dedicate herself to her career, but then she was more fortunate than some. She had Emily, who was determined to supply her with numerous nieces and nephews. For Susannah, Michelle and the little ones who were sure to follow would have to be enough.

Reminding herself that she was comfortable with her choices, Susannah quietly stepped away from the crib. For the next hour, she sat on her bed reading the details of the proposed marketing program the department had sent her. The full presentation was scheduled for Monday morning and she wanted to be informed and prepared.

When she finished reading the report, she tiptoed back to her desk, situated in the far corner of the living room, and replaced the file in her briefcase.

Once more she paused to check on her niece. Feeling just a little cocky, she returned to the bedroom convinced this babysitting business wasn't going to be so bad after all.

Susannah changed her mind at one-thirty when a piercing wail startled her out of a sound sleep. Not knowing how long Michelle had been at it, Susannah nearly fell out of bed in her rush to reach her niece.

"Michelle," she cried, stumbling blindly across the floor, her arms stretched out in front of her. "I'm coming.... There's no need to panic."

Michelle disagreed vehemently.

Turning on a light only made matters worse. Squinting to protect her eyes from the glare, Susannah groped her way to the crib, then let out a cry herself when she stubbed her toe on the leg of the coffee table.

Michelle was standing, holding on to the bars and looking as if she didn't have a friend in the world.

"What's the matter, sweetheart?" Susannah asked softly, lifting the baby into her arms.

A wet bottom told part of the story. And the poor kid had probably woken and, finding herself in a strange place, felt scared. Susannah couldn't blame her.

"All right, we'll try this diapering business again."

Susannah spread a thick towel on the bathroom counter, then gently placed Michelle on it. She was halfway through the changing process when the phone rang. Straightening, Susannah glanced around her, wondering what she should do. She couldn't leave Michelle, and picking her up and carrying her into the kitchen would be difficult. Whoever was calling at this time of night should know better! If it was important they could leave a message on her answering machine.

But after three rings, the phone stopped, followed almost immediately by a firm knock at her door.

Hauling Michelle, newly diapered, Susannah squinted

and checked the peephole to discover a disgruntled Nate on the other side.

"Nate," she said in surprise as she opened the door. She couldn't even guess what he wanted. And she wasn't too keen about letting him into her apartment at this hour.

He stood just inside the condo, barefoot and dressed in a red plaid housecoat. His hair was mussed, which made Susannah wonder about her own disheveled appearance. She suspected she looked like someone who'd walked out of a swamp.

"Is Michelle all right?" he barked, despite the evidence before him. Not waiting for a reply, he continued in an accusing tone, "You didn't answer the phone."

"I couldn't. I was changing her diaper."

Nate hesitated, then studied her closely. "In that case, are *you* all right?"

She nodded and managed to raise one hand. It was difficult when her arms were occupied with a baby. "I lived to tell about it."

"Good. What happened? Why was Michelle crying?"

"I'm not sure. Maybe when she woke up and didn't recognize her surroundings, she suffered an anxiety attack."

"And, from the look of us, caused a couple more."

Susannah would rather he hadn't mentioned that. Her long, tangled hair spilled over her shoulders and she, too, was barefoot. She'd been so anxious to get to Michelle that she hadn't bothered to reach for her slippers or her robe.

Michelle, it seemed, was pleased with all the unexpected attention, and when she leaned toward Nate, arms outstretched, Susannah marveled at how fickle an infant could be. After all, she was the one who'd fed and diapered her. Not Nate.

"It's my male charm," he explained delightedly.

"More likely, it's your red housecoat."

Whatever it was, Michelle went into his arms as if he were a long-lost friend. Susannah excused herself to retrieve her robe from the foot of her bed. By the time she got back, Nate was sitting on the sofa with his feet stretched out, supported by Susannah's mahogany coffee table.

"Make yourself at home," she muttered. Her mood wasn't always the best when she'd been abruptly wakened from a sound sleep.

He glanced up at her and grinned. "No need to be testy."

"Yes, there is," she said, but destroyed what remained of her argument by yawning loudly. Covering her mouth with the back of her hand, she slumped down on the chair across from him and flipped her hair away from her face.

His gaze followed the action. "You should wear your hair down more often."

She glared at him. "I always wear my hair up."

"I noticed. And frankly, it's much more flattering down."

"Oh, for heaven's sake," she cried, "are you going to tell me how to dress next?"

"I might."

He said it with such a charming smile that any sting there might have been in his statement was diluted.

"You don't have to stick with business suits every day, do you? Try jeans sometime. With a T-shirt."

She opened her mouth to argue with him, then decided not to bother. The arrogance he displayed seemed to be characteristic of handsome men in general, she'd noted. Because a man happened to possess lean good looks and could smile beguilingly, he figured he had the right to say anything he pleased to a woman—to comment on how she styled her hair, how she chose to dress or anything else. These were things he wouldn't dream of discussing if he were talking to another man.

"You aren't going to argue?"

"No," she said, and for emphasis shook her head.

That stopped him short. He paused and blinked, then sent her another of his captivating smiles. "I find that refreshing."

"I'm gratified to hear there's something about me you approve of." There were probably plenty of other things that didn't please him. Given any encouragement, he'd probably be glad to list them for her.

Sweet little traitor that she was, Michelle had curled up in Nate's arms, utterly content just to sit there and study his handsome face, which no doubt had fascinated numerous other females before her. The least Michelle could do was show some signs of going back to sleep so Susannah could return her to the crib and usher Nate out the door.

"I shouldn't have said what I did about your hair and clothes."

"Hey," she returned flippantly, "you don't need to worry about hurting my feelings. I'm strong. I've got a lot of emotional fortitude."

"Strong," he repeated. "You make yourself sound like an all-weather tire."

"I've had to be tougher than that."

His face relaxed into a look of sympathy. "Why?"

"I work with men just like you every day."

"Men just like me?"

"It's true. For the past seven years, I've found myself up against the old double standard, but I've learned to keep my cool."

He frowned as if he didn't understand what she was talking about. Susannah felt it was her obligation to tell him. Apparently Nate had never been involved in office politics. "Let me give you a few examples. If a male coworker has a cluttered desk, then everyone assumes he's a hard worker. If my desk is a mess, it's a sign of disorganization."

Nate looked as if he wanted to argue with her, but Susannah was just warming to her subject and she forged ahead before he had a chance to speak. "If a man in an office marries, it's good for the company because he'll settle down and become a more productive employee. If a woman marries, it's almost the kiss of death because management figures she'll get pregnant and quit. If a man leaves because he's been offered a better job, everyone's pleased for him because he's taking advantage of an excellent career opportunity. But if the same position is offered to a woman and she takes it, then upper management shrugs and claims women aren't dependable."

When she'd finished there was a short pause. "You have very definite feelings on the subject," he said at last.

"If you were a woman, you would, too."

His nod of agreement was a long time coming. "You're right, I probably would."

Michelle seemed to find the toes of her sleeper fascinating and was examining them closely. Personally, Susannah didn't know how anyone could be so wide-awake at this ungodly hour.

"If you turn down the lights, she might get the hint," Nate said, doing a poor job of smothering a yawn.

"You're beat," said Susannah. "There's no need for you to stay. I'll take her." She held out her arms to Michelle, who whimpered and clung all the more tightly to Nate. Susannah's feelings of inadequacy were reinforced.

"Don't worry about me. I'm comfortable like this," Nate told her.

"But…" She could feel the warmth invading her

cheeks. She lowered her eyes, regretting her outburst of a few minutes ago. She'd been standing on her soapbox again. "Listen, I'm sorry about what I said. What goes on at the office has nothing to do with our being neighbors."

"Then we're even."

"Even?"

"I shouldn't have commented on your hair and clothes." He hesitated long enough to envelop her in his smile. "Friends?"

Despite the intolerable hour, Susannah found herself smiling back. "Friends."

Michelle seemed to concur because she cooed loudly, kicking her feet.

Susannah stood and turned the lamp down to its lowest setting, then reached for Michelle's blanket, covering the baby. Feeling slightly chilled herself, she fetched the brightly colored afghan at the foot of the sofa, which Emily had crocheted for her last Christmas.

The muted light created an intimate atmosphere, and suddenly self-conscious, Susannah suggested, "Maybe I'll sing to her. That should help her go to sleep."

"If anyone sings, it'll be me," he said much too quickly.

Susannah's pride was a little dented, but remembering her limited repertoire of songs, she gestured toward him and said, "All right, Frank Sinatra, have a go."

To Susannah's surprise, Nate's singing voice was soothing and melodious. Even more surprisingly, he knew exactly the right kind of songs. Not lullabies, but easy-listening songs, the kind she'd heard for years on the radio. She felt her own eyes drifting closed and battled to stay awake. His voice dropped to a mere whisper that felt like a warm caress. Much too warm. And cozy, as if the three of them belonged together, which was ridiculous since she'd only just met Nate. He was her neighbor and nothing more. There hadn't been time for them to get to know each other, and Michelle was her *niece*, not her daughter.

But the domestic fantasy continued, no matter how hard she tried to dispel it. She couldn't stop thinking about what it would be like to share her life with a husband and children—and she could barely manage to keep her eyes open for more than a second or two. Perhaps if she rested them for a moment…

The next thing Susannah knew, her neck ached. She reached up to secure her pillow, then realized she didn't have one. Instead of being in bed, she was curled up in the chair, her head resting uncomfortably against the arm. Slowly, reluctantly, she opened her eyes and discovered Nate across from her, head tilted back, sleeping soundly. Michelle was resting peacefully in his arms.

It took Susannah a minute or so to orient herself. When she saw the sun breaking across the sky and spilling through her large windows, she closed her eyes again. It was morning. Morning! Nate had spent the night at her place.

Flustered, Susannah twisted her body into an upright position and rubbed the sleep from her face, wondering what she should do. Waking Nate was probably not the best idea. He was bound to be as unnerved as she was to discover he'd fallen asleep in her living room. To complicate matters, the afghan she'd covered herself with had somehow become twisted around her hips and legs. Muttering under her breath, Susannah yanked it about in an effort to stand.

Her activity disturbed Nate's restful slumber. He stirred, glanced in her direction and froze for what seemed the longest moment of Susannah's life. Then he blinked several times and glared at her as though he hoped she'd vanish into thin air.

Standing now, Susannah did her best to appear dignified, which was nearly impossible with the comforter still twisted around her.

"Where am I?" Nate asked dazedly.

"Ah…my place."

His eyes drifted shut. "I was afraid of that." The mournful look that came over Nate's face would have been comical under other circumstances. Only neither of them was laughing.

"I, ah, must've fallen asleep," she said, breaking the embarrassed silence. She took pains to fold the afghan, and held it against her stomach like a shield.

"Me, too, apparently," Nate muttered.

Michelle woke and struggled into a sitting position.

She looked around her and evidently didn't like what she saw, either. Her lower lip started to tremble.

"Michelle, it's okay," Susannah said quickly, hoping to ward off the scream she feared was coming. "You're staying with Auntie Susannah this weekend, remember?"

"I think she might be wet," Nate offered when Michelle began to whimper softly. He let out a muffled curse and hastily lifted the nine-month-old from his lap. "I'm positive she's wet. Here, take her."

Susannah reached for her niece and a dry diaper in one smooth movement, but it didn't help. Michelle was intent on letting them both know, in no uncertain terms, that she didn't like her schedule altered. Nor did she appreciate waking up in a stranger's arms. She conveyed her displeasure in loud boisterous cries.

"I think she might be hungry, too," Nate suggested, trying to brush the dampness from his housecoat.

"Brilliant observation," Susannah said sarcastically on her way to the bathroom, Michelle in her arms.

"My, my, you certainly get testy in the mornings," he said.

"I need coffee."

"Fine. I'll make us both a cup while I'm heating a bottle for Michelle."

"She's supposed to eat her cereal first," Susannah shouted. At least that was what Emily had insisted when she'd outlined her daughter's schedule.

"I'm sure she doesn't care. She's hungry."

"All right, all right," Susannah yelled from the bathroom. "Heat her bottle first if you want."

Yelling was a mistake, she soon discovered. Michelle clearly wasn't any keener on mornings than Susannah was. Punching the air with her stubby legs, her niece made diapering a nearly impossible task. Susannah grew more frustrated by the minute. Finally her hair, falling forward over her shoulders, caught Michelle's attention. She grasped it, pausing to gulp in a huge breath.

"Do you want me to get that?" she heard Nate shout.

"Get what?"

Apparently it wasn't important because he didn't answer her. But a moment later he was standing at the bathroom door.

"It's for you," he said.

"What's for me?"

"The phone."

The word bounced around in her mind like a ricocheting bullet. "Did…did they say who it was?" she asked, her voice high-pitched and wobbly. No doubt it was someone from the office and she'd be the subject of gossip for months.

"Someone named Emily."

"Emily," she repeated. That was even worse. Her sister was sure to be full of awkward questions.

"Hi," Susannah said as casually as possible into the receiver.

"Who answered the phone?" her sister demanded without preamble.

"My neighbor. Nate Townsend. He, ah, lives next door." That awkward explanation astonished even her. Worse, Susannah had been ready to blurt out that Nate had spent the night, but she'd stopped herself just in time.

"I haven't met him, have I?"

"My neighbor? No, you haven't."

"He sounds cute."

"Listen, if you're phoning about Michelle," Susannah hurried to add, anxious to end the conversation, "there's no need for concern. Everything's under control." That was a slight exaggeration, but what Emily didn't know couldn't worry her.

"Is that Michelle I hear crying in the background?" Emily asked.

"Yes. She just woke up and she's a little hungry." Nate was holding the baby and pacing the kitchen, waiting impatiently for Susannah to get off the phone.

"My poor baby," Emily moaned. "Tell me when you met your neighbor. I don't remember you ever mentioning anyone named Nate."

"He's been helping me out," Susannah said quickly. Wanting to change the subject, she asked, "How are you and Robert?"

Her sister sighed audibly. "Robert was so right. We needed this weekend alone. I feel a thousand times better and so does he. Every married couple should get away for a few days like this—but then everyone doesn't have a sister as generous as you to fill in on such short notice."

"Good, good," Susannah said, hardly aware of what she was supposed to think was so fantastic. "Uh-oh," she said, growing desperate. "The bottle's warm. I hate to cut you off, but I've got to take care of Michelle. I'm sure you understand."

"Of course."

"I'll see you tomorrow afternoon then. What time's your flight landing?"

"One-fifteen. We'll drive straight to your place and pick up Michelle."

"Okay, I'll expect you sometime around two." Another day with Michelle. She could manage for another twenty-four hours, couldn't she? What could possibly go wrong in that small amount of time?

Losing patience, Nate took the bottle and Michelle and returned to the living room. Susannah watched through the doorway as he turned on her television and plopped himself down as if he'd been doing it for years. His concentration moved from the TV long enough to place the rubber nipple in Michelle's eager mouth.

Her niece began greedily sucking, too hungry to care who was feeding her. Good heavens, Susannah thought, Michelle had spent the night in his arms. A little thing like letting this man feed her paled in comparison.

Emily was still chatting, telling her sister how romantic her first night in San Francisco had been. But Susannah barely heard. Her gaze settled on Nate, who looked rumpled, crumpled and utterly content, sitting in her living room, holding an infant in his arms.

That sight affected Susannah as few ever had, and she was powerless to explain its impact on her senses. She'd dated a reasonable number of men—debonair, rich, sophisticated ones. But the feeling she had now, this attraction, had taken her completely by surprise. Over the years, Susannah had always been careful to guard her heart. It hadn't been difficult, since she'd never met anyone who truly appealed to her. Yet this disheveled, disgruntled male, who sat in her living room feeding her infant niece with enviable expertise, attracted her more profoundly than anyone she'd ever met. It wasn't the least bit logical. Nothing could ever develop between them—they were as different as…as gelatin and concrete. The last thing she wanted was to become involved in a serious relationship. With some effort, she forced her eyes away from the homey scene.

When at last she was able to hang up the phone, Susannah moved into the living room, feeling weary. She brushed the tangled curls from her face, wondering if she should take Michelle from Nate so he could return to his own apartment. No doubt her niece would resist and humiliate her once more.

"Your sister isn't flying with Puget Air, is she?" he asked, frowning. His gaze remained on the television screen.

"Yes, why?"

Nate's mouth thinned. "You…we're in trouble here.

Big trouble. According to the news, maintenance workers for Puget Air are going on strike. By six tonight, every plane they own will be grounded."

Four

"If this is a joke," Susannah told him angrily, "it's in poor taste."

"Would I kid about this?" Nate asked mildly.

Susannah slumped down on the edge of the sofa and gave a ragged sigh. This couldn't be happening, it just couldn't. "I'd better call Emily." She assumed her sister was blissfully unaware of the strike.

Susannah was back a few minutes later.

"Well?" Nate demanded. "What did she say?"

"Oh, she knew all along," Susannah replied disparagingly, "but she didn't want to say anything because she was afraid I'd worry."

"How exactly does she intend to get home?"

"Apparently they booked seats on another airline on the off chance something like this might happen."

"That was smart."

"My brother-in-law's like that. I'm not to give the matter another thought," she said, quoting Emily. "My sister will be back Sunday afternoon as promised." If the Fates so decreed—and Susannah said a fervent prayer that they would.

But the Fates had other plans.

Sunday morning, there were bags under Susannah's eyes. She was mentally and physically exhausted, and convinced anew that motherhood was definitely not for her. Two nights into the ordeal, Susannah had noticed that the emotional stirring for a husband and children came to her only when Michelle was sleeping or eating. And with good reason.

Nate arrived around nine bearing gifts. He brought freshly baked cinnamon rolls still warm from the oven. He stood in her doorway, tall and lean, with a smile bright enough to dazzle the most dedicated career woman. Once more, Susannah was shocked by her overwhelming reaction to him. Her heart leaped to her throat, and she immediately wished she'd taken time to dress in something better than her faded housecoat.

"You look terrible."

"Thanks," she said, bouncing Michelle on her hip.

"I take it you had a bad night."

"Michelle was fussing. She didn't seem the least bit interested in sleeping." She wiped a hand over her face.

"I wish you'd called me," Nate said, taking her by

the elbow and leading her into the kitchen. He actually looked guilty because he'd had a peaceful night's rest. Ridiculous, Susannah thought.

"Call you? Whatever for?" she asked. "So you could have paced with her, too?" As it was, Nate had spent a good part of Saturday in and out of her apartment helping her. Spending a second night with them was above and beyond the call of duty. "Did I tell you," Susannah said, yawning, "Michelle's got a new tooth coming in—I felt it myself." Deposited in the high chair, Michelle was content for the moment.

Nate nodded and glanced at his watch. "When does your sister's flight get in?"

"One-fifteen." No sooner had the words left her lips than the phone rang. Susannah's and Nate's eyes met, and as it rang a second time she wondered how a telephone could sound so much like a death knell. Even before she answered it, Susannah knew it would be what she most dreaded hearing.

"Well?" Nate asked when she'd finished the call.

Covering her face with both hands, Susannah sagged against the wall.

"Say something."

Slowly she lowered her hands. "Help."

"Help?"

"Yes," she cried, struggling to keep her voice from cracking. "All Puget Air flights are grounded just the way the news reported, and the other airline Robert and

Emily made reservations with is overbooked. The earliest flight they can get is tomorrow morning."

"I see."

"Obviously you don't!" she cried. "Tomorrow is Monday and I've got to be at work!"

"Call in sick."

"I can't do that," she snapped, angry with him for even suggesting such a thing. "My marketing group is giving their presentation and I've got to be there."

"Why?"

She frowned at him. It was futile to expect someone like Nate to understand something as important as a sales presentation. Nate didn't seem to have a job; he didn't worry about a career. For that matter, he couldn't possibly grasp that a woman holding a management position had to strive twice as hard to prove herself.

"I'm not trying to be cute, Susannah," he said with infuriating calm. "I honestly want to know why that meeting is so important."

"Because it is. I don't expect you to appreciate this, so just accept the fact that I *have* to be there."

Nate cocked his head and idly rubbed the side of his jaw. "First, answer me something. Five years from now, will this meeting make a difference in your life?"

"I don't know." She pressed two fingers to the bridge of her nose. She'd had less than three hours' sleep, and Nate was asking impossible questions. Michelle, bless her devilish little heart, had fallen asleep in her high chair. Why shouldn't she? Susannah reasoned. She'd spent the entire night fussing, and was exhausted now. By the time Susannah had discovered the new tooth, she felt as if she'd grown it herself.

"If I were you, I wouldn't sweat it," Nate said with that same nonchalant attitude. "If you aren't there to hear their presentation, your marketing group will give it Tuesday morning."

"In other words," she muttered, "you're saying I don't have a thing to worry about."

"Exactly."

Nate Townsend knew next to nothing about surviving in the corporate world, and he'd obviously been protected from life's harsher realities. It was all too obvious to Susannah that he was a man with a baseball-cap mentality. He couldn't be expected to fully comprehend her dilemma.

"So," he said now, "what are you going to do?"

Susannah wasn't sure. Briefly, she closed her eyes in an effort to concentrate. *Impose discipline,* she said to herself. *Stay calm.* That was crucial. *Think slowly and analyze your objectives.* For every problem there was a solution.

"Susannah?"

She glanced at him; she'd almost forgotten he was there. "I'll cancel my early-morning appointments and go in for the presentation," she stated matter-of-factly.

"What about Michelle? Are you going to hire a sitter?"

A babysitter hired by the babysitter. A novel thought,

perhaps even viable, but Susannah didn't know anyone who sat with babies.

Then she made her decision. She would take Michelle to work with her.

And that was exactly what she did.

As she knew it would, Susannah's arrival at H&J Lima caused quite a stir. At precisely ten the following morning, she stepped off the elevator. Her black leather briefcase was clutched in one hand and Michelle was pressed against her hip with the other. Head held high, Susannah marched across the hardwood floor, past the long rows of doorless cubicles and shelves of foot-thick file binders. Several employees moved away from their desks to view her progress. A low rumble of hushed whispers followed her.

"Good morning, Ms. Brooks," Susannah said crisply as she walked into her office, the diaper bag draped over her shoulder like an ammunition pouch.

"Ms. Simmons."

Susannah noted that her assistant—to her credit—didn't so much as bat an eye. The woman was well trained; to all outward appearances, Susannah regularly arrived at the office with a nine-month-old infant attached to her hip.

Depositing the diaper bag on the floor, Susannah took her place behind a six-foot-wide walnut desk. Content for the moment, Michelle sat on her lap, gleefully viewing her aunt's domain.

"Would you like some coffee?" Ms. Brooks asked.

"Yes, please."

Her assistant paused. "Will your, ah..."

"This is my niece, Michelle, Ms. Brooks."

The woman nodded. "Will Michelle require anything to drink?"

"No, but thanks anyway. Is there anything urgent in the mail?"

"Nothing that can't wait. I canceled your eight and nine o'clock appointments," her assistant went on to explain. "When I spoke to Mr. Adams, he asked if you could join him for drinks tomorrow night at six."

"That'll be fine." The old lecher would love to do all their business outside the office. On this occasion, she'd agree to his terms, since she'd been the one to cancel their appointment, but she wouldn't be so willing a second time. She'd never much cared for Andrew Adams, who was overweight, balding and a general nuisance.

"Will you be needing me for anything else?" Ms. Brooks asked when she delivered the coffee.

"Nothing. Thank you."

As she should have predicted, the meeting was an unmitigated disaster. The presentation took twenty-two minutes, and in that brief time Michelle managed to dismantle Susannah's Cross pen, unfasten her blouse and pull her hair free from her carefully styled French twist. The baby clapped her hands at various inappropriate points and made loud noises. At the low point of the meeting, Susannah had been forced to leave her seat and dive under the conference table to retrieve her niece, who was cheerfully crawling over everyone's feet.

By the time she got home, Susannah felt like climbing back into bed and staying there. It was the type of day that made her crave something chocolate and excessively sweet. But there weren't enough chocolate chip cookies in the world to see her through another morning like that one.

To Susannah's surprise, Nate met her in the foyer outside the elevator. She took one look at him and resisted the urge to burst into tears.

"I take it things didn't go well."

"How'd you guess?" she asked sarcastically.

"It might be the fact you're wearing your hair down when I specifically remember you left wearing it up. Or it could be that your blouse is buttoned wrong and there's a gaping hole in the middle." His smile was mischievous. "I wondered if you were the type to wear a lacy bra. Now I know."

Susannah groaned and slapped a hand over her front. He could have spared her that comment.

"Here, kiddo," he said, taking Michelle out of Susannah's arms. "It looks like we need to give your poor aunt a break."

Turning her back, Susannah refastened her blouse and then brought out her key. Her once orderly, immaculate apartment looked as if a cyclone had gone through it. Blankets and baby toys were scattered from one end of the living room to the other. She'd slept on the couch in order to be close to Michelle, and her pillow and blankets were still there, along with her blue suit jacket, which she'd been forced to change when Michelle had tossed a spoonful of plums on the sleeve.

"What happened here?" Nate asked, looking in astonishment at the scene before him.

"Three days and three nights with Michelle and you need to ask?"

"Sit down," he said gently. "I'll get you a cup of coffee." Susannah did as he suggested, too grateful to argue with him.

Nate stopped just inside the kitchen. "What's this purple stuff all over the walls?"

"Plums," Susannah informed him. "I discovered the hard way that Michelle hates plums."

The scene in the kitchen was a good example of how her morning had gone. It had taken Susannah the better part of three hours to get herself and Michelle ready for the excursion to the office. And that was just the beginning.

"What I need is a double martini," she told Nate when he carried in two cups of coffee.

"It's not even noon."

"I know," she said, slowly lowering herself to the sofa. "Can you imagine what I'd need if it was two o'clock?"

Chuckling, Nate handed her the steaming cup. Michelle was sitting on the carpet, content to play with the very toys she'd vehemently rejected that morning.

Nate unexpectedly sat down next to her and looped

his arm over her shoulder. She tensed, but if he noticed, he chose to ignore it. He stretched his legs out on the coffee table and relaxed.

Susannah felt her tension mount. The memory of the meeting with marketing was enough to elevate her blood pressure, but when she analyzed the reasons for this anxiety, she discovered it came from being so close to Nate. It wasn't that Susannah objected to his touch; in reality, quite the opposite was true. They'd spent three days in close quarters, and contrary to everything she'd theorized about her neighbor, she'd come to appreciate his happy-go-lucky approach to life. But it was diametrically opposed to her own, and the fact that she could be so attracted to him was something of a shock.

"Do you want to talk about marketing's presentation?"

She released her breath. "No, I think this morning is best forgotten by everyone involved. You were right, I should have postponed the meeting."

Nate sipped his coffee and said, "It's one of those live-and-learn situations."

Pulling herself to a standing position at the coffee table, Michelle cheerfully edged her way around until she was stopped by Nate's outstretched legs. Then she surprised them both by reaching out one arm and granting him a smile that would have melted concrete.

"Oh, look," Susannah said proudly, "you can see her new tooth!"

"Where?" Lifting the baby onto his lap, Nate peered inside her mouth. Susannah was trying to show him where to look when someone, presumably her sister, rang impatiently from the lobby.

Susannah opened her door a minute later, and Emily flew in as if she'd sprouted wings. "My baby!" she cried. "Mommy missed you so-o-o much."

Not half as much as I missed you, Emily, she mused, watching the happy reunion.

Robert followed on his wife's heels, obviously pleased. The weekend away had apparently done them both good. Never mind that it had nearly destroyed Susannah's peace of mind *and* her career.

"You must be Nate," Emily said, claiming the seat beside Susannah's neighbor. "My sister couldn't say enough about you."

"Coffee anyone?" Susannah piped up eagerly, rubbing her palms together. The last thing she needed was her sister applying her matchmaking techniques to her and Nate. Emily strongly believed it was unnatural for Susannah to live the way she did. A career was fine, but choosing to forgo the personal satisfaction of a husband and family was beyond her sister's comprehension. Being fulfilled in that role herself, Emily assumed that Susannah was missing an essential part of life.

"Nothing for me," Robert answered.

"I'll bet you're eager to pack everything up and head home," Susannah said hopefully. Her eye happened to catch Nate's, and it was obvious that he was struggling not to laugh at her less-than-subtle attempt to usher her sister and family on their way.

"Susannah's right," Robert announced, glancing around the room. It was clear he'd never seen his orderly, efficient sister-in-law's home in such a state of disarray.

"But I've hardly had a chance to talk to Nate," Emily protested. "And I was looking forward to getting to know him better."

"I'll be around," Nate said lightly.

His gaze settled on Susannah, and the look he gave her made her insides quiver. For the first time she realized how much she wanted this man to kiss her. Susannah wasn't the type of person who looked at a handsome male and wondered how his mouth would feel on hers. She was convinced this current phenomenon had a lot to do with sheer exhaustion, but whatever the cause she found her eyes riveted to his.

Emily suddenly noticed what was happening. "Yes, I think you may be right, Robert," she said, and her voice contained more than a hint of amusement. "I'll pack Michelle's things."

Susannah's cheeks were pink with embarrassment by the time she tore her gaze away from Nate's. "By the way, did you know Michelle has an aversion to plums?"

"I can't say I did," Emily said, busily throwing her daughter's things together.

Nate helped disassemble the crib and the high chair, and it seemed no more than a few minutes had passed before Susannah's condo was once more her own. She stood in the middle of the living room savoring the silence. It was pure bliss.

"They're off," she said when she saw that Nate had stayed behind.

"Like a herd of turtles."

Susannah had heard that saying from the time she was a kid. She didn't find it particularly funny anymore, but she shared a smile with him.

"I have my life back now," she sighed. It would probably take her a month to recover, though.

"Your life is your own," Nate agreed, watching her closely.

Susannah would've liked to attribute the tears that flooded her eyes to his close scrutiny, but she knew better. With her arms cradling her middle, she walked over to the window, which looked out over Elliott Bay. A green-and-white ferry glided peacefully over the darker green waters. Rain tapped gently against the window, and the sky, a deep oyster-gray, promised drizzle for most of the afternoon.

Hoping Nate wouldn't notice, she wiped the tears from her face and drew in a deep calming breath.

"Susannah?"

"I... I was just looking at the Sound. It's so lovely in the fall." She could hear him approach her from behind, and when he placed his hands on her shoulders it was all she could do to keep from leaning against him.

"You're crying."

She nodded, sniffling because it was impossible to hold it inside any longer.

"It's not like you to cry, is it? What's wrong?"

"I don't know..." she said and hiccuped on a sob. "I can't believe I'm doing this. I love that little kid...we were just beginning to understand each other...and... dear heaven, I'm glad Emily came back when...she did." Before Susannah could recognize how much she was missing without a husband and family.

Nate ran his hands down her arms in the softest of caresses.

He didn't say anything for a long time, and Susannah was convinced she was making an absolute idiot of herself. Nate was right; it wasn't like her to dissolve into tears. This unexpected outburst must've been a result of the trauma she'd experienced that morning in her office, or the fact that she hadn't had a decent night's sleep in what felt like a month and, yes, she'd admit it, of meeting Nate.

Without saying another word, Nate turned her around and lifted her chin with his finger, raising her eyes to his. His look was so tender, so caring, that Susannah sniffled again. Her shoulders shook and she wiped her nose.

He brushed away the hair that clung to the sides of her damp face. His fingertips slid over each of her features as though he were a blind man trying to memorize her face. Susannah was mesmerized, unable to pull away. Slowly, as if denying himself the pleasure for as long as he could, he lowered his mouth.

When his lips settled on hers, Susannah released a barely audible sigh. She'd wondered earlier what it would be like when Nate kissed her. Now she knew. His kiss was soft and warm. Velvet smooth and infinitely gentle, and yet it was undeniably exciting.

As if one kiss wasn't enough, he kissed her again. This time it was Nate who sighed. Then he dropped his hands and stepped back.

Startled by his abrupt action, Susannah swayed slightly. Nate's arms righted her. Apparently he'd come to his senses at the same time she had. For a brief moment they'd decided to ignore their differences. The only thing they had in common was the fact that they lived in the same building, she reminded herself. Their values and expectations were worlds apart.

"Are you all right?" he asked, frowning.

She blinked, trying to find a way to disguise that she wasn't. Everything had happened much too fast; her heart was galloping like a runaway horse. She'd never been so attracted to a man in her life. "Of course I'm all right," she said with strained bravado. "Are you?"

He didn't answer for a moment. Instead, he shoved his hands in his pants pocket and moved away from her, looking annoyed.

"Nate?" she whispered.

He paused, scowling in her direction. Rubbing his hand across his brow, he twisted the ever-present baseball cap until it faced backward. "I think we should try that again."

Susannah wasn't sure what he meant until he reached for her. His first few kisses had been gentle, but this one was meant to take charge of her senses. His mouth slid over hers until she felt the starch go out of her knees. In an effort to maintain her balance, she gripped his shoulders, and although she fought it, she quickly surrendered to the swirling excitement. Nate's kiss was debilitating. She couldn't breathe, couldn't think, couldn't move.

Nate groaned, then his hands shifted to the back of her head. He slanted his mouth over hers. At length he released a jagged breath and buried his face in the soft curve of her neck. "What about now?"

"You're a good kisser."

"That's not what I meant, Susannah. You feel it, too, don't you? You must! There's enough electricity between us to light up a city block."

"No," she lied, and swallowed tightly. "It was nice as far as kisses go—"

"Nice!"

"Very nice," she amended, hoping to appease him, "but that's about it."

Nate didn't say anything for a long minute, a painfully long minute. Then, scowling at her again, he turned and walked out of the apartment.

Trembling, Susannah watched him go. His kiss had touched a chord within her, notes that had been long-silent, and now she feared the music would forever mark her soul. But she couldn't let him know that. They had nothing in common. They were too mismatched.

Now that she was seated in the plush cocktail lounge with her associate, Andrew Adams, Susannah regretted having agreed to meet him after hours. It was apparent from the moment she stepped into the dimly lit room that he had more on his mind than business. Despite the fact that Adams was balding and overweight, he would have been attractive enough if he hadn't seen himself as some kind of modern-day Adonis. Although Susannah struggled to maintain a businesslike calm, it was becoming increasingly difficult, and she wondered how much longer her good intentions would hold.

"There are some figures I meant to show you," Adams said, holding the stem of his martini glass with both hands and studying Susannah with undisguised admiration. "Unfortunately I left them at my apartment. Why don't we conclude our talk there?"

Susannah made a point of looking at her watch and frowning, hoping he'd get the hint. Something told her differently. "I'm afraid I won't have the time," she said. It was almost seven and she'd already spent an hour with him.

"My place is only a few blocks from here," he coaxed.

His look was much too suggestive, and Susannah was growing wearier by the minute. As far as she could see, this entire evening had been a waste of time.

The only thing that interested her was returning to her own place and talking to Nate. He'd been on her mind all day and she was eager to see him again. The truth was, she felt downright nervous after their last meeting, and wondered how they'd react to each other now. Nate had left her so abruptly, and she hadn't talked to him since.

"John Hammer and I are good friends," Adams

claimed, pulling his chair closer to her own. "I don't know if you're aware of that."

He didn't even bother to veil his threat—or his bribe, whichever it was. Susannah worked directly under John Hammer, who would have the final say on the appointment of a new vice president. Susannah and two others were in the running for the position. And Susannah wanted it. Badly. She could achieve her five-year goal if she got it, and in the process make H&J Lima history—by being the first female vice president.

"If you're such good friends with Mr. Hammer," she said, "then I suggest you give those figures to him directly, since he'll need to review them anyway."

"No, that wouldn't work," he countered sharply. "If you come with me it'll only take a few minutes. We'd be in and out of my place in, say, half an hour at the most."

Susannah's immediate reaction to situations such as this was a healthy dose of outrage, but she managed to control her temper. "If your apartment is so convenient, then I'll wait here while you go back for those sheets." As she spoke, a couple walked past the tiny table where she was seated with Andrew Adams. Susannah didn't pay much attention to the man, who wore a gray suit, but the blonde with him was striking. Susannah followed the woman with her eyes and envied the graceful way she moved.

"It would be easier if you came with me, don't you think?"

"No," she answered bluntly, and lowered her gaze to

her glass of white wine. It was then that she felt an odd sensation prickle down her spine. Someone was staring at her; she could feel it as surely as if she were being physically touched. Looking around, Susannah was astonished to discover Nate sitting two tables away. The striking blonde was seated next to him and obviously enjoying his company. She laughed softly and the sound was like a melody, light and breezy.

Susannah's breath caught in her chest, trapped there until the pain reminded her it was time to breathe again. When she did, she reached for her wineglass and succeeded in spilling some of the contents.

Nate's gaze centered on her and then moved to her companion. His mouth thinned and his eyes, which had been so warm and tender a day earlier, now looked hard. Almost scornful.

Susannah wasn't exactly thrilled herself. Nate was dating a beauty queen while she was stuck with Donald Duck.

Five

Susannah vented her anger by pacing the living room carpet. Men! Who needed them?

Not her. Definitely not her! Nate Townsend could take his rainy day kisses and stuff them in his baseball cap for all she cared. Only he hadn't been wearing it for Miss Universe. Oh no, with the other woman, he was dressed like someone out of *Gentlemen's Quarterly*. Susannah, on the other hand, rated worn football jerseys or faded T-shirts.

Susannah hadn't been home more than five minutes when there was a knock at her door. She whirled around. Checking the peephole, she discovered that her caller was Nate. She pulled back, wondering what she should do. He was the last person she wanted to see. He'd made a fool of her… Well, that wasn't strictly true. He'd only made her *feel* like a fool.

"Susannah," he said, knocking impatiently a second time. "I know you're in there."

"Go away."

Her shout was followed by a short pause. "Fine. Have it your way."

Changing her mind, she turned the lock and yanked open the door. She glared at him with all the fury she could muster—which just then was considerable.

Nate glared right back. "Who was that guy?" he asked with infuriating calm.

She was tempted to inform Nate that it wasn't any of his business. But she decided that would be churlish.

"Andrew Adams," she answered and quickly followed her response with a demand of her own. "Who was that woman?"

"Sylvia Potter."

For the longest moment, neither spoke.

"That was all I wanted to know," Nate finally said.

"Me, too," she returned stiffly.

Nate retreated two steps, and like precision clockwork Susannah shut the door. "Sylvia Potter," she echoed in a low-pitched voice filled with disdain. "Well, Sylvia Potter, you're welcome to him."

It took another fifteen minutes for the outrage to work its way through her system, but once she'd watched a portion of the evening news and read her mail, she was reasonably calm.

When Susannah really thought about it, what did she have to be so furious about? Nate Townsend didn't mean anything to her. How could he? Until a week ago, she hadn't even known his name.

Okay, so he'd kissed her a couple of times, and sure, there'd been electricity, but that was all. Electricity did not constitute a lifetime commitment. If Nate Townsend chose to date every voluptuous blonde between Seattle and New York it shouldn't matter to her.

But it did. And that infuriated Susannah more than anything. She didn't *want* to care about Nate. Her career goals were set. She had drive, determination and a positive mental attitude. But she didn't have Nate.

Jutting out her lower lip, she expelled her breath forcefully, ruffling the dark wisps of hair against her forehead. Maybe it was her hair color—perhaps Nate preferred blondes. He obviously did, otherwise he wouldn't be trying to impress Sylvia Potter.

Refusing to entertain any more thoughts of her neighbor, Susannah decided to fix herself dinner. An inspection of the freezer revealed a pitifully old chicken patty. Removing it from the cardboard box, Susannah took one look at it and promptly tossed it into the garbage.

Out of the corner of her eye she caught a movement on her balcony. She turned and saw a sleek Siamese cat walking casually along the railing as if he were strolling across a city park.

Although she remained outwardly calm, Susannah's heart lunged to her throat. Her condo was eight floors up. One wrong move and that cat would be history. Walking carefully to her sliding glass door, Susannah eased it open and called, "Here, kitty, kitty, kitty."

The cat accepted her invitation and jumped down from the railing. With his tail pointing skyward, he walked directly into her apartment and headed straight for the garbage pail, where he stopped.

"I bet you're hungry, aren't you?" she asked softly. She retrieved the chicken patty and stuck it in her microwave. While she stood waiting for it to cook, the cat, with his striking blue eyes and dark brown markings, wove around her legs, purring madly.

She'd just finished cutting the patty into bite-size pieces and putting it on a plate when someone pounded at her door. Wiping her fingers clean, she moved into the living room.

"Do you have my cat?" Nate demanded when she opened the door. He'd changed from his suit into jeans and a bright blue T-shirt.

"I don't know," she fibbed. "Describe it."

"Susannah, this isn't the time for silly games. Chocolate Chip is a valuable animal."

"Chocolate Chip," she repeated with a soft snicker, crossing her arms and leaning against the doorjamb. "Obviously you didn't read the fine print in the tenant's agreement, because it specifically states in section 12, paragraph 13, that no pets are allowed." Actually she didn't have a clue what section or what paragraph that clause was in, but she wanted him to think she did.

"If you don't tattle on me, then I won't tattle on you."

"I don't have any pets."

"No, you had a baby."

"But only for three days," she said. Talk about nitpicking people! He was flagrantly disregarding the rules and had the nerve to throw a minor infraction in her face.

"The cat belongs to my sister. He'll be with me for less than a week. Now, is Chocolate Chip here, or do I go into cardiac arrest?"

"He's here."

Nate visibly relaxed. "Thank God. My sister dotes on that silly feline. She flew up from San Francisco and left him with me before she left for Hawaii." As if he'd heard his name mentioned, Chocolate Chip casually strolled across the carpet and paused at Nate's feet.

Nate bent down to retrieve his sister's cat, scolding him with a harsh look.

"I suggest you keep your balcony door closed," she told him, striving for a flippant air.

"Thanks, I will." Chocolate Chip was tucked under his arm as Nate's gaze casually caught Susannah's. "You might be interested to know that Sylvia Potter's my sister." He turned and walked out her door.

"'Sylvia Potter's my sister,'" Susannah mimicked. It wasn't until she'd closed and locked her door that she recognized the import of what he'd said. "His sister," she repeated. "Did he really say that?"

Susannah was at his door before she stopped to judge the wisdom of her actions. When Nate answered her furious knock, she stared up at him, her eyes confused. "What was that you just said?"

"I said Sylvia Potter's my sister."

"I was afraid of that." Her thoughts were tumbling over one another like marbles in a bag. She'd imagined...she'd assumed....

"Who's Andrew Adams?"

"My brother?" she offered, wondering if he'd believe her.

Nate shook his head. "Try again."

"An associate from H&J Lima," she said, then hurried to explain. "When I canceled my appointment with him Monday morning, he suggested we get together for a drink to discuss business this evening. It sounded innocent enough at the time, but I should've realized it was a mistake. Adams is a known sleazeball."

An appealing smile touched the edges of Nate's mouth. "I wish I'd had a camera when you first saw me in that cocktail lounge. I thought your eyes were going to fall out of your face."

"It was your sister—she intimidated me," Susannah admitted. "She's lovely."

"So are you."

The man had obviously been standing out in the sun too long, Susannah decided. Compared to Sylvia, who was tall, blond and had curves in all the right places, Susannah felt about as pretty as a professional wrestler.

"I'm flattered that you think so." Susannah wasn't comfortable with praise. She was much too levelheaded to let flattery affect her. When men paid her compliments, she smiled and thanked them, but she treated their words like water running off a slick surface.

Except with Nate. Everything was different with him. She seemed to be accumulating a large stack of exceptions because of Nate. As far as Susannah could see, he had no ambition, and if she'd met him anyplace other than her building, she probably wouldn't have given him a second thought. Instead she couldn't stop thinking about him. She knew better than to allow her heart to be distracted this way, and yet she couldn't seem to stop herself.

"Do you want to come in?" Nate asked and stepped aside. A bleeping sound drew Susannah's attention to a five-foot-high television screen across the room. She'd apparently interrupted Nate in the middle of an action-packed video game. A video game!

"No," she answered quickly. "I wouldn't want to interrupt you. Besides I was…just about to make myself some dinner."

"You cook?"

His astonishment—no, shock—was unflattering, to say the least.

"Of course I do."

"I'm glad to hear it, because I seem to recall that you owe me a meal."

"I—"

"And since we seem to have gotten off on the wrong

foot tonight, a nice quiet dinner in front of the fireplace sounds like exactly what we need."

Susannah's thoughts were zooming at the speed of light. Nate was inviting himself to dinner—one she was supposed to whip up herself! Why did she so glibly announce that she could cook? Everything she'd ever attempted in the kitchen had been a disaster. Other than toast. Toast was her specialty. Her mind whirled with all the different ways she could serve it. Buttered? With honey? Jam? Cheese? The list was endless.

"You fix dinner and I'll bring over the wine," Nate said in a low seductive voice. "It's time we sat down together and talked. Deal?"

"I, ah, I've got some papers I have to read over tonight."

"No problem. I'll make it a point to leave early so you can finish whatever you need to."

His eyes held hers for a long moment, and despite everything Susannah knew about Nate, she still wanted time alone with him. She had some papers to review and he had to get back to his video game. A relationship like theirs was not meant to be. However, before she was even aware of what she was doing, Susannah nodded.

"Good. I'll give you an hour. Is that enough time?"

Once more, like a remote-controlled robot, she nodded.

Nate smiled and leaned forward to lightly brush his lips over hers. "I'll see you in an hour then."

He put his hand at her lower back and guided her out

the door. For a few seconds she did nothing more than stand in the hallway, wondering how she was going to get herself out of this one. She reviewed her options and discovered there was only one.

The Western Avenue Deli.

Precisely an hour later, Susannah was ready. A tossed green salad rested in the middle of the table in a crystal bowl, which had been a gift when she graduated from college. Her aunt Gerty had given it to her. Susannah loved her aunt dearly, but the poor soul had her and Emily confused. Emily would have treasured the fancy bowl. As it happened, this was the first occasion Susannah had even used it and now that she looked at it, she thought the bowl might have been meant for punch. Maybe Nate wouldn't notice. The stroganoff was simmering in a pan and the noodles were in a foil-covered dish, keeping warm in the oven.

Susannah drew in a deep breath, then frantically waved her hands over the simmering food to disperse the scent around the condo before she opened her door.

"Hi," Nate said. He held a bottle of wine.

His eyes were so blue, it was like looking into a clear, deep lake. When she spoke, her voice trembled slightly. "Hi. Dinner's just about ready."

He sniffed the air appreciatively. "Will red wine do?"

"It's perfect," she told him, stepping aside so he could come in.

"Shall I open it now?"

"Please." She led him into the kitchen.

He cocked an eyebrow. "It looks like you've been busy."

For good measure, Susannah had stacked a few pots and pans in the sink and set out an array of spices on the counter. In addition, she'd laid out several books. None of them had anything to do with cooking—she didn't own any cookbooks—but they looked impressive.

"I hope you like stroganoff," she said cheerfully.

"It's one of my favorites."

Susannah swallowed and nodded. She'd never been very good at deception, but then she'd rarely put her pride on the line the way she had this evening.

While she dished up the stroganoff, Nate expertly opened the wine and poured them each a glass. When everything was ready, they sat across the table from each other.

After one taste of the buttered noodles and the rich sauce, Nate said, "This is delicious."

Susannah kept her eyes lowered. "Thanks. My mother has a recipe that's been handed down for years." It was a half-truth that was stretched about as far it could go without snapping back and hitting her in the face. Yes, her mother did have a favorite family recipe, but it was for Christmas candies.

"The salad's excellent, too. What's in the dressing?"

This was the moment Susannah had dreaded. "Ah…" Her mind faltered before she could remember exactly what usually went into salad dressings. "Oil!" she cried, as if black gold had just been discovered in her living room.

"Vinegar?"

"Yes," she agreed eagerly. "Lots of that."

Planting his elbows on the table, he smiled at her. "Spices?"

"Oh, yes, those, too."

His mouth was quivering when he took a sip of wine.

Subterfuge had never been Susannah's strong suit. If Nate hadn't started asking her these difficult questions, she might've been able to pull off the ruse. But he obviously knew, and there wasn't any reason to continue it.

"Nate," she said, after fortifying herself with a sip of wine, "I… I didn't exactly cook this meal myself."

"The Western Avenue Deli?"

She nodded, feeling wretched.

"An excellent choice."

"H-how'd you know?" Something inside her demanded further abuse. Anyone else would have dropped the matter right then.

"You mean other than the fact that you've got enough pots and pans in your sink to have fed a small army? By the way, what could you possibly have used the broiler pan for?"

"I…was hoping you'd think I'd warmed the dinner rolls on it."

"I see." He was doing an admirable job of not laughing outright, and Susannah supposed she should be grateful for that much.

After taking a bite of his—unwarmed—roll, he asked, "Where'd you get all the spices?"

"They were a Christmas gift from Emily one year. She continues to hold out hope that a miracle will happen and I'll suddenly discover I've missed my calling in life and decide to chain myself to the stove."

Nate grinned. "For future reference, I can't see how you'd need poultry seasoning or curry powder for stroganoff."

"Oh." She should've quit when she was ahead. "So... you knew right from the first?"

Nate nodded. "I'm afraid so, but I'm flattered by all the trouble you went to."

"I suppose it won't do any more harm to admit that I'm a total loss in the kitchen. I'd rather analyze a profit-and-loss statement any day than attempt to bake a batch of cookies."

Nate reached for a second dinner roll. "If you ever do, my favorite are chocolate chip."

Perhaps he was the one who'd named his sister's cat, she mused. Or maybe chocolate chip cookies were popular with his whole family. "I'll remember that." An outlet for Rainy Day Cookies had recently opened on the waterfront and they were the best money could buy.

Nate helped her clear the table once they'd finished. While she rinsed the plates and put them in the dishwasher, Nate built a fire. He was seated on the floor in front of the fireplace waiting for her when she entered the room.

"More wine?" he asked, holding up the bottle.

"Please." Inching her straight skirt slightly higher, Susannah carefully lowered herself to the carpet beside him. Nate grinned and reached for the nearby lamp, turning it to the lowest setting. Shadows from the fire flickered across the opposite wall. The atmosphere was warm and cozy.

"All right," he said softly, close to her ear. "Ask away."

Susannah frowned, not sure what he meant.

"You've been dying of curiosity about me from the moment we met. I'm simply giving you the opportunity to ask me anything you want."

Susannah gulped her wine. If he could read her so easily, then she had no place in the business world. Yes, she was full of questions about him and had been trying to find a subtle way to bring some of them into the conversation.

"First, however," he said, "let me do this."

Before she knew what was happening, Nate had pressed her down onto the carpet and was kissing her. Kissing her deeply, drugging her senses with a mastery that was just short of arrogant. He'd caught her unprepared, and before she could raise any defenses, she was captured in a dizzying wave of sensation.

When he lifted his head, Susannah stared up at him, breathless and amazed at her own ready response. Before she could react, Nate slid one hand behind her. He unpinned her hair, then ran his fingers through it.

"I've been wanting to do that all night," he murmured.

Still she couldn't speak. He'd kissed and held her, but it didn't seem to affect his power of speech, while she felt completely flustered and perplexed.

"Yes, well," she managed to mutter, scrambling to a sitting position. "I...forget what we were talking about."

Nate moved behind her and pulled her against his chest, wrapping his arms around her and nibbling on the side of her neck. "I believe you were about to ask me something."

"Yes...you're right, I was... Nate, do you work?"

"No."

Delicious shivers were racing up and down her spine. His teeth found her earlobe and he sucked on it gently, causing her insides to quake in seismic proportions.

"Why not?" she asked, her voice trembling.

"I quit."

"But why?"

"I was working too hard. I wasn't enjoying myself anymore."

"Oh."

His mouth had progressed down the gentle slope of her neck to her shoulder, and she closed her eyes to the warring emotions churning inside her. Part of her longed to surrender to the thrill of his touch, yet she hungered to learn all she could about this unconventional man.

Nate altered his position so he was in front of her again. His mouth began exploring her face with soft kisses that fell like gentle raindrops over her eyes, nose, cheeks and lips.

"Anything else you want to know?" he asked, pausing.

Unable to do more than shake her head, Susannah sighed and reluctantly unwound her arms from around his neck.

"Do you want more wine?" he asked.

"No...thank you." It demanded all the fortitude she possessed not to ask him to keep kissing her.

"Okay," he said, making himself comfortable. He raised his knees and wrapped his arms around them. "My turn."

"Your turn?"

"Yes," he said with a lazy grin that did wicked things to her equilibrium. "I have a few questions for you."

Susannah found it difficult to center her attention on anything other than the fact that Nate was sitting a few inches away from her and could lean over and kiss her again at any moment.

"You don't object?"

"No," she said, gesturing with her hand.

"Okay, tell me about yourself."

Susannah shrugged. For the life of her, she couldn't think of a single thing that would impress him. She'd worked hard, climbing the corporate ladder, inching her way toward her long-range goals.

"I'm up for promotion," she began. "I started working for H&J Lima five years ago. I chose this company, although the pay was less than I'd been offered by two others."

"Why?"

"There's opportunity with them. I looked at the chain of command and saw room for steady advancement. Being a woman is both an asset and a detriment, if you know what I mean. I had to prove myself, but I was also aware of being the token woman on the staff."

"You mean you were hired because you were female?"

"Exactly. But I swallowed my pride and set about proving I could handle anything asked of me, and I have."

Nate looked proud of her.

"Five years ago, I decided I wanted to be the vice president in charge of marketing," she said, her voice gaining strength and conviction. "It was a significant goal, because I'd be the first woman to hold a position that high within the company."

"And?"

"And I'll find out in the next few weeks if I'm going to get it. I'll derive a great deal of satisfaction from knowing I earned it. I won't be their token female in upper management anymore."

"What's the competition like?"

Susannah slowly expelled her breath. "Stiff. Damn stiff. There are two men in the running, and both have been with the company as long as me, in one case longer. Both are older, bright and dedicated."

"You're bright and dedicated, too."

"That may not be enough," she murmured. Now that her dream was within reach, she yearned for it even more. She could feel Nate's eyes studying her.

"This promotion means a lot to you, doesn't it?"

"Yes. It's everything. From the moment I was hired, I've striven toward this very thing. And it's happening faster than I dared hope."

Nate was silent for a moment. He put another log on the fire, and although she hadn't asked for it, he replenished her wine.

"Have you ever stopped to think what would happen if you achieved your dreams and then discovered you weren't happy?"

"How could I not be happy?" she asked. She honestly didn't understand. For years she'd worked toward obtaining this vice presidency. Of course she was going to be happy! She'd be thrilled, elated, jubilant.

Nate's eyes narrowed. "Aren't you worried about there being a void in your life?"

Oh, no, he was beginning to sound like Emily. "No," she said flatly. "How could there be? Now before you start, I know what you're going to say, so please don't. Save your breath. Emily has argued with me about this from the time I graduated from college."

Nate looked genuinely puzzled. "Argued with you about what?"

"Getting married and having a family. But the roles of wife and mother just aren't for me. They never have been and they never will be."

"I see."

Susannah was convinced he didn't. "If I were a man, would everyone be pushing me to marry?"

Nate chuckled and his eyes rested on her for a tantalizing moment. "Trust me, Susannah, no one's going to mistake you for a man."

She grinned and lowered her gaze. "It's the nose, isn't it?"

"The nose?"

"Yes." She turned sideways and held her chin at a lofty angle so he could view her classic profile. "I think it's my best feature." The wine had obviously gone to her head. But that was all right because she felt warm and comfortable and Nate was sitting beside her. Rarely had she been more content.

"Actually I wasn't thinking about your nose at all. I was remembering that first night with Michelle."

"You mean when we both fell asleep in the living room?"

Nate nodded and reached for her shoulder, his eyes trapping hers. "It was the only time in my life I can remember having one woman in my arms and wanting another."

Six

"I've decided not to see him again," Susannah announced.

"I beg your pardon?" Ms. Brooks stopped in her tracks and looked at her boss.

Unnerved, Susannah made busywork at her desk. "I'm sorry, I didn't realize I'd spoken out loud."

Her assistant brought a cup of coffee to her desk and hesitated. "How late did you end up staying last night?"

"Not long," Susannah lied. It had, in fact, been past ten when she left the building.

"And the night before?" Ms. Brooks pressed.

"Not so late," Susannah fibbed again.

Eleanor Brooks walked quietly out of the room, but not before she gave Susannah a stern look that said she didn't believe her for one moment.

As soon as the door closed, Susannah pressed the tips of her fingers to her forehead and exhaled a slow steady breath. Dear heaven, Nate Townsend had her so twisted up inside she was talking to the walls.

Nate hadn't left her condo until almost eleven the night he'd come for dinner, and by that time he'd kissed her nearly senseless. Three days had passed and Susannah could still taste and feel his mouth on hers. The scent of his aftershave lingered in her living room to the point that she looked for him whenever she entered the room.

The man didn't even hold down a job. Oh, he'd had one, but he'd quit and it was obvious, to her at least, that he wasn't in any hurry to get another. He'd held her and kissed her and patiently listened to her dreams. But he hadn't shared any of his own. He had no ambition, and no urge to better himself.

And Susannah was falling head over heels for him.

Through the years, she had assumed she was immune to falling in love. She was too sensible for that, too practical, too career-oriented. Not once did she suspect she'd fall so hard for someone like Nate. Nate, with his no-need-to-rush attitude and tomorrow-will-take-care-of-itself lifestyle.

Aware of what was happening to her, Susannah had done the only thing she could—gone into hiding. For three days she'd managed to avoid Nate. He'd left a couple of messages on her answering machine, which she'd ignored. If he confronted her, she had a perfect excuse.

She was working. And it was true: she spent much of her time holed up in the office. She headed out early in the morning and arrived home late at night. The extra hours she was putting in served two distinct purposes: they showed her employer that she was dedicated, and they kept her from having to deal with Nate.

Her intercom buzzed, pulling Susannah from her thoughts. She reached over and hit the speaker button. "Yes?"

"Mr. Townsend is on the phone."

Susannah squeezed her eyes shut and her throat muscles tightened. "Take a message, please," she said, her voice little more than a husky whisper.

"He insists on speaking to you."

"Tell him I'm in a meeting and…unavailable."

It wasn't like Susannah to lie, and Eleanor Brooks knew it. She finally asked, "Is this the man you plan never to see again?"

The abruptness of her question caught Susannah off guard. "Yes…"

"I assumed as much. I'll tell him you're not available."

"Thank you." Susannah's hand was trembling as she released the intercom button. She hadn't dreamed Nate would call her at the office.

By eleven, a feeling of normalcy had returned. Susannah was gathering her notes for an executive meeting with the finance committee when her assistant came in. "Mr. Franklin phoned and canceled his afternoon appointment."

Susannah glanced up. "Did he want to reschedule?"

"Friday at ten."

She nodded. "That'll be fine." It was on the tip of her tongue to ask how Nate had responded earlier when told she was unavailable, but she resisted the temptation.

"Mr. Townsend left a message. I wrote it out for you."

Her assistant knew her too well, it seemed. "Leave it on my desk."

"You might want to read it," the older woman urged.

"I will. Later."

Halfway through the meeting, Susannah wished she'd followed her assistant's advice. Impatience filled her. She wanted this finance meeting over so she could hurry back to her desk and read the message from Nate. Figures flew overhead—important ones with a bearing on the outcome of the marketing strategy she and her department had planned. Yet, again and again, Susannah found her thoughts drifting to Nate.

That wasn't typical for her. When the meeting ended, she was furious with herself. She walked briskly back to her office, her low heels making staccato taps against the polished hardwood floor.

"Ms. Brooks," she said, as she went into the outer office. "Could you—"

Susannah stopped dead in her tracks. The last person she'd expected to see was Nate. He was sitting on the corner of her assistant's desk, wearing a Mariners T-shirt, faded jeans and a baseball cap. He tossed a baseball in the air and deftly caught it in his mitt.

Eleanor Brooks looked both unsettled and inordinately pleased. No doubt Nate had used some of his considerable male charm on the gray-haired grandmother.

"It's about time," Nate said, grinning devilishly. He leaped off the desk. "I was afraid we were going to be late for the game."

"Game?" Susannah repeated. "What game?"

Nate held out his right hand to show her his baseball mitt and ball—just in case she hadn't noticed them. "The Mariners are playing, and I've got two of the best seats in the place reserved for you and me."

Susannah's heart sank to the pit of her stomach. It was just like Nate to assume she could take off in the middle of the day on some lark. He obviously had no understanding of what being a responsible employee meant. It was bad enough that he'd dominated her thoughts during an important meeting, but suggesting they escape for an afternoon was too much.

"You don't honestly expect me to leave, do you?"

"Yes."

"I can't. I won't."

"Why not?"

"I'm working," she said, deciding that was sufficient explanation.

"You've been at the office every night this week. You need a break. Come on, Susannah, let your hair down long enough to have a good time. It isn't going to hurt. I promise."

He was so casual about the whole thing, as if obligation and duty were of little significance. It proved more than anything that he didn't grasp the concept of hard work being its own reward.

"It *will* hurt," she insisted.

"Okay," he said forcefully. "What's so important this afternoon?" To answer his own question, he walked around her assistant's desk. Then he leaned forward and flipped open the pages of her appointment schedule.

"Mr. Franklin canceled his three o'clock appointment," Ms. Brooks reminded her primly. "And you skipped lunch because of the finance meeting."

Susannah frowned at the older woman, wondering what exactly Nate had said or done that had turned her into a traitor on such short acquaintance.

"I have more important things to do," Susannah told them both stiffly.

"Not according to your appointment schedule," Nate said confidently. "As far as I can see, you haven't got an excuse in the world not to attend that baseball game with me."

Susannah wasn't going to stand there and argue with him. Instead she marched into her office and dutifully sat down at her desk.

To her chagrin both Nate and Ms. Brooks followed her inside. It was all Susannah could do not to bury her face in her hands and demand that they leave.

"Susannah," Nate coaxed gently, "you need a break. Tomorrow you'll come back rejuvenated and refreshed.

If you spend too much time at the office, you'll begin to lose perspective. An afternoon away will do you good."

Her assistant seemed about to comment, but Susannah stopped her with a scalding look. Before she could say anything to Nate, someone else entered her office.

"Susannah, I was just checking over these figures and I—" John Hammer stopped midsentence when he noticed the other two people in her office.

If there'd been an open window handy, Susannah would gladly have hurled herself through it. The company director smiled benignly, however, looking slightly embarrassed at having interrupted her. Now, it seemed, he was awaiting an introduction.

"John, this is Nate Townsend…my neighbor."

Ever the gentleman, John stepped forward and extended his hand. If he thought it a bit odd to find a man in Susannah's office dressed in jeans and a T-shirt, he didn't show it.

"Nate Townsend," he repeated, pumping his hand. "It's a pleasure, a real pleasure."

"Thank you," Nate said. "I'm here to pick up Susannah. We're going to a Mariners game this afternoon."

John removed the glasses from the end of his nose, and nodded thoughtfully. "An excellent idea."

"No, I really don't think I'll go. I mean…" She stopped when it became obvious that no one was paying any attention to her protests.

"Nate's absolutely right," John said, setting the file

on her desk. "You've been putting in a lot of extra hours lately. Take the afternoon off. Enjoy yourself."

"But—"

"Susannah, are you actually going to argue with your boss?" Nate prompted.

Her jaw sagged. "I…guess not."

"Good. Good." John looked as pleased as if he'd made the suggestion himself. He was smiling at Nate and nodding as if the two were longtime friends.

Her expression more than a little smug, Eleanor Brooks returned to her own office.

Nate glanced at his watch. "We'd better go now or we'll miss the opening pitch."

With heavy reluctance, Susannah scooped up her purse. She'd done everything within her power to avoid Nate, yet through no fault of her own, she was spending the afternoon in his company. They didn't get a chance to speak until they reached the elevator, but once the door glided shut, Susannah tried again. "I can't go to a baseball game dressed like this."

"You look fine to me."

"But I've got a business suit on."

"Hey, don't sweat the small stuff." His hand clasped hers and when the elevator door opened on the bottom floor, he led her out of the building. Once outside, he quickened his pace as he headed toward the stadium.

"I want you to know I don't appreciate this one bit," she said, forced to half run to keep pace with his long-legged stride.

"If you're going to complain, wait until we're inside and settled. As I recall, you get testy on an empty stomach." His smile could have caused a nuclear meltdown, but she was determined not to let it influence her. Nate had a lot of nerve to come bursting into her office, and as soon as she could catch her breath, she'd tell him so.

"Don't worry, I'm going to feed you," he promised as they waited at a red light.

His words did nothing to reassure her. Heaven only knew what John Hammer thought—although she had to admit that her employer's reaction had baffled her. John was as hardworking and dedicated as Susannah herself. It wasn't like him to fall in with Nate's offbeat idea of attending a ball game in the middle of the afternoon. In fact, it almost seemed as if John knew Nate, or had heard of him. Hardly ever had she seen her employer show such enthusiasm when introduced to anyone.

The man at the gate took their tickets and Nate directed her to a pair of seats right behind home plate. Never having attended a professional baseball game before, Susannah didn't realize how good these seats were—until Nate pointed it out.

She'd no sooner sat down in her place than he leaped to his feet and raised his right hand, glove and all. Susannah slouched as low as she could in the uncomfortable seat. The next thing she knew, a bag of peanuts whizzed past her ear.

"Hey!" she cried, and jerked around.

"Don't panic," Nate said, chuckling. "I'm just playing catch with the vendor." Seconds after the words left his mouth he expertly caught another bag.

"Here." Nate handed her both bags. "The hot dog guy will be by in a minute."

Susannah had no intention of sitting still while food was being tossed about. "I'm getting out of here. If you want to play ball, go on the field."

Once more Nate laughed, the sound husky and rich. "If you're going to balk at every little thing, I know a good way to settle you down."

"Do you think I'm a complete idiot? First you drag me away from my office, then you insist on throwing food around like some schoolboy. I can't even begin to guess what's going to happen next and—"

She didn't get any further, although her outrage was mounting with every breath she drew. Before she could guess his intention, Nate planted his hands on her shoulders, pulled her against him and gave her one of his dynamite-packed kisses.

Completely unnerved, she numbly lowered herself back into her seat and closed her eyes, her pulse roaring in her ears.

A little later, Nate was pressing a fat hot dog into her lifeless hands. "I had them put everything on it," he said.

A glance at the overstuffed bun informed her that "everything" included pickles, mustard, ketchup, onions and sauerkraut and one or two other items she wasn't sure she could identify.

"Now eat it before I'm obliged to kiss you again."

His warning was all the incentive she needed. Several minutes had passed since he'd last kissed her and she was still so bemused she could hardly think. On cue, she lifted the hot dog to her mouth, prepared for the worst. But to her surprise, it didn't taste half bad. In fact, it was downright palatable. When she'd polished it off, she started on the peanuts, which were still warm from the roaster. Warm and salty, and excellent.

Another vendor strolled past and Nate bought them each a cold drink.

The first inning was over by the time Susannah finished eating. Nate reached for her hand. "Feel better?" His eyes were fervent and completely focused on her.

One look certainly had an effect on Susannah. Whenever her eyes met his she felt as though she was caught in a whirlpool and about to be sucked under. She'd tried to resist the pull, but it had been impossible.

"Susannah?" he asked. "Are you okay?"

She managed to nod. After a moment she said, "I still feel kind of foolish…."

"Why?"

"Come on, Nate. I'm the only person here in a business suit."

"I can fix that."

"Oh?" Susannah had her doubts. What did he plan to do? Undress her?

He gave her another of his knowing smiles and casually excused himself. Puzzled, Susannah watched as he made his way toward the concession stand. Then he was back—with a Mariners T-shirt in one hand, a baseball cap in the other.

Removing her suit jacket, Susannah slipped the T-shirt over her head. When she'd done that, Nate set the baseball cap on her head, adjusting it so the bill dipped low over her forehead.

"There," he said, satisfied. "You look like one of the home team now."

"Thanks." She smoothed the T-shirt over her straight skirt and wondered how peculiar she looked. Funny, but it didn't seem to matter. She was having a good time with Nate, and it felt wonderful to laugh and enjoy life.

"You're welcome."

They both settled back in their seats to give their full attention to the game. The Seattle Mariners were down by one run at the bottom of the fifth inning.

Susannah didn't know all that much about baseball, but the crowd was lending vociferous support to the home team and she loved the atmosphere, which crackled with excitement, as if everyone was waiting for something splendid to happen.

"You've been avoiding me," Nate said halfway through the sixth inning. "I want to know why."

She couldn't very well tell him the truth, but lying seemed equally unattractive. Pretending to concentrate on the game, Susannah shrugged, hoping he'd accept that as explanation enough.

"Susannah?"

She should've known he'd force the issue. "Because

I don't like what happens when you kiss me," she blurted out.

"What happens?" he echoed. "The first time we kissed, you nearly dealt my ego a fatal blow. As I recall, you claimed it was a pleasant experience. I believe you described it as 'nice,' and said that was about it."

Susannah kicked at the litter on the cement floor with the toes of her pumps, her eyes downcast. "Yes, I do remember saying something along those lines."

"You lied?"

He didn't need to drill her to prove his point. "All right," she admitted, "I lied. But you knew that all along. You must have, otherwise…"

"Otherwise what?"

"You wouldn't be kissing me every time you want to coerce me into doing something I don't want to do."

Crow's-feet fanned out beside his eyes as he grinned, making him look naughty and angelic at once.

"You knew all along," she repeated, "so don't give me that injured-ego routine!"

"There's electricity between us, Susannah, and it's about time you recognized that. I did, from the very first."

"Sure. But there's a big difference between standing next to an electrical outlet and fooling around with a high-voltage wire. I prefer to play it safe."

"Not me." He ran a knuckle down the side of her face. Circling her chin, his finger rested on her lips, which parted softly. "No," he said in a hushed voice, studying her. "I always did prefer to live dangerously."

"I've noticed." Nerve endings tingled at his touch, and Susannah held her breath until he removed his hand. Only then did she breathe normally again.

The cheering crowd alerted her to the fact that something important had taken place on the field. Glad to have her attention diverted from Nate, she watched as a Mariner rounded the bases for a home run. Pleased, she clapped politely, her enthusiasm far more restrained than that of the spectators around her.

That changed, however, at the bottom of the ninth. The bases were loaded and Susannah sat on the edge of her seat as the designated hitter approached home plate.

The fans chanted, "Grand slam, grand slam!" and Susannah soon joined in. The pitcher tossed a fastball, and unable to watch, she squeezed her eyes shut. But the sound of the wood hitting the ball was unmistakable. Susannah opened her eyes and jumped to her feet as the ball flew into left field and over the wall. The crowd went wild, and after doing an impulsive jig, Susannah threw her arms around Nate's neck and hugged him.

Nate appeared equally excited, and when Susannah had her feet back on the ground, he raised his fingers to his mouth and let loose a piercing whistle.

She was laughing and cheering and even went so far as to cup her hands over her mouth and boisterously yell her approval. It was then that she noticed Nate watching her. His eyes were wide with feigned shock, as if he couldn't believe the refined and businesslike Susannah Simmons would lower herself to such uninhibited behavior.

His apparent censure instantly cooled her reactions, and she returned to her seat and demurely folded her hands and crossed her ankles, embarrassed now by her response to something as mindless as a baseball game. When she dared to glance in Nate's direction, she discovered him watching her intently.

"Nate," she whispered, disconcerted by his attention. The game was over and the people around them had started to leave their seats. Susannah could feel the color in her cheeks. "Why are you looking at me like that?"

"You amaze me."

More likely, she'd disgraced herself in his eyes by her wild display. She was mortified.

"You're going to be all right, Susannah Simmons," he said cryptically. "We both are."

"Susannah, I didn't expect to find you home on a Saturday," Emily said as she stepped inside her sister's apartment. "Michelle and I are going to the Pike Place Market this morning and decided to drop by and see you first. You don't mind, do you?"

"No. Of course not. Come in." Susannah brushed the disheveled hair from her face. "What time is it anyway?"

"Eight-thirty."

"That late, huh?"

Emily chuckled. "I forgot. You like to sleep in on the weekends, don't you?"

"Don't worry about it," she said on the tail end of a yawn. "I'll put on a pot of coffee and be myself in no time."

Emily and Michelle followed her into the kitchen. Once the coffee was brewing, Susannah took the chair across from her sister. Michelle gleefully waved her arms, and despite the early hour, Susannah found herself smiling at her niece's enthusiasm for life. She held out her arms to the baby and was pleasantly surprised when Michelle came happily into them.

"She remembers you," Emily said.

"Of course she does," Susannah said as she nuzzled her niece's neck. "We had some great times, didn't we, kiddo? Especially when it came to feeding you plums."

Emily chuckled. "I don't think I'll ever be able to thank you enough for keeping Michelle that weekend. It was just what Robert and I needed."

"Don't mention it." Susannah dismissed Emily's appreciation with a weak gesture of her hand. She was the one who'd profited from that zany weekend. It might've been several more weeks before she met Nate if it hadn't been for Michelle.

Emily sighed. "I've been trying to get hold of you, but you're never home."

"Why didn't you leave a message?"

Emily shook her head and her long braid swung back and forth. "You know I hate doing that. I get all tongue-tied and I can't seem to talk. You might phone *me* some-time, you know."

Over the past couple of weeks, Susannah had consid-ered it, but she'd been avoiding her sister because she knew that the minute she called, Emily was going to ply her with questions about Nate.

"Have you been working late every night?" Emily asked.

Susannah dropped her gaze. "Not exactly."

"Then you must've been out with Nate Townsend." Emily didn't give her time to respond, but immediately started jabbering away. "I don't mind telling you, Susan-nah, both Robert and I were impressed with your new neighbor. He was wonderful with Michelle, and from the way he was looking at you, I think he's interested. Now, please don't tell me to keep my nose out of this. You're twenty-eight, for heaven's sake, and that biologi-cal clock is ticking away. If you're ever going to settle down and get serious about a man, the time is now. And personally, I don't think you'll find anyone better than Nate. Why, he's…"

She paused to breathe, giving Susannah the chance she'd been waiting for. "Coffee?"

Emily blinked, then nodded. "You didn't listen to a word I said, did you?"

"I listened."

"But you didn't *hear* a single word."

"Sure I did," Susannah countered. "You're saying I'd be a fool not to put a ring through Nate Townsend's nose. You want me to marry him before I lose my last chance at motherhood."

"Exactly," Emily said, looking pleased that she'd conveyed her message so effectively.

Michelle squirmed and Susannah set her on the floor to crawl around and explore.

"Well?" Emily pressed. "What do you think?"

"About marrying Nate? It would never work," she said calmly, as though they were discussing something as mundane as stock options, "for more reasons than you realize. But to satisfy your curiosity I'll list a few. First and foremost I've got a career and he doesn't, and furthermore—"

"Nate's unemployed?" her sister gasped. "But how can he not work? I mean, this is an expensive complex. Didn't you tell me the condominium next to yours is nearly twice as large? How can he afford to live there if he doesn't have a job?"

"I have no idea."

Susannah forgot about Nate for the moment as her eyes followed Michelle, astonished by how much she'd missed her. She stood and got two cups from the cupboard.

"That's not decaffeinated, is it?" Emily asked.

"No."

"Then don't bother pouring me a cup. I gave up caffeine years ago."

"Right." Susannah should have remembered. Michelle crawled across the kitchen floor toward her and, using

Susannah's nightgown for leverage, pulled herself into a standing position. She smiled proudly at her achievement.

"Listen," Susannah said impulsively, leaning over to pick up her niece. "Why don't you leave Michelle with me? We'll take this morning to become reacquainted and you can do your shopping without having to worry about her."

There was a shocked silence. "Susannah?" Emily said. "Did I hear you correctly? I thought I just heard you volunteer to babysit."

Seven

The morning was bright and sunny, and unable to resist, Susannah opened the sliding glass door and let the salty breeze off Elliott Bay blow into her apartment. Sitting on the kitchen floor with a saucepan and a wooden spoon, Michelle proceeded to demonstrate her musical talents by pounding out a loud enthusiastic beat.

When the phone rang, Susannah knew it was Nate.

"Good morning," she said, pushing her hair behind her ears. She hadn't pinned it up when she got dressed, knowing Nate preferred it down, and she didn't try to fool herself with excuses for leaving it that way.

"Morning," he breathed into the phone. "Do you have a drummer visiting?"

"No, a special friend. I think she'd like to say hello. Wait a minute." Susannah put down the receiver and lifted Michelle from the floor. Holding the baby on her hip, she pressed the telephone receiver to the side of Michelle's face. Practically on cue, the child spouted an excited flow of gibberish.

"I think she said good morning," Susannah explained.

"Michelle?"

"How many other babies would pay me a visit?"

"How many Simmons girls are there?"

"Only Emily and me," she answered with a soft laugh, "but trust me, the two of us were enough for any one set of parents to handle."

Nate's responding chuckle was warm and seductive. "Are you in the mood for more company?"

"Sure. If you bring the Danish, I'll provide the coffee."

"You've got yourself a deal."

It wasn't until several minutes had passed that Susannah realized how little resistance she'd been putting up lately when it came to Nate. Since the baseball game, she'd given up trying to avoid him; she simply didn't have the heart for it, although deep down, she knew anything beyond friendship was impossible. Yet despite her misgivings, after that one afternoon with him she'd come away feeling exhilarated. Being with Nate was like recapturing a part of her youth that had somehow escaped her. But even though seeing him was fun, it wasn't meant to last, and Susannah reminded herself of that every time they were together. Nate Townsend was like an unexpected burst of sunshine on an overcast day, but soon the rain would come, the way it always did. Susannah wasn't going to be fooled into believing there could ever be anything permanent between them.

When Nate arrived, the reunion was complete. He lifted Michelle high in the air and Susannah smiled at the little girl's squeals of delight.

"Where's Emily?" he wanted to know.

"Shopping. She won't be more than an hour or so."

With Michelle in one arm, Nate moved into the kitchen, where Susannah was dishing up the pastries and pouring coffee. "She's grown, hasn't she?" she said.

"Is that another new tooth?" he asked, peering inside the baby's mouth.

"It might be," Susannah replied, taking a look herself.

Nate slipped his free arm around her shoulder and smiled at her. "Your hair's down," he murmured, his smile caressing her upturned face.

She nodded, not knowing how else to respond, although a dozen plausible excuses raced through her mind. But none of them would have been true.

"For me?"

Once more, she answered him with a slight nod.

"Thank you," he whispered, his face so close to her own that his words were like a kiss.

Susannah leaned into him, pressing herself against his solid length. When he kissed her, she could hardly stop herself from melting into his arms.

Michelle thought it was great fun to have two adults

for company. She wove her fingers into Susannah's hair and yanked until Susannah was forced to pull away from Nate.

Smiling, Nate disengaged the baby's hand from her aunt's hair and kissed Susannah again. "Hmm," he said when he lifted his head. "You taste better than any sweet roll ever could."

Unnerved, and suddenly feeling shy, Susannah busied herself setting the pastries on the table.

"Do you have plans for today?" he asked, taking a chair, Michelle gurgling happily on his lap.

Michelle was content for now, but from experience Susannah knew she'd want to be back on the floor soon. "I... I was planning to go to the office for an hour or so."

"I don't think so," Nate said flatly.

"You don't?"

"I'm taking you out." He surveyed her navy-blue slacks and the winter-white sweater she wore. "I don't suppose you have any jeans."

Susannah nodded. She knew she did, somewhere, but it was years since she'd worn them. As long ago as college, and maybe even her last year of high school. "I don't know if they'll fit, though."

"Go try them on."

"Why? What are you planning? Knowing you, I could end up on top of Mount Rainier looking over a crevasse, with no idea how I got there."

"We're going to fly a kite today," he said casually, as if it was something they'd done several times.

Susannah thought she'd misunderstood him. Nate obviously loved this kind of surprise. First a baseball game in the middle of a workday, and now kites?

"You heard me right. Now go find your jeans."

"But…kites…that's for kids. Frankly, Nate," she said, her voice gaining conviction, "I don't happen to have one hidden away in a closet. Besides, isn't that something parents do with their children?"

"No, it's for everyone. Adults have been known to have fun, too. Don't worry about a thing. I built a huge one and it's ready for testing."

"A kite?" she repeated, holding in the desire to laugh outright. She'd been in grade school when she'd last attempted anything so…so juvenile.

By the time Susannah had rummaged in her closet and found an old pair of jeans, Emily had returned for Michelle. Nate let her sister inside, but the bedroom door was cracked open, and Susannah could hear the conversation. She held her breath, first because her hips were a tiny bit wider than the last time she'd worn her jeans, and also because Susannah could never be sure what her sister was going to say. Or do.

It'd be just like Emily to start telling Nate how suitable Susannah would be as a wife. That thought was sobering and for a moment Susannah stopped wriggling into her pants.

"Nate," she heard her sister say, "it's so good of you to help with Michelle." In her excitement, her voice was a full octave higher than usual.

"No problem. Susannah will be out in a minute—she's putting on a pair of jeans. We're going to Gas Works Park to fly a kite."

There was a short pause. "Susannah wearing jeans and flying a kite? You mean she's actually going with you?"

"Of course I am. Don't look so shocked," Susannah said, walking into the room. "How did the shopping go?"

Emily couldn't seem to close her mouth. She stared at her sister to the point of embarrassment, then swung her gaze to Nate and back to Susannah again.

Susannah realized she must look different, wearing jeans and with her hair down, but it certainly didn't warrant this openmouthed gawking.

"Emily?" Susannah waved her hand in front of her sister's face in an effort to bring her back to earth.

"Oh…the shopping went just fine. I was able to get the fresh herbs I wanted. Basil and thyme and…some others." As though in a daze, Emily lifted the home-sewn bag draped over her arm as evidence of her successful trip to the market.

"Good," Susannah said enthusiastically, wanting to smooth over her sister's outrageous reaction. "Michelle wasn't a bit of trouble. If you need me to watch her again, just say so."

Her sister's eyes grew wider. She swallowed and nodded. "Thanks. I'll remember that."

* * *

The sky was as blue as Nate's eyes, Susannah thought, sitting with her knees tucked under her chin on the lush green grass of Gas Works Park. The wind whipped Nate's box kite back and forth as he scrambled from one hill to the next, letting the brisk breeze carry the multicolored crate in several directions. As it was late September, Susannah didn't expect many more glorious Indian summer days like this one.

She closed her eyes and soaked up the sun. Her spirits raced with the kites that abounded in the popular park. She felt like tossing back her head and laughing triumphantly, for no other reason than that it felt good to be alive.

"I'm beat," Nate said, dropping down on the grass beside her. He lay on his back, arms and legs spread-eagle.

"Where's the kite?"

"I gave it to one of the kids who didn't have one."

Susannah smiled. That sounded exactly like something Nate would do. He'd spent hours designing and constructing the box kite, and yet he'd impulsively given it away without a second thought.

"Actually I begged the kid to take it, before I keeled over from exhaustion," he amended. "Don't let anyone tell you otherwise. Flying a kite is hard work."

Work was a subject Susannah stringently avoided with Nate. From the first he'd been completely open with her. Open and honest. She was confident that if she quizzed him about his profession or lack of one, he'd answer her truthfully.

Susannah had decided that what she didn't know about him couldn't upset her. Nate apparently had plenty of money. He certainly didn't seem troubled by financial difficulties. But it was his attitude that worried her. He seemed to see life as a grand adventure; he leaped from one interest to another without rhyme or reason. Nothing appeared to be more important or vital than the moment.

"You're frowning," he said. He slipped a hand around her neck and pulled her down until her face was within inches of his own. "Aren't you having fun?"

She nodded, unable to deny the obvious.

"Then what's the problem?"

"Nothing."

He hesitated and the edges of his mouth lifted sensuously. "It's a good thing you didn't become an attorney," he said with a roguish grin. "You'd never be able to fool a jury."

Susannah was astonished that Nate knew she'd once seriously considered going into law.

He grinned at her. "Emily told me you'd thought about entering law school."

Susannah blinked a couple of times, then smiled, too. She was determined not to ruin this magnificent afternoon with her concerns.

"Kiss me, Susannah," he whispered. The humor had left his face and his gaze searched hers.

Her breath caught. She lifted her eyes and quickly glanced around. The park was crowded and children were everywhere.

"No," he said, cradling the sides of her face. "No fair peeking. I want you to kiss me no matter how many spectators there are."

"But—"

"If you don't kiss me, I'll simply have to kiss you. And, honey, if I do, watch out because—"

Not allowing him to finish, she lowered her mouth and gently skimmed her lips over his. Even that small sample was enough to send the blood racing through her veins. Whatever magic quality this man had should be bottled and sold over the counter. Susannah knew she'd be the first one in line to buy it.

"Are you always this stingy?" he asked when she raised her head.

"In public, yes."

His eyes were smiling and Susannah swore she could have drowned in his look. He exhaled, then bounded to his feet with an energy she had to envy.

"I'm starved," he announced, reaching out for her. Susannah placed her hand in his and he pulled her to her feet. "But I hope you realize," he whispered close to her ear, wrapping his arm around her waist, "my appetite isn't for food. I'm crazy about you, Susannah Simmons. Eventually we're going to have to do something about that."

* * *

"I hope I'm not too early," Susannah said as she entered her sister's home on Capitol Hill. When Emily had called to invite her to Sunday dinner, she hadn't bothered to disguise her intentions. Emily was dying to grill Susannah about her budding relationship with Nate Townsend. A week ago, Susannah would've found an excuse to get out of tonight's dinner. But after spending an entire Saturday with Nate, she was so confused that she was willing to talk this out with her sister, who seemed so much more competent in dealing with male/female relationships.

"Your timing's perfect," Emily said, coming out of the kitchen to greet her. She wore a full-length skirt with a bib apron, and her long hair was woven into a single braid that fell halfway down her back.

"Here." Susannah handed her sister a bottle of chardonnay, hoping it was appropriate for the meal.

"How thoughtful," Emily murmured, leading her back into the kitchen. The house was an older one, built in the early forties, with a large family kitchen. The red linoleum countertop was crowded with freshly canned tomatoes. Boxes of jars were stacked on the floor, along with a wicker basket filled with sun-dried diapers. A rope of garlic dangled above the sink and a row of potted plants lined the windowsill.

"Whatever you're serving smells wonderful."

"It's lentil soup."

Emily opened the oven and pulled out the rack, wadding up the skirt of her apron to protect her fingers. "I made a fresh apple pie. Naturally I used organically grown apples so you don't need to worry."

"Oh, good." That hadn't been a major concern of Susannah's.

"Where's Michelle?" Father and daughter were conspicuously absent.

Emily turned around, looking mildly guilty, and Susannah realized that her sister had gone to some lengths to provide time alone with her. No doubt she was anxious to wring out as much information about Nate as possible. Not that Susannah had a lot to tell.

"How was your day in the park?"

Susannah took a seat on the stool and made herself comfortable for the coming inquisition. "Great. I really enjoyed it."

"You like Nate, don't you?"

Like was the understatement of the year. Contrary to every ounce of sense she possessed, Susannah was falling in love with her neighbor. It wasn't what she wanted, but she hadn't been able to stop herself.

"Yes, I like him," she answered after a significant pause.

Emily seemed thrilled by her admission. "I thought as much," she said, nodding profoundly. She pushed a stool next to Susannah and sat down. Emily's hands were rarely idle, and true to form, she reached for her crocheting.

"I'm waiting," Susannah said, growing impatient.

"For what?"

"For the lecture."

Emily cracked a knowing smile. "I was gathering my thoughts. You were always the one who could evaluate things so well. I always had trouble with that and you aced every paper."

"School reports have very little to do with real life," Susannah reminded her. How much simpler it would be if she could just look up everything she needed to know about dealing with Nate.

"I knew that, but I wasn't sure you did."

Perhaps Susannah hadn't until she met Nate. "Emily," she said, her stomach tightening, "I need to ask you something…important. How did you know you loved Robert? What was it that told you the two of you were meant to share your lives?" Susannah understood that she was practically laying her cards faceup on the table, but she was past the point of subtlety. She wanted hard facts.

Her sister smiled and tugged at her ball of yarn before she responded. "I don't think you're going to like my answer," she murmured, frowning slightly. "It was the first time Robert kissed me."

Susannah nearly toppled from her perch on the stool, remembering her experience with Nate. "What happened?"

"We'd gone for a nature walk in the rain forest over on the Olympic Peninsula and had stopped to rest. Robert helped me remove my backpack, then he looked into my eyes and leaned over and kissed me." She sighed softly at the memory. "I don't think he intended to do it because he looked so shocked afterward."

"Then what?"

"Robert took off his own backpack and asked if I minded that he'd kissed me. Naturally I told him I rather liked it, and he sat down next to me and did it again— only this time it wasn't a peck on the lips but a full-blown kiss." Emily's shoulders sagged a little in a sigh. "The moment his lips touched mine I couldn't think, I couldn't breathe, I couldn't even move. When he finished I was trembling so much I thought something might be physically wrong with me."

"So would you say you felt…electricity?"

"Exactly."

"And you never had that with any of the other men you dated?"

"Never."

Susannah wiped a hand down her face. "You're right," she whispered. "I don't like your answer."

Emily paused in her crocheting to glance at her. "Nate kissed you and you felt something?"

Susannah nodded. "I was nearly electrocuted."

"Oh, Susannah, you poor thing!" She patted her sister's hand. "You don't know what to do, do you?"

"No," she admitted, feeling wretched.

"You never expected to fall in love, did you?"

Slowly Susannah shook her head. And it couldn't be happening at a worse time. The promotion was going to

be announced within the next week, and the entire direction of her life could be altered if she became involved
with Nate. She didn't even know if that was what either
of them wanted. Susannah felt mystified by everything
going on in her life, which until a few short weeks ago
had been so straightforward and uncluttered.

"Are you thinking of marriage?" Emily asked outright.

"Marriage," Susannah echoed weakly. It seemed the
natural conclusion when two people were falling in love.
She was willing to acknowledge her feelings, but she
wasn't completely confident Nate felt the same things
she did. Nor was she positive that he was ready to move
into something as permanent as a lifelong commitment.
She knew *she* wasn't, and the very thought of all this
was enough to throw her into a tizzy.

"I don't…know about marriage," Susannah said. "We
haven't discussed anything like that." The fact was, they
hadn't even talked about dating regularly.

"Trust me, if you leave it to Nate the subject of
marriage will never come up. Men never want to talk
about getting married. The topic is left totally up to us
women."

"Oh, come on—"

"No, it's true. From the time Eve slipped Adam the
apple, we've been stuck with the burden of taming men,
and it's never more difficult than when it comes to con-
vincing one he should take a wife."

"But surely Robert wanted to get married?"

"Don't be silly. Robert's like every other man alive. I had to convince him this was what he wanted. Subtlety is the key, Susannah. In other words, I chased Robert until he caught me." She stopped working her crochet hook to laugh at her own wit.

From the first day she met her brother-in-law, Susannah had assumed he'd taken one look at her sister and dropped to his knees to propose. It had always seemed obvious to Susannah that they were meant for each other, far more obvious than it was that Nate was right for her.

"I don't know, Emily," she said with a deep sigh. "Everything's so confused in my mind. How could I possibly be so attracted to this man? It doesn't make any sense! Do you know what we did yesterday afternoon when we'd finished at the park?" She didn't wait for a response. "Nate brought over his Nintendo game and Super Mario Brothers cartridge, and we played video games. Me! I can't believe it even now. It was a pure waste of time."

"Did you have fun?"

That was a question Susannah wanted to avoid. She'd laughed until her stomach hurt. They'd challenged each other to see who could achieve the higher score, and then had done everything possible to sabotage each other.

Nate had discovered a sensitive area behind her ear and taken to kissing her there just when she was about to outscore him. Fair was fair, however, and Susannah soon discovered that Nate had his own area of vulnerability. Without a qualm, she'd used it against him, effectively disrupting his game. Soon they both forgot Nintendo and became far more interested in learning about each other.

"We had fun" was all Susannah was willing to admit.

"What about the kite flying?"

Her sister didn't know when to quit. "Then, too," she said reluctantly. "And at the baseball game Thursday, as well."

"He took you to a Mariners game…on Thursday? But they played in the middle of the afternoon. Did you actually leave the office?"

Susannah nodded, without explaining the details of how Nate had practically kidnapped her. "Back to you and Robert," she said, trying to change the subject.

"You want to know how I convinced him he wanted to get married? It wasn't really that difficult."

For Emily it wouldn't have been, but for Susannah it would be another story entirely. The biggest problem was that she wasn't sure she *wanted* Nate to be convinced. However, she should probably learn these things for future reference. She'd listen to what her sister had to say and make up her mind later.

"Remember that old adage—the way to a man's heart is through his stomach? It's true. Men equate food with comfort and love—that's a well-known fact."

"Then I'm in trouble," Susannah said flatly. Good grief, she thought, Nate could cook far better than she could any day of the week. She couldn't attract him with her cooking. All she had in the way of looks was her classic profile. Painful as it was to accept, men simply weren't attracted to her.

"Now don't overreact. Just because you can't whip up a five-course meal doesn't mean your life is over before it even begins."

"My married life is. I can't put together soup and a sandwich and you know it."

"Susannah, I wish you'd stop demeaning yourself. You're bright and pretty, and Nate would be the luckiest man in the world if he were to marry you."

Now that they were actually discussing marriage, Susannah was having mixed feelings. "I...don't know if Nate's the marrying kind," she muttered. "For that matter, I don't know if I am."

Emily ignored that. "I'll start you out on something simple and we'll work our way up."

"I don't understand."

"Cookies," Emily explained. "There isn't a man alive who doesn't appreciate homemade cookies. There's something magical about them—really," she added when Susannah cast her a doubtful glance. "Cookies create an aura of domestic bliss—it sounds crazy, but it's true. A man can't resist a woman who bakes him cookies. They remind him of home and mother and a fire crackling in the fireplace." Emily paused and sighed. "Now, it's also true that men have been fighting this feeling since the beginning of time."

"What feeling?"

Emily rolled her eyes. "Domestic contentment. It's exactly what they need and want, but they fight it."

Susannah mulled over her sister's words. "Now that you mention it, Nate did say chocolate chip's his favorite."

"See what I mean?"

Susannah couldn't believe she was pursuing this subject with her sister. Okay, so she and Nate had shared some good times. But lots of people had good times together. She was also willing to admit there was a certain amount of chemistry between them. But that wasn't any reason to run to the nearest altar.

For the past few minutes, she'd been trying to sensibly discuss this situation between Nate and her with her sister, and before she even knew how it'd happened, Emily had her talking about weddings and chocolate chip cookies. At this rate Emily would have her married and pregnant by the end of the week.

"So how did dinner with your sister go?" Nate asked her later that same night. He'd been on the Seattle waterfront earlier in the day and had brought her back a polished glass paperweight made of ash from the Mount St. Helens volcano.

"Dinner was fine," she said quickly, perhaps too quickly. "Emily and I had a nice talk."

Nate put his arms around her, trapping her against the kitchen counter. "I missed you."

Swallowing tensely, she murmured, "I missed you, too."

He threaded his fingers though the length of her hair, pulling it away from her face and holding it there. "You wore it down again today," he whispered against her neck.

"Yes… Emily says she likes it better that way, too." Talking shouldn't be this difficult, but every time Nate touched her it was. Susannah's knees had the consistency of pudding and her resolve was just as weak. After analyzing her talk with Emily, Susannah had decided to let the situation between her and Nate cool for a while. Things were happening much too quickly. She wasn't ready, and she doubted Nate was, either.

When he kissed her lightly at the hollow of her throat, it was all she could do to remain in an upright position. As she braced her hands against his chest, she began to push him gently away. But when his lips traveled up the side of her neck, blazing a trail of moist kisses, she was lost. His mouth grazed the line of her jaw, slowly edging its way toward her lips, prolonging the inevitable until Susannah thought she'd dissolve at his feet.

When he finally kissed her mouth, they both sighed, caught in a swelling tide of longing. His mouth moved hungrily over hers. Then he tugged at her lower lip with his teeth, creating a whole new wave of sensation.

By the time Nate went back to his own apartment, Susannah was shaking from the inside out. She'd walked all the way to the kitchen before she was conscious of her intent. She stared at the phone for a long moment. Calling Emily demanded every ounce of courage she had. With a deep calming breath, she punched out her sister's number.

"Emily," she said when her sister answered on the second ring, "do you have a recipe for chocolate chip cookies?"

Eight

The recipe for chocolate chip cookies was safely tucked away in a kitchen drawer. The impulse to bake them had passed quickly and reason had returned.

Monday morning, back at the office, Susannah realized how close she'd come to the edge of insanity. The vice presidency was almost within her grasp, and she'd worked too long and too hard to let this promotion slip through her fingers simply because she felt a little weak in the knees when Nate Townsend kissed her. To even contemplate anything beyond friendship was like…like amputating her right hand because she had a sliver in her index finger. She'd been overreacting, which was understandable, since she'd never experienced such a strong attraction to a man before.

"There's a call for you on line one," Ms. Brooks told

her. She paused, then added dryly, "It sounds like that nice young man who stopped by last week."

Nate. Squaring her shoulders—and her resolve—Susannah picked up the phone. "This is Susannah Simmons."

"Good morning, beautiful."

"Hello, Nate," she said stiffly. "What can I do for you?"

He chuckled. "That's a leading question if there ever was one. Trust me, honey, you don't want to know."

"Nate," she breathed, briefly closing her eyes. "Please. I'm busy. What do you want?"

"Other than your body?"

Hot color leaped into her cheeks and she gave a distressed gasp. "We'd better put an end to this conversation—"

"All right, all right, I'm sorry. I just woke up and I was lying here thinking how nice it would be if we could escape for the day. Could I tempt you with a drive to the ocean? We could dig for clams, build a sand castle, and then make a fire and sing our favorite camp songs."

"As a matter of interest, I've been up for several hours. And since you've obviously forgotten, I do have a job—an important one. At least it's important to me. Now exactly what is the purpose of this call, other than to embarrass me?"

"Lunch."

"I can't today. I've got an appointment."

"Okay." He sighed, clearly frustrated. "How about dinner, just you and me?"

"I'm working late and was planning on sending out for something. Thanks, anyway."

"Susannah," he said in a burst of impatience, "are we going to go through this again? You should've figured out by now that avoiding me won't change anything."

Perhaps not, she reasoned, but it would certainly help. "Listen, Nate, I really am busy. Perhaps we should continue this conversation another time."

"Like next year—I know you. You'd be willing to bury your head in the sand for the next fifteen years if I didn't come and prod you along. I swear, I've never met a more stubborn woman."

"Goodbye, Nate."

"Susannah," he persisted, "what about dinner? Come on, change your mind. We have a lot to talk about."

"No. I wasn't lying—I do have to work late. The fact is, I can't go outside and play today—or tonight."

"Ouch," Nate cried. "That hurt."

"Perhaps it hit too close to home."

A short silence followed. "Maybe it did," he murmured thoughtfully. "But before we hang up, I do want to know when I can see you again."

Susannah leaned forward and stretched her arm across the desk to her calendar, flipping the pages until she found a blank space. "How about lunch on Thursday?"

"All right," he said, "I'll see you Thursday at noon."

For a long moment after they'd hung up, Susannah kept her hand on the receiver. As crazy as it seemed, spending the afternoon with Nate at the beach sounded far too appealing. The way he made her think and feel was almost frightening. The man was putting her whole career in jeopardy. Something had to be done, only Susannah wasn't sure what.

An hour later, Ms. Brooks tapped on her door and walked inside, carrying a huge bouquet of red roses. "These just arrived."

"For me?" Surely there was some mistake. No one had ever sent her flowers. There'd never been any reason. There wasn't now.

"The card has your name on it," her assistant informed her. She handed the small white envelope to Susannah.

Not until Eleanor had left the room did Susannah read the card. The roses were from Nate, who wrote that he was sorry for having disturbed her earlier. She was right, he told her, now wasn't the time to go outside and play. He'd signed it with his love. Closing her eyes, Susannah held the card to her breast and fought down a swelling surge of emotion. The least he could do was stop being so damn wonderful. Then everything would be easier.

As it turned out, Susannah finished work relatively early that evening and returned home a little after seven. Her apartment was dark and empty—but it was that way every night and she didn't understand why it should matter to her now. Yet it did.

It was when she stood outside Nate's door and knocked that she realized how impulsive her behavior had become since she'd met him. She was doing everything in her power to avoid him, and yet she couldn't stay away.

"Susannah," he said when he opened the door. "This is a pleasant surprise."

She laced her fingers together. "I… I just wanted you to know how much I appreciated the roses. They're lovely and the gesture was so thoughtful."

"Come in," he said, stepping inside. "I'll put on some coffee."

"No, thanks. I've got to get back, but I wanted to thank you for the flowers…and to apologize if I sounded waspish on the phone. Monday mornings aren't exactly my best time."

Grinning, he leaned against the doorjamb and crossed his arms over his broad chest. "Actually, I'm the one who owed you an apology. I should never have phoned you this morning. I was being selfish. You do have an important job and these are anxious days for you. Didn't you tell me you'd hear about that promotion within the next week or two?"

Susannah nodded.

"You might find this hard to believe, but I don't want to say or do anything to take that away from you. You're a dedicated, hardworking employee and you deserve to be the first female vice president of H&J Lima."

His confidence in her was reassuring, but it confused

her, too. From everything she'd witnessed about Nate, she could only conclude that he didn't appreciate hard work and its rewards.

"If I do get the promotion," she said, watching him closely, "things will change between you and me. I… I won't have a lot of free time for a while."

"Does that mean you won't be able to go outside and play as often?" he asked, his mouth curving into a sensuous smile. He was taunting her with the words she'd used earlier that day.

"Exactly."

"I can accept that. Just…" He hesitated.

"What?" Nate was frowning and that wasn't like him. He wore a saucy grin as often as he donned a baseball cap. "Tell me," she demanded.

"I want you to do everything possible to achieve your dreams, Susannah, but there are plenty of pitfalls along the way."

Now it was her turn to frown. She wasn't sure she understood what he was talking about.

"All I'm saying," he elaborated, "is that you shouldn't lose sight of who you are because this vice presidency means so much to you. And most important, count the cost." With that he stepped forward, gazed hungrily into her eyes and kissed her lightly on the lips. Then he stepped back reluctantly.

For a second Susannah teetered, then she moved forward into his arms as if that was the most natural place in the world for her to be. Even now, she didn't entirely understand what he meant, but she couldn't mistake the tenderness she heard in his voice. Once her head had cleared and she wasn't wrapped up in this incredible longing he created every time he touched her, she'd mull over his words.

Susannah woke around midnight, and rolling over, adjusted her pillow. The illuminated dial on her clock radio told her she'd only been sleeping for a couple of hours. She yawned, wondering what had woken her out of a sound peaceful slumber. Closing her eyes, she tucked the blankets more securely over her shoulders, determined to sleep. She tried visualizing herself accepting the promotion to vice president. Naturally, there'd be a nice write-up about her in the evening paper and possibly a short piece in a business journal or two.

Susannah's eyes drifted open as she recalled Nate's words reminding her not to forget who she was. Who *was* she? A list of possible replies skipped easily through her mind. She was Susannah Simmons, future vice president in charge of marketing for the largest sporting-goods store in the country. She was a daughter, a sister, an aunt… And then it hit her. *She was a woman.* That was what Nate had been trying to tell her. It was the same message Emily had tried to get across to her on Sunday. From the time Susannah had set her goals, she'd dedicated her life to her career and pushed aside every feminine part of herself. Now was the time for her to deal with that aspect of her life.

* * *

It was the following evening after work. Susannah was leaning against the kitchen counter, struggling to remove the heavy food mixer from its reinforced cardboard box. Emily's recipe for chocolate chip cookies made three dozen. After her trip to the grocery, plus a jaunt to the hardware store for the mixer, cookie sheets and measuring utensils, these cookies were costing her $4.72 apiece.

Price be damned. She was setting out to prove something important—although she wasn't sure exactly what. She would've preferred to dismiss all her sister's talk about cookies being equated with warmth and love as a philosophy left over from an earlier generation. Susannah didn't actually believe Emily's theory, but she wanted to give it a try. Susannah didn't know why she was doing this anymore. All she knew was that she had this urge to bake chocolate chip cookies.

Emily had eagerly given her the recipe, and Susannah had read it carefully. Just how difficult could baking cookies be?

Not very, she determined twenty minutes later when everything was laid out on her extended counter. Pushing up the sleeves of her shirt, she turned on the radio to keep her company. Next she tied the arms of an old shirt around her waist, using that as an apron. Emily always seemed to wear one when she worked in the kitchen and if her sister did, then it must be the thing to do.

The automatic mixer was blending the butter and

white sugar nicely and, feeling extraordinarily proud of herself, Susannah cracked the eggs on the edge of the bowl with a decided flair.

"Damn," she cried when half the shell fell into the swirling blades. She glared at it a moment, watching helplessly as the beater broke the fragile shell into a thousand bits. Shrugging, she figured a little extra protein—or was it calcium?—wasn't going to hurt anyone. Finally she turned off the mixer and stirred in the flour, then the chocolate chips.

The oven was preheated exactly as the recipe required when Susannah slipped the shiny new cookie sheet inside. She closed the oven door with a swing of her hip and set the timer for twelve minutes.

Sampling a blob of dough from the end of her finger, she had to admit it was tasty. At least as good as Emily's. But Susannah considered it best not to let anyone know her secret ingredient was eggshell.

With a sense of genuine satisfaction, she poured herself a cup of coffee and sat down at the table with the evening paper.

A few minutes later she smelled smoke. Suspiciously sniffing the air, she set the paper aside. It couldn't possibly be her cookies—they'd been in the oven less than five minutes. To be on the safe side, however, she reached for a towel and opened the oven door.

She was immediately assaulted by billowing waves of smoke, followed by flames that licked out at her. Gasping in horror, she dropped the towel and gave a piercing scream. "Fire! Fire!"

The smoke alarm blared, and she thought she'd never heard anything louder in her life. Like a madwoman, Susannah raced for the door, throwing it open in an effort to allow the smoke to escape. Then she ran back to the table and hurled her coffee straight into the belly of the oven. Coughing hoarsely, she slammed the door shut.

"Susannah!" Breathless, Nate burst into her condominium.

"I started a fire," she shouted above the deafening din of the smoke alarm. Her voice still sounded raspy.

"Where?" Nate circled her table several times, looking frantically for the source of her panic.

"In the oven." Standing aside, she covered her face with her hands, not wanting to look.

A few minutes later, Nate took her in his arms. The smoke alarm was off. Two blackened sheets of charred cookies were angled into the sink. "Are you all right?"

Somehow she managed a nod.

"You didn't burn yourself?"

She didn't have so much as a blister and told him so.

Gently he brushed the hair away from her face, and expelled his breath, apparently to ease his tension. "Okay, how did the fire get started?"

"I don't know," she said dismally. "I… I did everything the recipe said, but when I put the cookies in the oven they…they caught on fire." Her voice quavered as she spoke.

"The cookies weren't responsible for the fire," he corrected her. "The cookie sheets were the culprits. They must've been new—it seems, ah, you forgot to remove the paper covering."

"Oh," she whispered. Her shoulders were shaking with the effort to repress her sobs.

"Susannah, there's no reason to cry. It was a reasonable mistake. Here, sit down." Gently he lowered her onto the kitchen chair and knelt in front of her, taking her hands in his and rubbing them. "It isn't the biggest disaster in the world."

"I know that," she wailed, unable to stop herself. "You don't understand. It was sort of a test...."

"A test?"

"Yes. Emily claims men love cookies...and I was baking them for you." She didn't go on to add that Emily also claimed that men loved the women who baked those cookies. "I can't cook... I started a fire...and I dropped part of the eggshell in the batter and...and left it.... I wasn't going to tell anyone."

Her confession must have shocked Nate because he stood up and left the room. Burying her face in her hands, Susannah endeavored to regain her composure and was doing an admirable job of it when Nate returned, holding a box of tissue.

Effortlessly lifting her into his arms, he pulled out the chair and sat down, holding her securely on his lap. "Okay, Betty Crocker, explain yourself."

She wiped her face dry with the tissue, feeling rather

silly at the way she was reacting. So she'd burned a couple of cookie sheets and ruined a batch of chocolate chip cookies. Big deal, she told herself with as much bravado as she could muster. "Explain what?"

"The comment about men loving cookies. Were you trying to prove something to me?"

"Actually, it was Emily I wanted to set straight," she whispered.

"You said you were baking them for my benefit."

"I was. Yesterday you said I shouldn't forget who I was, I should find myself, and… I think this sudden urge to bake was my response to that." Susannah suspected she wasn't making much sense. "Believe me, after today, I know I'm never going to be worth a damn in the kitchen."

"I don't remember suggesting you 'find yourself' in the kitchen," Nate said, looking confused.

"Actually, that part was Emily's idea," she admitted. "She's the one who gave me the recipe. My sister seems to believe a woman can coerce a man into giving up his heart and soul if she can bake chocolate chip cookies."

"And you want my heart and soul?"

"Of course not! Don't be ridiculous."

He hesitated for a moment and seemed to be considering her words. "Would it come as a surprise if I said I wanted yours?"

Susannah barely heard him; she wasn't in the mood to talk about heart and soul right now. She'd just shown how worthless she was in the kitchen. Her lack in that area hadn't particularly troubled her—until now. She'd made a genuine effort and fallen flat on her face. Not only that, having Nate witness her defeat had badly dented her pride. "When I was born something must've been missing from my genes," she murmured thoughtfully. "Obviously. I can't cook, and I don't sew, and I can hardly tell one end of a knitting needle from the other. I can't do any of the things that…normal people associate with the female gender."

"Susannah." He said her name on a disgruntled sigh. "Did you hear what I just said?"

She shook her head. She understood the situation perfectly. Some women had it and others didn't. Unfortunately, she was in the latter group.

"I was telling you something important. But I can see you're going to force me to say it without words." Cupping her face, Nate directed her mouth to his. But he didn't only kiss her. The hot moist tip of his tongue traced the sensitive line of her lips until she shivered with a whole new realm of unexplored sensations. All her disheartened thoughts dissolved instantly. She forgot to think, to breathe, to do anything but tremble in his arms. The fire in her oven was nothing compared to the one Nate had started in her body. Without conscious volition, she wrapped her arms around his neck and slanted her mouth over his, surrendering to the hot currents of excitement he'd created. She opened herself to him, granting him anything he wanted. His tongue found hers, and Susannah whimpered at the shock of pleasure she received. Her response was innocent and abandoned, unskilled and unknowing, yet eager.

"There," he whispered, supporting his forehead against hers, while he drew in deep breaths. His husky voice was unsteady.

He seemed to think their kiss was enough to prove everything. Susannah slowly opened her eyes. She took a steadying breath herself, one that made her tremble all the way to her toes. If she was going to say anything, it would be to whisper his name repeatedly and ask why he was doing this and then plead with him never to stop.

He threaded his fingers through her hair and kissed her again with a mastery that caused her to cling to him as if he were a life raft in a stormy sea. Unable to keep still, Susannah ran her palms along his neck and onto his shoulders and down the length of his arms. He must have liked her touch because he groaned and deepened the kiss even more.

"Unfortunately I don't think you're ready to hear it yet," he said.

"Hear what?" she asked, when she could find her voice.

"What I was telling you."

She puckered her brow. "What was that?"

"Forget the cookies. You're more than enough woman for any man."

She blinked, not understanding him. She barely understood herself.

"I never meant for you to test who you are. All I suggested was that you take care not to lose sight of your own personality. Goals are all well and good, even necessary, but you should always calculate the cost."

"Oh." Her mind was still too hazy to properly assimilate his meaning.

"Are you going to be all right?" he asked, as he grazed her cheek with his fingertips. He kissed Susannah's eyelids, closing them.

All she could do was nod.

"John Hammer would like to see you right away," Ms. Brooks told Susannah when she walked into her office Thursday morning.

Susannah's heart flew into her throat and stayed there for an uncomfortable moment. This was it. The day for which she'd been waiting five long years.

"Did he say what he wanted?" she asked, making an effort to appear at least outwardly calm.

"No," Ms. Brooks replied. "He just asked me to tell you he wanted to talk to you at your convenience."

Susannah slumped into her high-backed office chair. She propped her elbows on the desk and hid her face in her hands, trying to put some order to her muddled thoughts. "At my convenience," she repeated in a ragged whisper. "I didn't get the promotion. I just know it."

"Susannah," her assistant said sternly, calling her by her first name—something she rarely did. "I think you might be jumping to conclusions."

Susannah glared at her, annoyed by the woman's obtuseness. "If he planned to appoint me vice president, he would've called me into his office late in the afternoon. That's how it's done. Then he'd go through this long spiel about me being a loyal employee and what an asset I am to the company and all that stuff. Wanting to talk to me *now* means... Well, you know what it means."

"I can't say I do," Ms. Brooks said primly. "My suggestion is that you pull yourself together and get over to Mr. Hammer's office before he changes his mind."

Susannah got to her feet and stiffened her spine. But no matter how hard she tried she couldn't seem to stop shaking.

"I'll be waiting here when you get back," Ms. Brooks told her on her way out the door. She smiled then, an encouraging gesture that softened her austere features. "Break a leg, kid."

"I probably will, whatever happens," she muttered. If she didn't get this promotion, she was afraid she'd fall apart. Assuming a calm manner, she decided not to worry until she knew for sure.

John Hammer stood when she was announced. Susannah walked into his office, and the first thing she noticed was that the two men who were her competition hadn't been called. The company president smiled benignly and motioned toward a chair. Susannah sat on the edge of the cushion, doing her best to disguise how nervous she was.

A smile eased over her boss's face. "Good morning, Susannah..."

True to her word, Susannah's assistant was waiting for her when she strolled back to her office.

"Well?"

Eleanor Brooks followed her to her desk and watched as Susannah carefully sat down.

"What happened?" she demanded a second time. "Don't just sit there. Talk!"

Susannah's gaze slowly moved from the phone to her assistant. Then she started to chuckle. The laughter came from deep within her and she had to cover her mouth with her palms. When she could talk, she wiped the tears from the corners of her eyes.

"The first thing he did was ask me if I wanted to trade offices while mine was being repainted."

"What?"

Susannah thought Ms. Brooks's expression probably reflected her own when Mr. Hammer had asked that question. "That was my reaction, too," Susannah exclaimed. "I didn't understand what he meant. Then he said he was going to have my office redone, because he felt it was only right that the vice president in charge of marketing have a brand-new office."

"You got the promotion?" Eleanor Brooks clapped her hands in sheer delight, then pressed them over her lips.

"I got it," Susannah breathed, squeezing her eyes shut. "I actually got it."

"Congratulations."

"Thank you, thank you." Already she was reaching for the phone. She had to tell Nate. Only a few days before, he'd said she should go after her dreams, and now everything was neatly falling into place.

There was no answer at his apartment and, dejected, she replaced the receiver. But the need to talk to him consumed her, and she tried again every half hour until she thought she'd go crazy.

At noon, she was absorbed in her work when Ms. Brooks announced that her luncheon date had arrived.

"Send him in," Susannah said automatically, irritated that her concentration had been broken.

Nate strolled casually into her office and plopped himself down in the chair opposite her desk.

"Nate," she cried, leaping to her feet. "I've been trying to get hold of you all morning. What are you doing here?"

"We're going out to lunch, remember?"

Nine

"Nate!" Susannah ran around her desk until she stood directly in front of him. "John Hammer called me into his office this morning," she explained breathlessly. "I got the promotion! You're looking at the vice president in charge of marketing for H&J Lima."

For a moment Nate said nothing. Then he slowly repeated, "You got the promotion?"

"Yes," she told him. "I got it." In her enthusiasm, Susannah nodded several times, with a vigor that almost dislocated her neck. She was smiling so hard, her face ached.

Throwing back his head, Nate let out a shout that must have shaken the ceiling tile. Then he locked his arms around her waist, picked her up and swung her around, all the while howling with delight.

Susannah laughed with him. She'd never experienced joy more profoundly. The promotion hadn't seemed real to her until she'd shared it with Nate. The first person she'd thought to tell had been him. He'd become the very center of her world, and it was time to admit she was in love with him.

Nate had stopped whirling her around, but he continued to clasp her middle so that her face was elevated above his own.

Breathless with happiness, Susannah smiled down on him and on impulse buried her fingers in his hair. She couldn't resist him, not now, when she was filled with such exhilaration. Her mouth was trembling when she kissed him. She made a soft throaty sound of discovery and pleasure. Her gaze fell to the sensual lines of his mouth, and she remembered how she'd felt when he'd held and reassured her after the cookie disaster. She lowered her lips once more, lightly rocking her head back and forth, creating a friction that was so hot, she thought she'd catch fire.

In an unhurried movement, Nate lowered her to the ground and slid his arms around her. "Susannah," he moaned, kissing the corner of her mouth with exquisite care.

With a shudder, she opened her mouth to him. She wanted him to kiss her the way he had in the past. Deep, slow, moist, kisses that made her forget to breathe. She yearned for the taste and scent of him. This was the happiest moment of her life, and only a small part of it could be attributed to the promotion. Everything else was Nate and the growing love she felt for him each time they were together.

Someone coughed nervously in the background, and Nate broke off the kiss and glanced past her to the open door.

"Ms. Simmons," her assistant said, smiling broadly.

"Yes?" Breaking away from Nate, Susannah smoothed the hair at the sides of her head and struggled to replace her business facade.

"I'll be leaving now. Ms. Andrews will be answering your calls."

"Thank you, Ms. Brooks," Nate muttered, but there was little appreciation in his tone.

Susannah chastised him with a look. "We'll... I'll be leaving directly for my lunch appointment."

"I'll tell Ms. Andrews."

"This afternoon, I'd like you to call a meeting of my staff," Susannah said, "and I'll announce the promotion."

Eleanor Brooks nodded, but her smiling eyes landed heavily on Nate. "I believe everyone's already guessed from the...commotion that came from here a few minutes ago."

"I see." Susannah couldn't help smiling, too.

"There isn't an employee here who isn't happy about your news."

"I can think of two," Susannah said under her breath, considering the men she'd been competing against. Nate squeezed her hand, and she knew he'd heard her sardonic remark.

Her assistant closed the door on her way out, and the minute she did, Nate reached for Susannah to bring her back into the shelter of his arms. "Where were we?"

"About to leave for lunch, as I recall."

Nate frowned. "That's not the way I remember it."

Susannah laughed and hugged him tightly. "We both forgot ourselves for a while there." She broke away again and reached for her purse, hooking the long strap over her shoulder. "Are you ready?"

"Anytime you are." But the eager look in his eyes told her he was talking about something other than lunch.

Susannah could feel the color working its way up her neck and suffusing her face. "Nate," she whispered, "behave yourself. Please."

"I'm doing the best I can under the circumstances," he whispered back, his eyes filled with mischief. "In case you haven't figured it out yet, I'm crazy about you, woman."

"I… I'm pretty keen on you myself."

"Good." He tucked his arm around her waist and led her out of the office and down the long hallway to the elevator. Susannah was sure she could feel the stares of her staff, but for the first time, she didn't care what image she projected. Everything was right in her world, and she'd never been happier.

Nate chose the restaurant, Il Bistro, which was one of the best in town. The atmosphere was festive, and playing the role of gentleman to the hilt, Nate wouldn't allow her to even look at the menu, insisting that he'd order for her.

"Nate," she said once the waiter had left the table, "I want to pay for this. It's a business lunch."

His thick brows arched upward. "And how are you going to rationalize *that* when your boss questions you about it, my dear?" He wiggled his eyebrows suggestively.

"There's a reason I agreed to go to lunch with you—other than celebrating my promotion, which I didn't even know about until this morning." As she'd explained to Nate earlier, her life was going to change with this promotion. New responsibility would result in a further commitment of time and energy to the company, and could drastically alter her relationship with Nate. If anything, she wanted them to grow closer, not apart. This advancement had the potential to make or break them, and Susannah was looking for a way to keep them together. She thought she'd found it.

"A reason?" Nate questioned.

They were interrupted by the waiter as he produced a bottle of expensive French wine for their inspection. He removed the cork and poured a sample into Nate's glass to taste. When Nate nodded in approval, the waiter filled their glasses and discreetly retreated.

"Now, you were saying?" Nate continued, studying her. His mouth quirked up at the edges.

Gathering her resolve, Susannah reached across the

table and took Nate's hand. "You've always been open and honest with me. I want you to know how much I value that. When I asked you if you had a job, you told me you'd had one until recently and that you'd quit." She waited for him to elaborate on his circumstances, but he didn't, so she went on. "It's obvious you don't need the money, but there's something else that's obvious, too."

Nate removed his fingers from hers and twirled the stem of the wineglass between his open palms. "What's that?"

"You lack purpose."

His eyes rose to meet hers and his brow creased in query.

"You have no direction," she said. "Over the past several weeks, I've watched you flit from one interest to another. First it was baseball, then it was video games and kite flying, and tomorrow, no doubt, it'll be something completely different."

"Traveling," he concluded for her. "I was thinking of doing some serious sightseeing. I have a hankering to stroll the byways of Hong Kong."

"Hong Kong," she repeated, gesturing with one hand. "That's exactly what I mean." Her heart slowed to a sluggish beat at the thought of his being gone for any length of time. She'd become accustomed to having Nate nearby, to sharing bits and pieces of her day with him. Not only had she fallen in love with Nate Townsend, he'd quickly become her best friend.

"Do you think traveling is wrong?" he asked.

"Not wrong," she returned swiftly. "But what are you going to do once you've run out of ways to entertain yourself and places to travel? What are you going to do when you've spent all your money?"

"I'll face that when the time comes."

"I see." She lowered her gaze, wondering if she was only making matters worse. There wasn't much she could say to counter his don't-worry attitude.

"Susannah, you make it sound like the end of the world. Trust me, wealth isn't all that great. If I run out of money, fine. If I don't, that's all right, too."

"I see," she murmured miserably.

"Why are you so worried?" he asked in a gentle voice.

"It's because I care about you, I guess." She paused to take a deep breath. "We may live in the same building, but our worlds are totally opposite. My future is charted, right down to the day I retire. I know what I want and how to get there."

"I thought I did once, too, but then I learned how unimportant it all was."

"It doesn't have to be like that," she told him, her voice filled with determination. "Listen, there's something important I'm going to propose, but I don't want you to answer me now. I want you to give yourself time to think about it. Promise me you'll at least do that."

"Are you suggesting we get married?" he teased.

"No." Flustered, she smoothed out the linen napkin in her lap, her fingers lingering there to disguise her nervousness. "I'm offering you a job."

"You're doing what?" He half rose out of his seat.

Embarrassed, Susannah glanced nervously around and noted that several people had stopped eating and were gazing in their direction. "Don't look so aghast. A job would make a lot of difference in your attitude toward life."

"And exactly what position are you offering me?" Now that the surprise had worn off, he appeared amused.

"I don't know yet. We'd have to figure something out. But I'm sure there'd be a position that would fit your qualifications."

The humor drained from his eyes, and for a long moment Nate said nothing. "You think a job would give me purpose?"

"I believe so." In her view, it would help him look beyond today and toward the future. Employment would give Nate a reason to get out of bed in the morning, instead of sleeping in until nine or ten every day.

"Susannah—"

"Before you say anything," she interrupted, holding up her hand, "I want you to think it over seriously. Don't say anything until you've had a chance to consider my offer."

His eyes were more serious than she could ever remember seeing them—other than just before he kissed her. His look was almost brooding.

Their meal arrived, and the lamb was as delicious as Nate had promised. He was unusually quiet during the remainder of the meal, but that didn't alarm her. He was reflecting on her job offer, which was exactly what she wanted. She hoped he'd come to the right decision. Loving him the way she did, she longed to make his world as right as her own.

Despite Nate's protests, Susannah paid for their lunch. He walked her back to her office, standing with her on the sidewalk while they exchanged a few words of farewell. Susannah kissed him on the cheek and asked once more that he consider her offer.

"I will," he promised, running his finger lightly down the side of her face.

He left her then, and Susannah watched as he walked away, letting her gaze linger on him for several minutes.

"Any messages?" she asked Dorothy Andrews, who was sitting in her assistant's place.

"One," Dorothy said, without looking up. "Emily— she didn't leave her full name. She said she'd catch you later."

"Thanks." Susannah went into her office and, sitting down at her desk, punched out her sister's telephone number.

"Emily, this is Susannah. You phoned?"

"I know I probably shouldn't have called you at the office, but you never seem to be home and I had something important to ask you," her sister said, talking so fast she ran her words together.

"What's that?" Already Susannah was reaching for a file, intending to read while her sister spoke. It sometimes took Emily several minutes to get around to the reason for any call.

Her sister hesitated. "I've got a bunch of zucchini left from my garden, and I was wondering if you wanted some."

"About as much as I want a migraine headache." After her disaster with the chocolate chip cookies, Susannah planned to never so much as read a recipe again.

"The zucchini are excellent," Emily prompted, as if that would be enough to induce Susannah into agreeing to take a truckload.

Her sister hadn't phoned her to ask about zucchini; Susannah would have staked her promotion on it. That was merely a lead-in for some other request, and no doubt Susannah would have to play a guessing game. Mentally, she scanned a list of possible favors and decided to jump in with both feet.

"Zucchini are out, but I wouldn't mind looking after Michelle again, if you need me to."

"Oh, Susannah, would you? I mean, it'd work out so well if you could take her two weeks from this Saturday."

"All night?" As much as she loved her niece, another overnight stretch was more than Susannah wanted to contemplate. Still, Nate would probably be more than willing to lend a hand. No doubt she'd need it.

"Oh, no, not for the night, just for dinner. Robert's boss is taking us out to eat, and it wouldn't be appropriate if we brought Michelle along. Robert got a big promotion."

"Congratulate him for me, okay?"

"I'm so proud of him," Emily said. "I think he must be the best accountant in Seattle."

Susannah toyed with the idea of letting her sister in on her own big news, but she didn't want to take anything away from her brother-in-law. She could tell them both in two weeks when they dropped off Michelle.

"I'll be happy to keep Michelle for you," Susannah said, and discovered, as she marked the date on her calendar, how much she actually meant that. She might be a disaster waiting to happen in the kitchen, but she didn't do half badly with her niece. The time might yet come when she'd consider having a child of her own—not now, of course, but sometime in the future. "All right, I've got you down for the seventeenth."

"Susannah, I can't tell you how much this means to me," Emily said.

When Susannah arrived home that evening she was tipsy. The staff meeting that afternoon had gone wonderfully well. After five, she'd been taken out for a drink by her two top aides, to celebrate. Several others from her section had unexpectedly dropped by the cocktail lounge and insisted on buying her drinks, too. By seven, Susannah was flushed and excited, and from experience, she knew it was time to call it quits and phone for a taxi.

Dinner probably would have cut the effects of the

alcohol, but she was more interested in getting home. After a nice hot bath, she'd fix herself some toast and be done with it.

She hadn't been back more than half an hour when her phone rang. Dressed in her robe and sipping tea in the kitchen, she grabbed the receiver.

"Susannah, it's Nate. Can I come over?"

Glancing down at her robe and fuzzy slippers, she decided it wouldn't take her long to change.

"Give me five minutes."

"All right."

Dressed in slacks and a sweater, she opened the door at his knock. "Hi," she said cheerfully, aware that her mouth had probably formed a crooked grin despite her efforts to smile naturally.

Nate barely looked at her. His hands were thrust deep in his pockets, and his expression was disgruntled as he marched into her apartment. He didn't take a seat but paced the carpet in front of her fireplace. Obviously something was going on.

She sat on the edge of the sofa, watching him, feeling more than a little reckless and exhilarated from her promotion and the celebration afterward. She was amused, too, at Nate's peculiar agitation.

"I suppose you want to talk to me about the job offer," she said, surprised by how controlled her voice sounded.

He paused, splayed his fingers through his thick hair and nodded. "That's exactly what I want to talk about."

"Don't," she said, smiling up at him.

His forehead puckered in a frown. "Why not?"

"Because I'd like you to give long and careful consideration to the proposal."

"I need to explain something to you first."

Susannah wasn't listening. There were far more important things she had to tell him. "You're personable, bright and attractive," she began enthusiastically. "You could be anything you wanted, Nate. Anything."

"Susannah…"

She waved a finger at him and shook her head. "There's something else you should know."

"What?" he demanded.

"I'm in love with you." Her glorious confession was followed by a loud yawn. Unnerved, she covered her mouth with the tips of her fingers. "Oops, sorry."

Nate's eyes narrowed suspiciously. "Have you been drinking?"

She pressed her thumb and index finger together and held them up for his inspection. "Just a little, but I'm more happy than anything else."

"Susannah!" He dragged her name out into the sigh. "I can't believe you."

"Why not? Do you want me to shout it to all of Seattle? Because I will. Watch!" She waltzed into the kitchen and jerked open the sliding glass door.

Actually, some of the alcohol had worn off, but she experienced this irrepressible urge to tell Nate how much she'd come to care for him. They'd skirted around the subject long enough. He didn't seem to want to admit it, but she did, especially now, fortified as she was with her good fortune. This day had been one of the most fantastic of her life. After years of hard work, everything was falling into place, and she'd found the most wonderful man in the world to love—even if he *was* misguided.

The wind whipped against her on the balcony, and the multicolored lights from the waterfront below resembled those on a Christmas tree. Standing at the railing, she cupped her hands around her mouth and shouted, "I love Nate Townsend!" Satisfied, she whirled to face him and opened her arms as wide as she could. "See? I announced it to the world."

He joined her outside and slid his arms around her and closed his eyes. Susannah had expected him to show at least *some* emotion.

"You don't look very happy about it," she challenged.

"You're not yourself," he said as he released her.

"Then who am I?" Fists digging into her hips, she glared up at him, her eyes defiant. "I feel like me. I bet you think I'm drunk, but I'm not."

He didn't reply. Instead he threw an arm over her shoulder and urged her into the kitchen. Then, quickly and efficiently, he started to make coffee.

"I gave up caffeine," she muttered.

"When was this? You had regular coffee today at lunch," he said.

"Just now." She giggled. "Come on, Nate," she cried, bending forward and snapping her fingers. "Loosen up."

"I'm more concerned about sobering *you* up."

"You could kiss me."

"I could," he agreed, "but I'm not going to."

"Why not?" She pouted, disappointed by his refusal.

"Because if I do, I may not be able to stop."

Sighing, she closed her eyes. "That's the most romantic thing you've ever said to me."

Nate rubbed his face and leaned against the kitchen counter. "Have you had anything to eat since lunch?"

"One stuffed mushroom, a water chestnut wrapped in a slice of bacon and a piece of celery filled with cheese."

"But no dinner?"

"I was going to make myself some toast, but I wasn't hungry."

"After a stuffed mushroom, a celery stick and a water chestnut? I can see why not."

"Are you trying to be cute with me? Oh, just a minute, there was something I was supposed to ask you." She pulled herself up short and covered one eye, while she tugged at her memory for the date her sister had mentioned. "Are you doing anything on the seventeenth?"

"The seventeenth? Why?"

"Michelle's coming over to visit her auntie Susannah and I know she'll want to see you, too."

Nate looked even more disturbed, but he hadn't seemed particularly pleased about anything from the moment he'd arrived.

"I've got something else that night."

"Oh, well, I'll make do. I have before." She stopped

abruptly. "No, I guess I haven't, but Michelle and I'll be just fine, I think..."

The coffee had finished dripping into the glass pot. Nate poured a cup and, scowling, handed it to her.

"Oh, Nate, what's wrong with you? You've been cranky since you got here. We should be kissing by now and all you seem to do is ignore me."

"Drink your coffee."

He stood over her until she'd taken the first sip. She grimaced at the heat. "You know what I drank tonight? I've never had them before and they tasted so good. Shanghai Slungs."

"They're called Singapore Slings."

"Oh." Maybe she was more confused than she thought.

"Come on, drink up, Tokyo Rose."

Obediently Susannah did as he said. The whole time she was sipping her coffee, she was watching Nate, who moved restlessly about her kitchen, as if unable to stand still. He was disturbed about something, and she wished she knew what.

"Done," she announced when she'd finished her coffee, pleased with herself and this minor accomplishment. "Nate," she said, growing concerned, "do you love me?"

He turned around to face her, his eyes serious. "So much I can't believe it myself."

"Oh, good," she said with an expressive sigh. "I was beginning to wonder."

"Where are your aspirin?" He was searching through

her cupboards, opening and closing the ones closest to the sink.

"My aspirin? Did telling me how you feel give you a headache?"

"No." He answered her with a gentle smile. "I want to have it ready for you in the morning because you're going to need it."

Her love for him increased tenfold. "You are so thoughtful!"

"Take two tablets when you wake up. That should help." He crouched in front of her and took both her hands in his. "I'm leaving tomorrow and I won't be back for a couple of days. I'll call you, all right?"

"You're going away to think about my job offer, aren't you? That's a good idea—when you come back you can tell me your decision." She was forced to stop in order to yawn, a huge jaw-breaking yawn that depleted her strength. "I think I should go to bed, don't you?"

The next thing Susannah knew, her alarm was buzzing angrily. With the noise came a piercing pain that shot straight through her temple. She groped for the clock, turned it off and sighed with relief. Sitting up in bed proved to be equally overwhelming and she groaned.

When she'd managed to maneuver herself into the kitchen, she saw the aspirin bottle and remembered that Nate had insisted on setting it out the night before.

"Bless that man," she said aloud and winced at the sound of her own voice.

By the time she arrived at the office, she was operating on only three cylinders. Eleanor Brooks didn't seem to be any better off than Susannah was. They took one look at each other and smiled knowingly.

"Your coffee's ready," her assistant informed her.

"Did you have a cup yourself?"

"Yes."

"Anything in the mail?"

"Nothing that can't wait. Mr. Hammer was in earlier. He told me to give you this magazine and said you'd be as impressed as he was." Susannah glanced at the six-year-old issue of *Business Monthly*, a trade magazine that was highly respected in the industry.

"It's several years old," Susannah noted, wondering why her employer would want her to read it now.

"Mr. Hammer said there was a special feature in there about your friend."

"My friend?" Susannah didn't understand.

"Your friend," Eleanor Brooks repeated. "The one with the sexy eyes—Nathaniel Townsend."

Ten

Susannah waited until Eleanor had left the office before opening the magazine. The article on Nathaniel Townsend was the lead feature. The picture showed a much younger Nate standing in front of a shopping-mall outlet for Rainy Day Cookies, the most successful cookie chain in the country. He was holding a huge chocolate chip cookie.

Rainy Day Cookies were Susannah's absolute favorite. There were several varieties, but the chocolate chip ones were fantastic.

Two paragraphs into the article, Susannah thought she was going to be physically ill. She stopped reading and closed her eyes to the waves of nausea that lapped against her. Pressing a hand to her stomach, she resolutely focused her attention on the article, storing away the details of Nate's phenomenal success in her numb mind.

He had started his cookie company in his mother's kitchen while still in college. His specialty was chocolate chip cookies, and they were so popular, he soon found himself caught up in a roller-coaster ride that had led him straight to the top of the corporate world. By age twenty-eight, Nate Townsend was a multimillionaire.

Now that she thought about it, an article she'd read six or seven months ago in the same publication had said the company was recently sold for an undisclosed sum, which several experts had estimated to be a figure so staggering Susannah had gasped out loud.

Bracing her elbows on the desk, Susannah took several calming breaths. She'd made a complete idiot of herself over Nate, and worse, he had let her. She suspected this humiliation would stay with her for the rest of her life.

To think she'd baked the cookie king of the world chocolate chip cookies, and in the process nearly set her kitchen on fire. But that degradation couldn't compare to yesterday's little pep talk when she'd spoken to him about drive, ambition and purpose, before—dear heaven, it was too much—she'd offered him a job. How he must have laughed at that.

Eleanor Brooks brought in the mail and laid it on the corner of Susannah's desk. Susannah looked up at her and knew then and there that she wasn't going to be able to cope with the business of the day.

"I'm going home."

"I beg your pardon?"

"If anyone needs me, tell them I'm home sick."

"But…"

Susannah knew she'd shocked her assistant. In all the years she'd been employed by H&J Lima, Susannah had never used a single day of her sick leave. There'd been a couple of times she probably *should* have stayed home, but she'd insisted on working anyway.

"I'll see you Monday morning," she said on her way out the door.

"I hope you're feeling better then."

"I'm sure I will be." She needed some time alone to lick her wounds and gather the scattered pieces of her pride. To think that only a few hours earlier she'd drunkenly declared her undying love to Nate Townsend!

That was the worst of it.

When Susannah walked into her apartment she felt as if she was stumbling into a bomb shelter. For the moment she was hidden from the world outside. Eventually she'd have to go back and face it, but for now she was safe.

She picked up the afghan her sister had crocheted for her, wrapped it around her shoulders and sat staring sightlessly into space.

What an idiot she'd been! What a fool! Closing her eyes, she leaned her head against the back of the sofa and drew in several deep breaths, releasing the anger and hurt before it fermented into bitterness. She refused to dwell on the might-have-beens and the if-onlys, opting instead for a more positive approach. *Next time*, she would know enough not to involve her heart. *Next time*, she'd take care not to make such a fool of herself.

It astonished her when she awoke an hour later to realize she'd fallen asleep. Tucking the blanket more securely around her, she analyzed her situation.

Things weren't so bad. She'd achieved her primary goal and was vice president in charge of marketing. The first female in the company's long history to hold such a distinguished position, she reminded herself. Her life was good. If on occasion she felt the yearning for a family of her own, there was always Emily, who was more than willing to share. Heaving a sigh, Susannah told herself that she lacked for nothing. She was respected, hardworking and healthy. Yes, life was good.

Her head ached and her stomach didn't feel much better, but at noon, Susannah heated some chicken noodle soup and forced that down. She was putting the bowl in the dishwasher when the telephone rang. Ms. Brooks was the only one who knew she was home, and her assistant would call her only if it was important. Susannah answered the phone just as she would in her office.

"Susannah Simmons."

"Susannah, it's Nate."

She managed to swallow a gasp. "Hello, Nate," she said as evenly as possible. "What can I do for you."

"I called the office and your assistant said you'd gone home sick."

"Yes. I guess I had more to drink last night than I realized. I had one doozy of a hangover when I woke up this morning." But she didn't add how her malady had worsened once she read the article about him.

"Did you find the aspirin on the kitchen counter?"

"Yes. Now that I think about it, you were by last night, weren't you?" She was thinking fast, wanting to cover her tracks. "I suppose I made a fool of myself," she said, instilling a lightness in her tone. "I didn't say anything to embarrass you—or me, did I?"

He chuckled softly. "You don't remember?"

She did, but she wasn't going to admit it. "Some of it, but most of the evening's kind of fuzzy."

"Once I'm back in Seattle I'll help you recall every single word." His voice was low, seductive and filled with promise.

That was one guarantee, however, that Susannah had no intention of accepting.

"I…probably made a complete idiot of myself," she mumbled. "If I were you, I'd forget anything I said. Obviously, I can't be held responsible for it."

"Susannah, Susannah, Susannah," Nate said gently. "Let's take this one step at a time."

"I…think we should talk about it later, I really do… because it's all too obvious I wasn't myself." Tears pooled at the corners of her eyes. Furious at this display of emotion, she wiped them aside with the back of her hand.

"You're feeling okay now?"

"Yes...no. I was about to lie down."

"Then I'll let you," Nate said. "I'll be back Sunday. My flight should arrive early afternoon. I'd like us to have dinner together."

"Sure," she said, without thinking, willing to agree to just about anything in order to end this conversation. She was still too raw, still bleeding. By Sunday, she'd be able to handle the situation far more effectively. By Sunday, she could disguise her pain.

"I'll see you around five then."

"Sunday," she echoed, feeling like a robot programmed to do exactly as its master requested. She had no intention of having dinner with Nate, none whatsoever. He'd find out why soon enough.

The only way Susannah made it through Saturday was by working. She went to her office and sorted through the mail Ms. Brooks had left on her desk. News of her promotion was to be announced in the Sunday business section of the *Seattle Times*, but apparently word had already leaked out, probably through her boss; there was a speaking invitation in the mail, for a luncheon at a conference of local salespeople who had achieved a high level of success. The request was an honor and Susannah sent a note of acceptance to the organizer. She considered it high praise to have been asked. The date of the conference was the seventeenth, which was only two weeks away, so she spent a good part of the morning making notes for her speech.

On Sunday, Susannah woke feeling sluggish and out

of sorts. She recognized the source of her discomfort almost instantly. This afternoon, she would confront Nate. For the past two days, she'd gone over in her mind exactly what she planned to say, how she'd act.

Nate arrived at four-thirty. She answered his knock, dressed in navy blue slacks and a cream shell-knit sweater. Her hair was neatly rolled into a chignon.

"Susannah." His gaze was hungry as he stepped across the threshold and reached for her.

It was too late to hide her reaction by the time she realized he intended to kiss her. He swept her into his arms and eagerly pressed his mouth over hers. Despite everything that he'd failed to tell her, Susannah felt an immediate excitement she couldn't disguise.

Nate slipped his fingers into her hair, removing the pins that held it in place, while he leisurely moved his mouth over hers.

"Two days have never seemed so long," he breathed, then nibbled on her lower lip.

Regaining her composure, she broke away, her shoulders heaving. "Would you like some coffee?"

"No. The only thing I want is you."

She started to walk away from him, but Nate caught her, hauling her back into the warm shelter of his arms. He linked his hands at the small of her back and gazed down at her, his eyes soft and caressing. Gradually, his expression altered.

"Is everything all right?" he asked.

"Yes…and no," she admitted dryly. "I happened upon

an article in an old issue of *Business Monthly*. Does that tell you anything?"

He hesitated, and for a moment Susannah wondered if he was going to say anything or not.

"So you know?"

"That you're the world's cookie king, or once were— yes, I know."

His eyes narrowed slightly. "Are you angry?"

She sighed. A good deal depended on her delivery, and although she'd practiced her response several times, it was more difficult than she'd expected. She was determined, however, to remain calm and casual.

"I'm more embarrassed than amused," she said. "I wish you'd said something before I made such a fool of myself."

"Susannah, you have every right to be upset." He let her go and rubbed the back of his neck as he began to walk back and forth between the living room and kitchen. "It isn't like it was a deep dark secret. I sold the business almost six months ago, and I was taking a sabbatical—hell, I needed one. I'd driven myself as far as I could. My doctor thinks I was on the verge of a complete physical collapse. When I met you, I was just coming out of it, learning how to enjoy life again. The last thing I wanted to do was sit down and talk about the past thirteen years. I'd put Rainy Day Cookies behind me, and I was trying to build a new life."

Susannah crossed her arms. "Did you ever intend to tell me?"

"Yes!" he said vehemently. "Thursday. You were so sweet to have offered me a job and I knew I had to say something then, but you were..."

"Tipsy," she finished for him.

"All right, tipsy. You have to understand why I didn't. The timing was all wrong."

"You must have got a good laugh from the cookie disaster," she said, surprised at how steady her voice remained. Her poise didn't even slip, and she was proud of herself.

The edges of his mouth quivered, and it was apparent that he was struggling not to laugh.

"Go ahead," she said, waving her hand dramatically. "I suppose those charred cookies and the smoldering cookie sheets were pretty comical. I don't blame you. I'd probably be in hysterics if the situation were reversed."

"It isn't that. The fact that you made those cookies was one of the sweetest things anyone's ever done for me. I want you to know I was deeply touched."

"I didn't do it for you," she said, struggling to keep the anger out of her voice. "It was a trial by fire—" Hearing what she'd said, Susannah closed her eyes.

"Susannah—"

"You must've got a real kick out of that little pep talk I gave you the other day, too. Imagine *me* talking to *you* about drive, motivation and goals."

"That touched me, too," he insisted.

"Right on the funny bone, I'll bet." She faked a laugh

herself just to prove what a good sport she was. Still, she wasn't exactly keen on being the brunt of one.

Nate paused, then gestured at her. "I suppose it looks bad considered from your point of view."

"Looks bad," she echoed, with a short hysterical laugh. "That's one way of putting it!"

Nate strode from one end of the room to the other. If he didn't stop soon, he was going to wear a path in the carpet.

"Are you willing to put this misunderstanding behind us, Susannah, or are you going to hold it against me? Are you willing to ruin what we have over a mistake?"

"I don't know yet." Actually she did, but she didn't want him to accuse her of making snap decisions. It would be so easy for Nate to talk his way out of this. But Susannah had been humiliated. How could she possibly trust him now? He'd thought nothing of hiding an important portion of his life from her.

"How long will it be before you come to a conclusion about us?"

"I don't know that, either."

"I guess dinner is out?"

She nodded, her face muscles so tight, they ached.

"Okay, think everything through. I trust you to be completely fair and unbiased. All I want you to do is ask yourself one thing. If the situation were reversed, how would you have handled it?"

"All right." She'd grant him that much, although she

already knew what she would have done—and it wasn't keep up a charade the way he had.

"There's something else I want you to think about," he said when she held open the door for him.

"What?" Susannah was frantic to get him out of her home. The longer he stayed, the more difficult it was to remain angry with him.

"This." He kissed her then and it was the type of kiss that drove to the very depths of her soul. His mouth on hers was hot, the kiss deep and moist and so filled with longing that her knees almost buckled. Tiny sounds interrupted the moment, and Susannah realized she was the one making them.

When Nate released her, she backed away and nearly stumbled. Breathing hard, she leaned against the doorframe and heaved in giant gulps of oxygen.

Satisfied, Nate smiled infuriatingly. "Admit it, Susannah," he whispered and ran his index finger over her collarbone. "We were meant for each other."

"I… I'm not willing to admit anything."

His expression looked forlorn. It was no doubt calculated to evoke sympathy, but it wouldn't work. Susannah wouldn't be fooled a second time.

"You'll phone me?" he pressed.

"Yes." When the moon was in the seventh house, which should be somewhere around the time the government balanced the budget. Perhaps a decade from now.

For two days, Susannah's life returned to a more normal routine. She went in to the office early and worked late, doing everything she could to avoid Nate, although she was sure he'd wait patiently for some signal from her. After all, he, too, had his pride; she was counting on that.

When she arrived home on Wednesday, there was a folded note taped to her door. Susannah stared at it for several thundering heartbeats, then finally reached for it.

She waited until she'd put her dinner in the microwave before she read it. Her heart was pounding painfully hard as she opened the sheet and saw three words: "Call me. Please."

Susannah gave a short hysterical laugh. Ha! Nate Townsend could tumble into a vat of melted chocolate chips before she'd call him again. Guaranteed he'd say or do something that would remind her of what a fool she'd been! And yet... Damn, but it was hard to stay angry with him!

When the phone rang she was still ambivalent. Jumping back, she glared at it before answering.

"Hello," she said cautiously, quaveringly.

"Susannah? Is that you?"

"Oh, hi, Emily."

"Good grief, you scared me. I thought you were sick. You sounded so weak."

"No. No, I'm fine."

"I hadn't talked to you in a while and I was wondering how you were doing."

"Fine," she repeated.

"Susannah!" Her sister's tone made her name sound like a warning. "I know you well enough to realize something's wrong. I also know it probably has to do with Nate. You haven't mentioned him the last few times we've talked, but before you seemed to be overflowing with things you wanted to say about him."

"I'm not seeing much of Nate these days."

"Why not?"

"Well, being a multimillionaire keeps him busy."

Emily paused to gulp in a breath, then gasped, "I think there must be a problem with the phone. I thought you just said—"

"Ever been to Rainy Day Cookies?"

"Of course. Hasn't everyone?"

"Have you made the connection yet?"

"You mean Nate..."

"...is Mr. Chocolate Chip himself."

"But that's marvelous! That's wonderful. Why, he's famous... I mean his cookies are. To think that the man who developed Rainy Day Cookies actually helped Robert carry out Michelle's crib. I can't wait until he hears this."

"Personally, I wasn't all that impressed." It was difficult to act indifferent when her sister was bubbling over with such enthusiasm. Emily usually only got excited about something organic.

"When did you find out?" Emily asked, her voice almost accusing, as if Susannah had been holding out on her.

"Last Friday. John Hammer gave me a magazine that

had an article about Nate in it. The issue was a few years old, but the article told me everything Nate should have."

A brief sound of exclamation followed. "So you just found out?"

"Right."

"And you're angry with him?"

"Good heavens, no. Why should I be?" Susannah was afraid Emily wouldn't appreciate the sarcasm.

"He probably planned on telling you," Emily argued, defending Nate. "I don't know him all that well, but he seemed straightforward enough to me. I'm sure he intended to explain the situation when the time was right."

"Perhaps," Susannah said, but as far as she was concerned, that consolation was too little, too late. "Listen, I've got something in the microwave, so I've got to scoot." The excuse was feeble, but Susannah didn't want to continue discussing Nate. "Oh, before I forget," she added quickly. "I've got a speaking engagement on the seventeenth, but I'll be finished before five-thirty so you can count on me watching Michelle."

"Great. Listen, if you want to talk, I'm always here. I mean that. What are sisters for if not to talk?"

"Thanks, I'll remember that."

Once she replaced the receiver, Susannah was left to deal, once more, with Nate's three-word note. By all rights, she should crumple it up and toss it in the garbage. She did, feeling a small—very small—sense of satisfaction.

Out of sight, out of mind, or so the old adage went.

Only this time it wasn't working. Whenever she turned around, the sight of the telephone seemed to pull at her.

Her dinner was ready, but as she gazed down at the unappetizing entrée, she considered throwing it out and going to the Western Avenue Deli for a pastrami on rye instead. That would serve two purposes; first, it would take her away from the phone, which seemed to be luring her to its side; and second, she'd at least have a decent meal.

Having made her decision, she was already in the living room when there was a knock at the door. Susannah groaned, knowing even before she answered it that her visitor had to be Nate.

"You didn't call," he snapped the minute she opened the door.

He stormed inside without waiting for an invitation, looking irritated but in control. "Just how long were you planning to keep me waiting? It's obvious you're going to make me pay for the error of my ways, which to a certain point I can understand. But we've gone well past that point. So what are you waiting for? An apology? Okay—I'm sorry."

"Ah—"

"You have every reason to be upset, but what do you want? Blood? Enough is enough. I'm crazy about you, Susannah, and you feel the same about me, so don't try to fool me with this indifference routine, because I can see right through it. Let's put this foolishness behind us and get back on track."

"Why?" she demanded.

"Why what?"

"Why did you wait to tell me? Why couldn't you have said something sooner?"

He gave her a frown that suggested they were rehashing old news, then started his usual pacing. "Because I wanted to put Rainy Day Cookies out of my mind. I'd made the business my entire world." He stopped and whirled to face her. "I recognized a kindred spirit in you. Your entire life is wrapped up in some sporting goods company—"

"Not just *some* sporting goods company" she returned, indignant. "H&J Lima is the largest in the country."

"Forgive me, Susannah, but that doesn't really impress me. What about your *life?* Your whole world revolves around how far you can climb up the corporate ladder. Let me tell you that once you're at the top, the view isn't all that great. You forget what it means to appreciate the simple things in life. I did."

"Are you telling me to stop and smell the flowers? Well, I've got news for you, Nate Townsend. I like my life just the way it is. I consider it insulting that you think you can casually walk into my world and my career and tell me I'm headed down the road to destruction, because I'll tell you right now—" she paused to take a deep breath "—I don't appreciate it."

Nate's expression tightened. "I'm not talking about flowers, Susannah. I want you to look out this window at Puget Sound and see the lovely view with ferryboats and snowcapped mountains. Life, abundant life, is more than that. It's meaningful relationships. Connecting with other people. Friends. Fun. We'd both lost sight of that. It happened to me first, and I can see you going in the same direction."

"That's fine for you, but I—"

"You need the same things I do. We need each other."

"Correction," she said heatedly. "As I told you, I like my life just the way it is, thank you. And why shouldn't I? My five-year goals have been achieved, and there are more in the making. I can go straight to the top with this company, and that's exactly what I want. As for needing relationships, you're wrong about that, too. I got along fine before I met you, and the same will be true when you're out of my life."

The room went so still that for a second Susannah was convinced Nate had stopped breathing.

"*When* I'm out of your life," he echoed. "I see. So you've made your decision."

"Yes," she said, holding her head high. "It was fun while it lasted, but if I had to choose between you and the vice presidency, the decision wouldn't be difficult at all. I'm sure you'll encounter some other young woman who needs to be saved from herself and her goals. As far as I can see, from your perspective, our relationship was more of a rescue mission. Now that you know how the cookie crumbles—the pun's intended—perhaps you'll leave me to my sorry lot."

"Susannah, would you listen to me?"

"No." She held up her hand for effect. "I'll try to be happy," she said, a heavy note of mockery in her voice.

For a moment, Nate said nothing. "You're making a mistake, but that's something you're going to have to learn on your own."

"I suppose you're planning on being around to pick up the pieces when I fall apart?"

His blue eyes bored into hers. "I might be, but then again, I might not."

"Well, you needn't worry, because either way, you've got a long wait."

Eleven

"Ms. Simmons, Mr. Hammer, it's an honor to meet you."

"Thank you," Susannah said, smiling politely at the young man who'd been sent to greet her and her boss. The Seattle Convention Center was filled to capacity. The moment Susannah realized her audience was going to be so large, her stomach was attacked by a bad case of nerves. Not the most pleasant conditions under which to be eating lunch.

"If you'll come this way, I'll show you to the head table."

Susannah and John Hammer followed the young executive toward the front of the crowded room. There were several other people already seated on the stage. Susannah recognized the mayor and a couple of city councillors, along with the King County executive and two prominent local businessmen.

She was assigned the chair to the right of the podium. John was assigned the place beside her. After shaking hands with the conference coordinator, she greeted the others and took her seat. Almost immediately, the caterers started serving lunch, which consisted of an elegantly prepared salad tossed with a raspberry vinaigrette, wild rice and broiled fresh salmon with a teriyaki glaze.

She didn't think she could manage even a bite while sitting in front of so many people. Glancing out over the sea of unfamiliar faces, she forced herself to remain calm and collected. She was, after all, one of the featured speakers for the afternoon, and she'd come well prepared.

There was a slight commotion to her right, but the podium blocked her view.

"Hi, gorgeous. No one told me you were going to be here."

Nate. Susannah nearly swallowed her forkful of salmon whole. It stuck in her throat and she would've choked had she not reached for her water and hurriedly gulped some down.

Twisting around in her chair, she came eye to eye with him. "Hello, Nate," she said as nonchalantly as she could. Her smile was firmly in place.

"I thought Nate Townsend might be here," John whispered, looking pleased with himself.

"I see you've taken to following me around now," Nate taunted as he took his seat, two chairs down from John's.

Susannah ignored his comment and both men, studiously returning to her salmon, hoping to suggest that her meal was far more appealing than their conversation.

"Have you missed me?"

It was ten agonizing days since she'd last seen Nate. Avoiding him hadn't been easy. He'd made sure of that. The first night she'd come home to an Italian opera played just loud enough to be heard through her kitchen wall. The sound of the music was accompanied by the tangy scent of his homemade spaghetti sauce. The aroma of simmering tomatoes and herbs mingled with the pungent scent of hot garlic and butter.

Evidently Nate assumed the way to *her* heart was through her stomach. She'd nearly succumbed then, but her conviction was strong and she'd hurried to a favorite Italian restaurant to alleviate her sudden craving for pasta.

By the weekend, Susannah could've sworn Nate had whipped up every recipe in an entire cookbook, each one more enticing than the last. Susannah had never eaten as many restaurant meals as she had in the past week.

When Nate realized she couldn't be bought so easily with fine food, wine and song, he'd tried another tactic, this one less subtle.

A single red rose was waiting outside her door when

she arrived home from the office. There wasn't any note with it, just a perfect fresh flower. She picked it up and against her better judgment took it inside with her, inhaling the delicate scent. The only person who could have left it was Nate. Then, in a flurry of righteousness, she'd taken the rose and put it back where she found it. Five minutes later, she jerked open her door and to her dismay discovered the flower was still there, looking forlorn and dejected.

Deciding to send him her own less-than-subtle message, Susannah dropped the rose outside Nate's door. She hoped he'd understand once and for all that she refused to be bought!

Nate, however, wasn't dissuaded. The rose was followed the next evening by a small box of luscious chocolates. This time Susannah didn't even bring them inside, but marched them directly to Nate's door.

"No," she said now, forcing her thoughts back to the present and the conference. She surveyed the crowded, noisy room. "I haven't missed you in the least."

"You haven't?" He looked dashed. "But I thought you were trying to make it up to me. Why else would you leave those gifts outside my door?"

For just a second her heart thumped wildly. Then she gave him a fiery glare and diligently resumed her meal, making sure she downed every bite. If she didn't, Nate would think she was lovesick for want of him.

Her boss tilted his head toward her, obviously pleased with himself. "I thought it would be a nice surprise for you to be speaking with Nate. Fact is, I arranged it myself."

"How thoughtful," Susannah murmured.

"You have missed me, haven't you?" Nate asked again, balancing on two legs of his chair in an effort to see her.

Okay, she was willing to admit she'd been a bit lonely, but that was to be expected. For several weeks, Nate had filled every spare moment of her time with silliness like baseball games and kite flying. But she'd lived a perfectly fine life before she met him, and now she'd gone back to that same serene lifestyle without a qualm. Her world was wonderful. Complete. She didn't need him to make her a whole person. Nate was going to a lot of trouble to force her to admit she was miserable without him. She wasn't about to do that.

"I miss you," he said, batting his baby blues at her. "The least you could do is concede that you're as lonely and miserable as me."

"But I'm not," she answered sweetly, silently acknowledging the lie. "I have a fantastic job and a promising career. What else could I want?"

"Children?"

She leaned forward and spoke across the people between them. "Michelle and I have loads of fun together, and when we get bored with each other, she goes home to her mother. In my opinion that's the perfect way to enjoy a child."

The first speaker approached the podium, and Susannah's attention was diverted to him. He was five minutes into his greeting when Susannah felt something hit her arm. She darted a glance at Nate, who was holding up a white linen napkin. *"What about a husband?"* was inked across the polished cloth.

Groaning, Susannah prayed no one else had seen his note, especially her boss. She rolled her eyes and emphatically shook her head. It was then that she noticed how everyone was applauding and looking in her direction. She blinked, not understanding, until she realized that she'd just been introduced and they were waiting for her to stand up and give her talk.

Scraping back her chair, she stood abruptly and approached the podium, not daring to look at Nate. The man was infuriating! A lesser woman would have dumped the contents of her water glass over his smug head. Instead of venting her irritation, she drew in a deep calming breath and gazed out over her audience. That was a mistake. There were so many faces, and they all had their eyes trained on her.

Her talk had been carefully planned and memorized. But to be on the safe side, she'd brought the typed sheets with her. She had three key points she intended to share, and had illustrated each one with several anecdotes. Suddenly her mind was blank. It took all her courage not to bolt and run from the stage.

"Go get 'em, Susannah," Nate mouthed, smiling up at her.

His eyes were so full of encouragement and faith that

the paralysis started to leave her. Although she'd memorized her speech, she stared down at the written version. The instant she read the first sentence she knew she was going to be fine.

For the next twenty minutes she spoke about the importance of indelibly marking a goal on one's mind and how to minimize difficulties and maximize strengths. She closed by explaining the significance of building a mental ladder to one's dreams. She talked about using determination, discipline, dedication and demeanor as the rungs of this ladder to success.

Despite Nate's earlier efforts to undermine her dignity and poise, she was pleased by the way her speech was received. Many of her listeners nodded at key points in her talk, and Susannah knew she was reaching them. When she came to the end, she felt good, satisfied with her speech and with herself.

As she turned to go back to her seat, her gaze caught Nate's. He was smiling as he applauded, and the gleam in his eyes was unmistakably one of respect and admiration. The warm, caressing look he sent her nearly tripped her heart into overdrive. Yet he'd maddened her with his senseless questions, distracted her, teased and taunted her with his craziness and then written a note on a napkin. But when she finished her speech, the first person she'd looked at, whether consciously or unconsciously, was Nate.

Once Susannah was seated, she saw that her hands were trembling. But she couldn't be sure if it was a release from the tension that had gripped her when she first started to speak, or the result of Nate's tender look.

Nate was introduced next, and he walked casually to the podium. It would serve him right, Susannah thought, if she started writing messages on her napkin and holding them up for him to read while he gave his talk. She was immediately shocked by the childishness of the idea. Five minutes with Nate seemed to reduce her mentality to that of a ten-year-old.

With a great deal of ceremony, or so it seemed to Susannah, Nate retrieved his notes from inside his suit jacket. It was all she could do to keep from laughing out loud when she saw that everything he planned to say had been jotted on the back of a single index card. So this was how seriously he'd taken that afternoon's address. It looked as if he'd scribbled a couple of notes while she was delivering her speech. He hadn't given his lecture a second thought until five minutes before he was supposed to stand at the podium.

But Nate proved her wrong, as seemed to be his habit. The minute he opened his mouth, he had the audience in the palm of his hand. Rarely had she heard a more dynamic speaker. His strong voice carried to the farthest corners of the huge hall, and although he used the microphone, Susannah doubted he really needed it.

Nate told of his own beginnings, of how his father had died the year he was to enter college, so that the funds he'd expected to further his education were no longer available. It was the lowest point of his life and out of it had come his biggest success. Then he explained that his mother's chocolate chip cookies had always been everyone's favorite. Because of his father's untimely death, she'd taken a job in a local factory, and Nate, eager to find a way to attend university in the fall, had started baking the cookies and selling them to tourists for fifty cents each.

Halfway through the summer he'd made more than enough money to see him through his first year of school. Soon a handful of local delis had contacted him, wanting to include his cookies as part of their menus. These requests were followed by others from restaurants and hotels.

Nate went to school that first year and took every business course available to him. By the end of the following summer, he had set up a kitchen with his mother's help and opened his own business, which thrived despite his mistakes. The rest was history. By the time he graduated from college, Nate was already a millionaire and his mother was able to retire comfortably. To his credit, he'd resisted the temptation to abandon his education. It had served him well since, and he was glad he'd stuck with it, even though everyone around him seemed to be saying he knew more, from personal experience, than most of the authors of the textbooks did. A fact he was quick to dispute.

Susannah was enthralled. She'd assumed Nate would be telling this audience what he'd been beating her over the head with from the moment they'd met—that the drive to succeed was all well and good, but worthless if in the process one forgot to enjoy life. However, if that thought was on Nate's mind, he didn't voice it. Susannah suspected he'd reserved that philosophy for her and her alone.

When he returned to his seat, the applause was thunderous. The first thing he did was look at Susannah, who smiled softly, as touched by his story as the rest of the audience was. Not once had he patted himself on the back, or taken credit for the phenomenal success of Rainy Day Cookies. Susannah would almost have preferred it if his talk had been a boring rambling account of his prosperous career. She didn't want to feel so much admiration for him. It would be easier to get Nate out of her life and her mind if she didn't.

The luncheon ended a few minutes later. Gathering up her things, Susannah hoped to make a speedy escape. She should've known Nate wouldn't allow that. Several people had hurried up to the podium to talk to him, but he excused himself and moved to her side.

"Susannah, could we talk for a minute?"

She made a show of glancing at her watch, then at her boss. "I have another appointment," she said stiffly. She secured the strap of her purse over her shoulder and offered him what she hoped was a regretful smile.

"Your speech was wonderful."

"Thank you. So was yours," she said, then mentioned the one thing that had troubled her. "You never told me about your father's death."

"I've never told you I love you, either, but I do."

His words, so casual, so calm and serene, were like

a blow to her solar plexus. Susannah felt the tears form in her eyes and tried to blink them back. "I... I wish you hadn't said that."

"The way I feel about you isn't going to change."

"I...really have to go," she said, turning anxiously toward John Hammer. All she wanted to do was escape with her heart intact.

"Mr. Townsend," a woman bellowed from the audience. "You're going to be at the auction tonight, aren't you?"

Nate's gaze slid reluctantly from Susannah to the well-dressed woman on the floor. "I'll be there," he called back.

"I'll be looking for you," she said and laughed girlishly.

Susannah decided the other woman's laugh resembled the sound an unwell rooster would make. She was tempted to ask Nate exactly what kind of auction he planned to attend where he expected to run into someone who yelled questions across a crowded room. But she ignored the urge, which was just as well.

"Goodbye, Nate," she said, moving away.

"Goodbye, my love." It wasn't until she was walking out of the Convention Center that Susannah realized how final his farewell had sounded.

It was what she wanted, wasn't it? As far as she was concerned, Nate had proved he wasn't trustworthy; he had an infuriating habit of keeping secrets. So now that he wasn't going to see her again, there was absolutely no reason for her to complain. At least that was what

Susannah told herself as she headed home, making a short side trip to the Seattle waterfront.

Within a couple of hours, Emily and Robert would be dropping off Michelle before they went to dinner with Robert's employer. Once the baby was with her, Susannah reminded herself, she wouldn't have a chance to worry about Nate or anyone else.

By the time Emily arrived with her family, Susannah was in a rare mood. She felt light-headed and witty, as though she'd downed something alcoholic, but the strongest thing she'd had all day was coffee.

"Hi," she said cheerfully, opening the door. Michelle looked at her with large round eyes and grabbed for her mother's collar.

"Sweetheart, this is your auntie Susannah, remember?"

"Emily, the only thing she remembers is that every time you bring her here, you leave," Robert said, carrying in the diaper bag and a sack full of blankets and toys.

"Hello, Robert," Susannah murmured, kissing him on the cheek. The action surprised her as much as it did her brother-in-law. "I understand congratulations are in order."

"For you, too."

"Yes, well, it wasn't that big a deal," she said, playing down her own success.

"Not according to the article in the paper."

"Oh," Emily said, whirling around. "Speaking of the paper, I read Nate's name today."

"Yes…we were both speakers at a conference this afternoon."

Emily seemed impressed, but Susannah couldn't be sure if it was because of her or Nate.

"That wasn't what I read about him," Emily continued, focusing her attention on removing the jacket from Michelle's arms. The child wasn't being cooperative. "Nate's involved in the auction."

"Da-da!" Michelle cried once her arms were free.

Robert looked on proudly. "She finally learned my name. Michelle's first and only word," he added, beaming. "Da-da loves his baby, yes, he does."

It was so unusual to hear Robert using baby talk that for an instant, Susannah didn't catch what her sister was saying. "What was that?"

"I'm trying to tell you about the auction," Emily said again, as if that should explain everything. At Susannah's puzzled look, she added, "His name was in an article about the auction to benefit the Children's Home Society."

The lightbulb that clicked on inside Susannah's head was powerful enough to search the night sky. "Not the *bachelor* auction?" Her question was little more than a husky murmur. No wonder the woman who'd shouted to Nate at the luncheon had been so brazen! She was going to bid on him.

Slowly, hardly conscious of what she was doing, Susannah lowered herself onto the sofa next to her sister.

"He didn't tell you?"

"No, but then why should he? We're nothing more than neighbors."

"Susannah!"

Her sister had the annoying ability to turn Susannah's name into an entire statement just by the way she said it.

"Honey," Robert said, studying his watch, "it's quarter to seven. We'd better leave now if we're going to be at the restaurant on time. I don't want to keep my boss waiting."

Emily's glance at Susannah promised a long talk later. At least Susannah had several hours during which to come up with a way of warding off her sister's questions.

"Have a good time, you two," Susannah said lightheartedly, guiding them toward the door, "and don't worry about a thing."

"Bye, Michelle," Emily said as she waved from the doorway.

"Tell Mommy goodbye." Since the baby didn't seem too inclined to do so, Susannah held up the chubby hand and waved it for her.

As soon as Emily and Robert had left, Michelle started whimpering softly. Susannah took one look at her niece and her spirits plummeted. Who was she trying to fool? Herself? She'd been miserable and lonely from the moment she'd rejected Nate. Michelle sniffled, and Susannah felt like crying right along with her.

So the notorious Nate Townsend had done it again— he hadn't even bothered to mention the bachelor auction. Obviously he'd agreed to this event weeks in advance and it had never even occurred to him to tell her. Oh, sure, he swore undying love to her, but he was willing to let some strange woman buy him. Men, she was quickly learning, were not to be trusted.

The more Susannah thought back to their previous conversations, the angrier she became. When she'd asked Nate about helping her out with Michelle, he'd casually said he had "something else" this evening. He sure did. Auctioning off his body to the highest bidder!

"I told him I didn't want to see him again," Susannah announced to her niece, her fervor causing her to raise her voice. "That man was trouble from the night we met. You were with me at the time, remember? Don't we wish we'd known then what we know now?"

Michelle's shoulders began to shake, with the effort to either cry or keep from crying. Susannah didn't know which.

"He has this habit of hiding things from me—important information. But I'm telling you right now that I'm completely over that man. Any woman who wants him tonight can have him, because I'm not interested."

Michelle buried her face against Susannah's neck.

"I know exactly how you feel, kid," she said, stalking the carpet in front of the large picture window. She stared out at the lights and sounds of the city at night. "It's like you've lost your best friend, right?"

"Da-da."

"He's with your mommy. I thought Nate was my friend once," she said sadly to the baby. "But I learned the hard way what he really is—nothing earth shattering, don't misunderstand me. But he let me make a complete idiot of myself. And…and he doesn't trust me enough to tell me anything important."

Michelle looked at Susannah wide-eyed, apparently enthralled with her speech. In an effort to keep the baby appeased, she continued chattering. "I hope he feels like a fool on the auction block tonight," she said as she imagined him standing in front of an auditorium full of screaming women. She slowly released a sigh, knowing that with his good looks, Nate would probably bring in top money. In past auctions, several of the men had gone for thousands of dollars. All for an evening in the company of one of Seattle's eligible bachelors.

"So much for love and devotion," she muttered. Michelle watched her solemnly, and Susannah felt it was her duty as the baby's aunt to give her some free advice. "Men aren't all they're cracked up to be. You'd be wise to figure that out now."

Michelle gurgled cheerfully, obviously in full agreement.

"I for one don't need a man. I'm totally happy living on my own. I've got a job, a really good job, and a few close friends—mostly people I work with—and of course your mother." Michelle raised her hand to Susannah's face and rubbed her cheek where a tear had streaked a moist trail.

"I know what you're thinking," Susannah added, although it was unnecessary to explain all that to anyone so young. "If I'm so happy, then why am I crying? Darned if I know. The problem is I can't help loving him and that's what makes this so difficult. Then he had to go and write that note on a napkin." She brought her fingers to her mouth, trying to calm herself. "He asked me if I was willing to live my life without a husband... on a napkin he asked me that. Can you imagine what the caterers are going to think when they read it? And we were sitting at the head table, no less."

"Da-da."

"He asked about that, too," Susannah said, sniffling as she spoke. She was silent a moment and when she began again her voice trembled slightly. "I never thought I'd want children, but then I didn't realize how much I could love a little one like you." Holding the baby against her breast, Susannah closed her eyes to the pain that clawed at her. "I'm so mad at that man."

Fascinated by Susannah's hair, Michelle reached up and tugged it free from the confining pins.

"I wore it up this afternoon to be contrary—and to prove to myself that I'm my own woman. Then he was there and the whole time I was speaking I wished I'd left it down—just because Nate prefers it that way. Oh, honestly, Michelle, I think I may be ready to go off the deep end here. Any advice you'd care to give me?"

"Da-da."

"That's what I thought you'd say." Forcing in a deep breath, Susannah tried to control the tears that sprang to her eyes. She hadn't expected to cry.

"I really believed that once I was promoted to vice president everything would be so wonderful and, well, it *has* been good, but I feel…empty inside. Oh, Michelle, I don't know if I can explain it. The nights are so long and there are only so many hours I can work without thinking about getting home and the possibility of seeing Nate. I… I seem to have lost my drive. Here I was talking to all these people today about determination and drive and discipline, and none of it seemed real. Then…then on the way home I was walking along the waterfront and I saw an old college friend. She's married and has a baby a little older than you and she looked so happy." She paused long enough to rub the back of her hand under her nose. "I told her all about my big promotion and Sally seemed genuinely happy for me, but I felt this giant hole inside."

"Da-da."

"Michelle, can't you learn another word? Please. How about Auntie? It's not so difficult. Say it after me. Auntie."

"Da-da."

"Nate's probably going to meet some gorgeous blonde and fall madly in love with her. She'll bid thousands of dollars for him and he'll be so impressed he won't even mind when she—" Susannah stopped, her mind whirling. "You won't believe what I was thinking," she said to Michelle, who was studying her curiously. "It's completely crazy, but…perhaps not."

Michelle waved her arms and actually seemed interested in hearing about this insane idea that had popped into Susannah's head. It was impossible. Absurd. But then she'd made a fool of herself over Nate so many times that once more certainly wasn't going to hurt.

It took several minutes to get Michelle back into her coat. Susannah would've sworn the thing had more arms than an octopus.

After glancing at the balance in her checkbook, she grabbed her savings-account records and, carrying Michelle, headed to the parking garage. She'd been saving up to pay cash for a new car, but bidding for Nate was more important.

The parking lot outside the theater where the bachelor auction was being held was full, and Susannah had a terrible time finding a place to leave her car. Once she was inside the main entrance, the doorman was hesitant to let her into the auditorium, since Michelle was with her and neither one of them had a ticket.

"Ma'am, I'm sorry, I can't let you in there without a ticket and a bidding number—besides I don't think married women are allowed."

"I'll buy one and this is my niece. Now, either you let me in there or…or you'll… I'll… I don't know what I'll do. Please," she begged. "This is a matter of life and death." Okay, so that was a slight exaggeration.

While the doorman conferred with his supervisor, Susannah looked through the swinging doors that led into the theater. She watched as several women raised their hands, and leaped enthusiastically to their feet to show their numbers. A television crew was there taping the proceedings, as well.

Susannah was impatiently bouncing Michelle on her hip when the doorman returned.

"Ma'am, I'm sorry, but my supervisor says the tickets are sold out."

Susannah was about to argue with him when she heard the master of ceremonies call out Nate's name. A fervent murmur rose from the crowd.

Desperate times demanded desperate measures, and instead of demurely going back outside, Susannah rushed to the swinging doors, shoved them open and hurried down the narrow aisle.

As soon as the doorman saw what she'd done, he ran after her, shouting, "Stop that woman!"

The master of ceremonies ceased speaking, and a hush fell over the room as every head in the place turned toward Susannah, who was clutching Michelle protectively to her chest. She'd made it halfway down the center aisle before the doorman caught up with her. Susannah cast a wretched pleading glance at Nate, who had shielded his eyes from the glare of the lights and was staring at her.

Michelle cooed and with her pudgy hand, pointed toward Nate.

"Da-da! Da-da!" she cried, and her voice echoed loudly in the auditorium.

Twelve

An immediate uproar rose from the theater full of women. Nothing Susannah did could distract Michelle from pointing toward Nate and calling him Da-da. For his part, Nate appeared to be taking all the commotion in his stride. He walked over to the master of ceremonies, whom Susannah recognized as Cliff Dolittle, a local television personality, and whispered something in his ear.

"What seems to be the problem?" Cliff asked the doorman.

"This lady doesn't have a ticket or a bidding number," he shouted back. He clutched Susannah's upper arm and didn't look any too pleased with this unexpected turn of events.

"I may not have a number, but I've got $6010.12 I'd like to bid for this man," she shouted.

Her announcement was again followed by a hubbub of whispering voices, which rolled over the theater like a wave crashing onto the shore. That six thousand was the balance in Susannah's savings account, plus all the cash she had with her.

A noise from the back of the room distracted her, and that was when she realized the television crew had the cameras rolling. Every single detail of this debacle was being documented.

"I have a bid of $6010.12," Cliff Dolittle announced, sounding a little shocked. "Going once, going twice—" he paused and scanned the female audience "—sold to the lady who gate-crashed this auction. The one with the baby in her arms."

The doorman released Susannah and reluctantly directed her to where she was supposed to pay. It seemed that everyone was watching her and whispering. Several of the women were bold enough to shout bits of advice to her.

A man with a camera balanced on his shoulder hurried toward her. Loving the attention, Michelle pointed her finger at the lens and cried "Da-da" once more for all the people who would soon be viewing this disaster at home.

"Susannah, what are you doing here?" Nate whispered, joining her when she'd reached the teller's booth.

"You know what really irritates me about this?" she

said, her face bright with embarrassment. "I probably could've had you for three thousand, only I panicked and offered every penny I have. Me, the marketing wizard. I'll never be able to hold my head up again."

"You're not making any sense."

"And you are? One moment you're saying you love me and the next you're on the auction block, parading around for a bunch of women."

"That comes to $6025.12," the white-haired woman in the teller's booth told her.

"I only bid $6010.12," Susannah protested.

"The extra money is the price of the ticket. You weren't supposed to bid without one."

"I see."

Unzipping her purse and withdrawing her checkbook while balancing Michelle on her hip proved to be difficult.

"Here, I'll take her." Nate reached for Michelle, who surprised them both by protesting loudly.

"What have you been telling her about me?" Nate teased.

"The truth." With considerable ceremony, Susannah wrote out the check and ripped it from her book. Reluctantly she slid it across the counter to the woman collecting the fees.

"I'll write you a receipt."

"Thank you," Susannah said absently. "By the way, what exactly am I getting for my hard-earned money?"

"One evening with this young man."

"One evening," Susannah repeated grimly. "If we go out to dinner does he pay or do I?"

"I do," Nate answered for her.

"It's a good thing, because I don't have any money left."

"Have you eaten?"

"No, and I'm starved."

"Me, too," he told her, smiling sheepishly, but the look in his eyes said he wasn't talking about snacking on crêpes suzette. "I can't believe you did this."

"I can't, either," she said, shaking her head in wonder. "I'm still reeling with the shock." Later, she'd probably start trembling and not be able to stop. Never in her life had she done anything so bold. Love apparently did things like that to a woman. Before she met Nate she'd been a sound, logical, dedicated businesswoman. Six weeks later, she was smelling orange blossoms and thinking about weddings and babies—all because she was head over heels in love!

"Come on, let's get out of here," Nate said, tucking his arm around her waist and leading her toward the theater doors.

Susannah nodded. The doorman seemed relieved that she was leaving his domain.

"Susannah," Nate said, once they were in the parking lot. He turned and placed his hands on her shoulders, then closed his eyes as if gathering his thoughts. "You were the last person I expected to see tonight."

"Obviously," she returned stiffly. "When we're married, I'm going to have to insist that you keep me informed of your schedule."

Nate's head snapped up. "When we're married?"

"You don't honestly believe I just spent six thousand dollars for one dinner in some fancy restaurant, did you?"

"But—"

"And there'll be children, as well. I figure that two are about all I can handle, but we'll play that by ear."

For the first time since she'd met him, Nate Townsend seemed speechless. His mouth made several movements in an attempt to talk, but nothing came out.

"I suppose you're wondering how I plan to manage my career," she said, before he could ask the question. "I'm not sure what I'm going to do yet. Since I'm looking at the good side of thirty, I suppose we could delay having children for a few more years."

"I'm thirty-three. I want a family soon."

Nate's voice didn't sound at all like it normally did, and Susannah peered at him carefully, wondering if the shock had been too much for him. It had been for her! And she was going to end up on the eleven-o'clock news. "Fine, we'll plan on starting our family right away," she agreed. "But before we do any more talking about babies, I need to ask you something important. Are you willing to change messy diapers?"

A smile played at the edges of his mouth as he nodded.

"Good." Susannah looked at Michelle, who'd laid her

head against her aunt's shoulder and closed her eyes. Apparently the events of the evening had tired her out.

"What about dinner?" Nate asked, tenderly brushing the silky hair from the baby's brow. "I don't think Michelle's going to last much longer."

"Don't worry about it. I'll buy something on the way home." She paused, then gestured weakly with her hand. "Forget that. I... I don't have any money left."

Nate grinned widely. "I'll pick up some takeout and meet you back at your place in half an hour."

Susannah smiled her appreciation. "Thanks."

"No," Nate whispered, his eyes locked with hers. "Thank *you*."

He kissed her then, slipping his hand behind her neck and tilting her face up to meet his. His touch was so potent Susannah thought her heart would beat itself right out of her chest.

"Nate." Her eyes remained shut when his name parted her lips.

"Hmm?"

"I really do love you."

"Yes, I know. I love you, too. I knew it the night you bought the stroganoff from the Western Avenue Deli and tried to make me think you'd whipped it up yourself."

She opened her eyes and raised them to his. "But I didn't even realize it then. We barely knew each other."

He kissed the tip of her nose. "I was aware from the first time we met that my life was never going to be the same."

His romantic words stirred her heart and she wiped a tear from the corner of her eye. "I... I'd better take Michelle home," she said, and sniffled.

Nate's thumb stroked the moisture from her cheek before he kissed her again. "I won't be long," he promised.

He wasn't. Susannah had no sooner got Michelle home and into her sleeper when there was a light knock at the door.

Hurriedly, she tiptoed across the carpet and opened it. She brought her finger to her lips as she let Nate inside.

"I got Chinese."

She nodded. "Great."

She paused on her way into the kitchen and showed him Michelle, who was sleeping soundly on the end of the sofa. Susannah had taken the opposite cushion and braced it against the side so there wasn't any chance she could fall off.

"You're going to be a good mother," he whispered, kissing her forehead.

It was silly to get all misty-eyed over Nate's saying that, but she did. She succeeded in disguising her emotion by walking into the kitchen and getting two plates from the cupboard. Opening the silverware drawer, she took out forks.

Nate set the large white sack on the table and lifted out five wire-handled boxes. "Garlic chicken, panfried noodles, ginger beef and two large egg rolls. Do you think that'll be enough?"

"Were you planning on feeding the Seventh Infantry?" she teased.

"You said you were hungry." He opened all the boxes but one.

Susannah filled her plate and sat next to Nate, propping her feet on the chair opposite hers. The food was delicious, and after the first few mouthfuls she decided if Nate could eat with chopsticks she should try it, too. Her efforts had a humbling effect on her.

Watching her artless movements, Nate laughed, then leaned over and kissed the corner of her mouth.

"What's in there?" she asked pointing a chopstick at the fifth box.

He shrugged. "I forget."

Curious, Susannah picked up the container and opened it. Her breath lodged in her throat as she raised her eyes to Nate's. "It's a black velvet box."

"Oh, yes, now that you mention it I remember the chef saying something about black velvet being the special of the month." He went on expertly delivering food to his mouth with the chopsticks.

Susannah continued to stare at the velvet box as if it would leap out and open itself. It was the size of a ring box.

Nate waved a chopstick in her direction. "You might as well take it out and see what's inside."

Wordlessly she did as he suggested. Once the box was free, she set the carton aside and lifted the lid. She gasped when she saw the size of the diamond. For one wild moment she couldn't breathe.

"I picked it up when I was in San Francisco," Nate told her, with no more emotion than if he'd been discussing the weather.

The solitary diamond held her gaze as effectively as a magnet. "It's the most beautiful ring I've ever seen."

"Me, too. I took one look at it and told the jeweler to wrap it up."

He acted so casual, seeming far more interested in eating his ginger beef and noodles than talking about anything as mundane as an engagement ring.

"I suppose I should tell you that while I was in San Francisco, I made an offer for the Cougars. They're a professional baseball team, in case you don't know."

"The baseball team? You're going to own a professional baseball team?" Any news he hit her with, it seemed, was going to be big.

He nodded. "I haven't heard back yet, but if that doesn't work out, I might be able to interest the owner of the New York Wolves in selling."

He made it all sound as if he were buying a car instead of something that cost millions of dollars.

"But whatever happens, we'll make Seattle our home."

Susannah nodded, although she wasn't sure why.

"Here." He set his plate aside and took the ring box from her limp hand. "I suppose the thing to do would be to place this on your finger."

Once again, Susannah nodded. Her meal was sitting

like a ton of lead in the pit of her stomach. From habit, she held out her right hand. He grinned and reached for her left one.

"I had to guess the size," he said, deftly removing the diamond from its lush bed. "I had the jeweler make it a size five, because your fingers are dainty." The ring slipped on easily, the fit perfect.

Susannah couldn't stop staring at it. Never in all her life had she dreamed she'd ever have anything so beautiful. "I...don't dare go near the water with this," she whispered, looking down at her hand. Lowering her eyes helped cover her sudden welling up of tears. The catch in her voice was telltale enough.

"Not go near the water...why?"

"If I accidentally fell in," she said, managing a light laugh, "I'd sink from the weight of the diamond."

"Is it too big?"

Quickly she shook her head. "It's perfect."

Catching her unawares, Nate pressed his mouth to her trembling lips, kissing what breath she had completely away. "I planned to ask you to marry me the night I came back from the trip. We were going out for dinner, remember?"

Susannah nodded. That had been shortly after she'd read the article in *Business Monthly* about Nate. The day it felt as though her whole world was rocking beneath her feet.

"I know we talked briefly about your career, but I have something else I need to tell you."

Susannah nodded, because commenting at this point was becoming increasingly impossible.

"What would it take to lure you away from H&J Lima?"

The diamond on her ring finger seemed incentive enough, but she wasn't going to let him know that quite yet. "Why?"

"Because I'm starting a kite company. Actually, it's going to be a nationwide franchise. I've got plans to open ten stores in strategic cities around the country to see how it flies." He stopped to laugh at his pun. "But from the testing we're doing, this is going to be big. However—" he drew in a deep breath "—I'm lacking one important member of my team. I need a marketing expert, and was wondering if you'd like to apply for the job."

"I suppose," she said, deciding to play his game. "But I'd want top salary, generous bonuses, a four-day week, a health and retirement plan and adequate maternity leave."

"The job's yours."

"I don't know, Nate, there could be problems," she said, cocking her head to one side, implying that she was already having second thoughts. "People are going to talk."

"Why?"

"Because I intend to sleep with the boss. And some old fuddy-duddy's bound to think that's how I got the job."

"Let them." He laughed, reaching for her and pulling her into his lap. "Have I told you I'm crazy about you?"

Smiling into his eyes, she nodded. "There's one thing I want cleared up before we go any further, Nate Townsend. No more secrets. Understand?"

"I promise." He spit on the end of his fingertips and used the same fingers to cross his heart. "I used to do that when I was a kid. It meant I was serious."

"Well," Susannah murmured, "since you seem to be in a pledging mood, there are a few other items I'd like to have you swear to."

"Such as?"

"Such as…" she whispered, and lowered her mouth to a scant inch above his. Whatever thoughts had been in her mind scattered like autumn leaves in a brisk wind. Her tongue outlined his lips, teasing and taunting him as he'd taught her to do.

"Susannah…"

Whatever he meant to say was interrupted by the door. Susannah lifted her head. It took a moment to clear her muddled thoughts before she realized it must be her sister and brother-in-law returning from their celebration dinner with Robert's boss.

She tried to move from Nate's lap, but he groaned in protest and tightened his arms around her. "Whoever it is will go away," he said close to her ear.

"Nate—"

"Go back to doing what you were just doing and forget whoever's at the door."

"It's Emily and Robert."

Nate moaned and released her.

Susannah had no sooner unlocked the door than Emily flew in as though she were being pursued by a banshee. She marched into the living room and stopped suddenly. Robert followed her, looking nearly as frenzied as his wife. Sane sensible Robert!

"What's wrong?" Susannah asked, her heart leaping with concern.

"You're asking *us* that?" Robert flared.

"Now, Robert," Emily said, gently placing her hand on her husband's forearm. "There's no need to be so angry. Stay calm."

"Me? Angry?" he cried, facing his wife. "In the middle of our after-dinner drink you let out a shriek that scared me out of ten years of my life and now you're telling me not to be angry?"

"Emily," Susannah tried again, "what's wrong?"

"Where's Nate?" Robert shouted. One corner of her brother-in-law's mouth curved down in a snarl. He raised his clenched fist. "I'd like ten minutes alone with that man. Give me ten minutes."

"Robert!" Emily and Susannah cried simultaneously.

"Did someone say my name?" Nate asked, as he strolled out of the kitchen.

Emily threw herself in front of her husband, patting his heaving chest with her hands. "Now, honey, settle down. There's no need to get so upset."

Susannah was completely confused. She'd never

heard her brother-in-law raise his voice before. What-ever had happened had clearly unsettled him to the point of violence.

"He's not getting away with this," Robert shouted, straining against his wife's restricting hands.

"Away with what?" Nate said with a calm that seemed to inflame Robert even more.

"Taking my daughter away from me!"

"What?" Susannah cried. It astonished her that Michelle could be sleeping through all this commotion. But fortunately the baby seemed oblivious to what was happening.

"You'd better start at the beginning," Susannah said, leading everyone into the kitchen. "There's obviously been some kind of misunderstanding. Now sit down and I'll put on some decaffeinated coffee and we can sort this out in a reasonable manner."

Her brother-in-law pulled out a chair and put his elbows on the table, supporting his head in his hands.

"Why don't you start?" Susannah said, looking at her sister.

"Well," Emily began, taking in a deep breath, "as I told you, we were having dinner with Robert's boss and—"

"They know all that," Robert interrupted. "Tell them about the part when we were having a drink in the cocktail lounge."

"Yes," Emily said, heaving a great sigh. "That does seem to be where the problem started, doesn't it?"

Susannah shared a look with Nate, wondering if he was as lost as she was. Neither Emily nor Robert was making any sense.

"Go on," Susannah encouraged.

"As I explained, we were all sitting in the cocktail lounge having a drink. There was a television set in the corner of the room. I hadn't been paying much attention to it, but I looked up and I saw you and Michelle on the screen."

"Then she gave a scream that was loud enough to curdle a Bloody Mary," Robert explained. "I got everyone to be quiet while the announcer came on. He said you'd taken *my daughter* to this…this bachelor auction. They showed Michelle pointing her finger at Nate and calling him Da-da."

"That was when Robert let out a fierce yell," Emily said.

"Oh, no." Susannah slumped into a chair, wanting to find a hole to crawl into and hibernate for the next ten years. Maybe by then Seattle would have forgotten how she'd disgraced herself.

"Did they say anything else?" Nate wanted to know, doing a poor job of disguising his amusement.

"Only that the details would follow at eleven."

"I demand an explanation!" Robert said, frowning at Nate.

"It's all very simple," Susannah rushed to explain. "See… Nate's wearing a suit that's very similar to yours.

Same shade of brown. From the distance, Michelle obviously mistook him for you."

"She did?" Robert muttered.

"Of course," Susannah went on. "Besides, Da-da is the only word she can say...." Her voice trailed off.

"Michelle knows who her daddy is," Nate said matter-of-factly. "You don't need to worry that—"

"Susannah," Emily broke in, "when did you get that diamond? It looks like an engagement ring."

"It is," Nate said, reaching to the middle of the table for the last egg roll. He looked at Susannah. "You don't mind, do you?"

"No. Go ahead."

"What channel was it?" Nate asked between bites.

Emily told him.

"Must be a slow news day," Susannah mumbled.

"Gee, Susannah," said Emily, "I always thought if you were going to make the television news it would be because of some big business deal. I never dreamed it would be over a man. Are you going to tell me what happened?"

"Someday," she said, expelling her breath. She'd never dreamed it would be over a man, either, but this one was special. More than special.

"Well, since we're going to be brothers-in-law I guess I can forget about this unfortunate incident," Robert said generously, having regained his composure.

"Good. I'd like to be friends," Nate said, holding out his hand for Robert to shake.

"You're going to be married?" Emily asked her sister.

Susannah exchanged a happy smile with Nate and nodded.

"When?"

"Soon," Nate answered for her. His eyes told her the sooner the better.

She felt the heat crawl into her face, but she was as eager as Nate to get to the altar.

"Not only has Susannah agreed to be my wife, she's also decided to take on the position of marketing director for Windy Day Kites."

"You're leaving H&J Lima?" Robert asked, as if he couldn't believe his ears.

"Had to," she said. She moved to Nate's side, wrapped her arms around his waist and smiled up at him. "The owner made me an offer I couldn't refuse."

Nate's smile felt like a summer's day. Susannah closed her eyes, basking in the warmth of this man who'd taught her about love and laughter and rainy day kisses.

Thirteen

Michelle Davidson arrived at her aunt and uncle's waterfront home just before six. Although she'd been to the house countless times, its beauty never failed to impress her. The place was even lovelier at Christmas, illuminated by string upon string of sparkling lights. The figures on the lawn—the reindeer and St. Nick and everything else—were downright magical.

Michelle's favorite was the young boy running with his kite flying high above his head. Her uncle's kites were what had launched Windy Day Toys all those years ago. Michelle didn't have any memory of those early days, of course. She'd been much too young.

Her aunt Susannah had worked with Uncle Nate for seven years. In that time, the company had gone from one successful venture to another. The first major success had been with kites, and then there was a series of outdoor games, geared toward getting kids outside instead of sitting in front of a TV or a computer screen. Buried Treasure came next and then a game called Bugs that caught national attention.

In the meantime Aunt Susannah had three children in quick succession and became a stay-at-home mother for a while. Despite her initial doubts, she'd loved it. Michelle's own mother had three children in addition to her, all born within a few months of their Townsend cousins. When her youngest sibling, Glory, entered kindergarten, Michelle's mother and Aunt Susannah had formed Motherhood, Inc.

The two sisters had introduced a series of baby products that were environmentally friendly, starting with cloth diapers and organic baby food. They'd recognized the desire of young mothers all across the country for alternatives to disposable diapers and ways to feed their babies wholesome food.

"Michelle! Michelle!"

Ten-year-old Junior was out the door and racing toward her even before Michelle had made it up the driveway. Eight-year-old Emma Jane was directly behind him. Tessa, who was twelve, was far too aloof, too cool, to show any excitement over Michelle's visit. That was all right, because Michelle knew exactly how Tessa felt. Michelle had hated it when her parents had insisted on hiring a sitter, so she couldn't very well blame Tessa now.

"Michelle." Aunt Susannah waited for her by the entrance. "I really appreciate your doing this," she said. Two large evergreen wreaths decorated the front doors, and a fifteen-foot-high Christmas tree dominated the entry, with gifts stacked all around.

Her aunt finished fastening an earring. "How'd it go at the office today?"

"People heard that we're related," Michelle confessed.

Junior and Emma Jane sat down beneath the massive Christmas tree and began sorting through the gifts— obviously an activity they indulged in often.

"I suppose everyone was likely to find out sooner or later," Aunt Susannah said, turning toward the stairs. "Nate, hurry up or we're going to be late for dinner."

"I ended up telling everyone that it was because of me that you met Uncle Nate."

At that, Tessa came out of the library. "You were?"

"It's true," Michelle said, accustomed to looks of astonishment after her coworkers' reactions earlier in the day.

"How come no one's ever mentioned *this* before?" Tessa demanded.

Aunt Susannah glanced at Michelle, frowning slightly. "It was a long time ago, sweetie."

"All you said was that you met Dad when you lived in that condo building in downtown Seattle."

"That's how we did meet." Susannah called upstairs again. "Nate!"

"I'll be right down," Nate shouted from the landing.

"Michelle?" Tessa asked, looking to her for the explanation that wasn't being offered by her mother.

"I'll tell you all about it," Michelle whispered.

"Us, too," Emma Jane said.

"Of course," Michelle promised.

Nate Townsend bounded down the stairs, looking as handsome and debonair as always. He really was a wonderful uncle—energetic, funny and a terrific cook.

"Honey, we need to leave right now."

"I know." He opened the hall closet and took out Susannah's coat and his own. He helped Susannah on with hers, then reached over to kiss each of the kids.

"Be good," he said. "And Michelle, if you're going to tell them the story of your aunt and me, don't leave out the part about how you nearly ruined my reputation at the Seattle Bachelor Auction."

"Or the fact that I spent far too much money to buy you," Susannah muttered. "I could've got you for half of what I paid."

Nate chuckled. "That's what you think. And, hey, I was worth every penny."

"Honey, we—"

"Have fun," Michelle interrupted, steering her aunt and uncle toward the entrance. Once they were on their way, she closed the door—and found her three cousins watching her expectantly.

"Now, where were we?" she murmured.

"Tell us everything," Tessa insisted.

"Can we have dinner first?" Junior asked.

"No," Tessa answered.

"Can you tell us while we eat?" Emma Jane asked.

"I do believe I can," Michelle said and the three followed her into the kitchen. "This is one of the most romantic and wonderful love stories I've ever heard—and to think it all started because of me."

* * * * *

The First Man You Meet

One

It had been one of those days.

One of those nightmarish days in which nothing had gone right. Nothing. Shelly Hansen told herself she should have seen the writing on the wall that morning when she tripped over the laces of her high-top purple running shoes as she hurried from the parking lot to her dinky office. She'd torn a hole in the knee of her brand-new pants and limped ingloriously into her building. The day had gone steadily downhill from there, with a package lost by the courier and—worst of all—the discovery that her bank account was overdrawn because a client's check had bounced.

By the time she returned to her apartment that evening she was in a black mood. All she needed to make her day complete was to have her mother pop in unannounced with a man in tow, convinced she'd found the perfect mate for Shelly.

She could only hope that wouldn't happen, but it was exactly the kind of thing Shelly had come to expect from her dear, sweet *desperate* mother. Shelly was twenty-eight now and still single, and her mother tended to view her unmarried status as a situation to be remedied. Since her father had decided not to retire, and her two brothers were both living out of state, Shelly had become the focus of her mother's obsessions. Marriage, closely followed by grandchildren, were the first and second items on Faith Hansen's agenda for her only daughter.

Never mind that Shelly felt content with her life just the way it was. Never mind that she wasn't interested in marriage and children...at least not yet. That time would come, she was sure, not now, but someday soon—or rather, some *year* soon.

For the moment, Shelly was absorbed in her career. She was proud of her work as a video producer, although she continually suffered the cash-flow problems of the self-employed. Her relaxation DVDs—seascapes, mountain scenes, a flickering fire in a brick fireplace, all with a background of classical music—were selling well. Her cat-sitting DVD had recently caught the attention of a major distributor, and she couldn't help believing she was on the brink of real success.

That was the good news.

Her mother hounding her to get married was the bad.

Tossing her woven Mexican bag and striped blue

jacket onto the sofa, Shelly ventured into the kitchen and sorted through the packages in her freezer until she found something that halfway appealed to her for dinner. The frozen entrée was in the microwave when the doorbell chimed.

Her mother. The way her day was going, it *had* to be her mother. Groaning inwardly, she decided she'd be polite but insistent. Friendly but determined, and if her mother began talking about husbands, Shelly would simply change the subject.

But it wasn't Faith Hansen who stood outside her door. It was Elvira Livingston, the building manager, a warm, delightful but insatiably curious older woman.

"Good evening, dear," Mrs. Livingston greeted her. She wore heavy gold earrings and a billowing, bright yellow dress, quite typical attire. She clutched a large box protectively in both hands. "The postman dropped this off. He asked if I'd give it to you."

"For me, Mrs. L.?" Perhaps today wasn't a total loss, after all.

Elvira nodded, holding the package as though she wasn't entirely sure she should surrender it until she got every bit of relevant data. "The return address is California. Know anyone by the name of Millicent Bannister?"

"Aunt Milly?" Shelly hadn't heard from her mother's aunt in years.

"The package is insured," Mrs. Livingston noted, shifting the box just enough to examine the label again.

Shelly held out her hands to receive the package, but her landlady apparently didn't notice.

"I had to sign for it." This, too, seemed to be of great importance. "And there's a letter attached," Mrs. Livingston added.

Shelly had the impression that the only way she'd ever get her hands on the parcel was to let Mrs. Livingston open it first.

"I certainly appreciate all the trouble you've gone to," Shelly said, gripping the sides of the box and giving a firm tug. Mrs. Livingston released the package reluctantly. "Uh, thanks, Mrs. L. I'll talk to you soon."

The older woman's face fell with disappointment as Shelly began to close the door. Obviously, she was hoping for an invitation to stay. But Shelly wasn't in the mood for company, especially not the meddlesome, if well-meaning, Elvira Livingston.

Shelly sighed. This was what she got for renting an apartment with "character." She could be living in a modern town house with a sauna, pool and workout room in a suburban neighborhood. Instead she'd opted for a brick two-story apartment building in the heart of Seattle. The radiators hissed at all hours of the night in perfect harmony with the plumbing that groaned and creaked. But Shelly loved the polished hardwood floors, the high ceilings with their delicate crystal light fixtures and the bay windows that overlooked Puget Sound. She could do without the sauna and other amenities, even if it meant occasionally dealing with an eccentric busy-body like Mrs. Livingston.

Eagerly she carried the package into the kitchen and set it on her table. Although she wondered what Aunt Milly had sent her, she carefully peeled the letter free, then just as carefully removed the plain brown wrapper.

The box was an old one, she noticed, the cardboard heavier than that currently used by stores. Shelly gently pried off the lid. She found layers of tissue paper wrapped around…a dress. Shelly pushed aside the paper and lifted the garment from its box. She gasped in surprise as the long white dress gracefully unfolded.

This wasn't just any dress. It was a wedding dress, an exquisitely sewn lace-and-satin wedding dress.

Surely it couldn't have been Aunt Milly's… No, that couldn't be… It wasn't possible.

Anxious now, her heart racing, Shelly refolded the dress and placed it back in the box. She reached for the envelope and saw that her hands were trembling as she tore it open.

My Dearest Shelly,

I trust this letter finds you happy and well. You've frequently been in my thoughts the past few days. I suppose you could blame Dr. Phil for that. Though now that I think about it, it may have been Oprah. As you'll have gathered, I often watch those talk shows these days. John would have disapproved, but he's been gone eight years now. Of course, if I wanted to, I'd watch them if he were still alive. John could disapprove all he wanted, but it wouldn't do him a bit of good. Never did. He knew it and loved me, anyway.

I imagine you're wondering why I'm mailing you my wedding dress and what Dr. Phil and Oprah have to do with it. (Yes, that is indeed my infamous wedding dress.) I suspect the sight of it has put the fear of God into you. I wish I could've been there to see your face when you realized what I was sending you. No doubt you're familiar with the story; everyone in the family's known about it for years. Since you're fated to marry the first man you meet once the dress is in your hands, your instinct is probably to burn the thing immediately!

Now that I reconsider, I'm certain it was Dr. Phil. He had a show recently featuring pets as companions to the elderly, lifting their spirits and the like. The man being interviewed brought along a cute little Scottish terrier and that was when the old seamstress drifted into my mind. Her name was Mrs. McDonald—or was it McDonnell? At any rate, I must have fallen asleep, because the next thing I knew the six-o'clock news was on.

While I slept I had a dream about you. This was no ordinary dream, either. I saw you plain as day, standing beside a tall young man, your blue eyes bright and shining. You were so happy, so truly in love. But what astonished me was the wedding dress you were wearing.

Mine.

The very dress the old Scottish woman sewed for me all those years ago. It seemed to me I was receiving a message of some sort and that I'd best not ignore it. Neither should you! You're about to embark on the grandest adventure of your life, my dear. Keep me informed!

Believe me, Shelly, I know what you're thinking. I well remember my own thoughts the day that seamstress handed me the wedding dress. I'd ordered something completely different from her—a simple evening gown—so I was shocked to say the least. Marriage was the *last* thing on my mind! I had a career, back in the days when it was rare for a woman to attend college, let alone graduate from law school.

You and I are a great deal alike, Shelly. We value our independence. It takes a special kind of man to be married to women like us. And you, my dear niece, are about to meet that one special man just the way I did.

All my love,
Aunt Milly

P.S. You're only the second person to wear the dress. Never before have I felt anything like this. Perhaps it's the beginning a new tradition!

With hands that trembled even more fiercely now, Shelly folded the letter and slid it back into the envelope. Her heart was pounding, and she could feel the sweat beading her forehead.

The phone rang then, and more from instinct than any desire to talk, Shelly picked up the receiver.

"Hello." It hadn't dawned on her until that moment that the caller might be her mother, wanting to bring over a man for her to meet. Any man her mother introduced would only add to the growing nightmare, but—

"Shelly, it's Jill. Are you all right? You sound... strange."

"Jill." Shelly was so relieved that her knees went weak. "Thank heaven it's you."

"What's wrong?"

Shelly hardly knew where to begin. "My aunt Milly's wedding dress just arrived. I realize that won't mean anything to you unless you've heard the family legend about my aunt Milly and uncle John."

"I haven't."

"Of course you haven't, otherwise you'd understand what I'm going through," Shelly snapped, then felt guilty for being short-tempered with her best friend. Making an effort to compose herself, she explained, "I've just been mailed a wedding dress—one that's been in my family for over sixty years—with the clear understanding that I'll be wearing it soon myself."

"You didn't even tell me you were dating anyone." Jill hadn't managed to disguise the hurt in her voice.

"I'm *not!* And I'm not getting married, either. If anyone should know that, it's you."

"Then your aunt intends you to wear it when you do get married."

"There's more to it than that," Shelly cried. "Listen. Aunt Milly—who's really my mother's aunt, a few years older than my grandmother—became an attorney just after the Second World War. She worked hard to earn her law degree and had decided to dedicate her life to her career."

"In other words, she'd planned never to marry."

"Exactly."

"But apparently she did."

"Yes, and the story of how that happened has been in the family for years. It seems Aunt Milly had all her clothes professionally made. As the story goes, she took some lovely white material to an old Scottish woman who had a reputation as the best seamstress around. Milly needed an evening dress for some formal event that was coming up—business-related, of course. The woman took her measurements and told her the dress would be finished by the end of the week."

"And?" Jill prompted when Shelly hesitated.

"And…when Milly returned for the dress the old woman sat her down with a cup of tea."

"The dress wasn't ready?"

"Oh, it was ready, all right, only it wasn't the dress Aunt Milly had ordered. The Scottish woman said she was gifted with the 'sight.'"

"She was clairvoyant?"

"So she claimed," Shelly said, breathing in deeply. "The old woman told my aunt that when she began the dress a vision came to her. A clear vision that involved Milly. This vision showed Milly getting married. The old woman was so convinced of it that she turned what was supposed to be a simple evening dress into an elaborate wedding gown, with layers of satin and lace and lots of pearls."

"It sounds beautiful," Jill said with a sigh.

"Of course it's beautiful—but don't you see?"

"See what?"

It was all Shelly could do not to groan with frustration. "The woman insisted my aunt Milly would marry within the year. It happened, too, just the way that seamstress said, right down to the last detail."

Jill sighed again. "That's the most romantic story I've heard in ages."

"It isn't romance," Shelly argued, "it's fate interrupting one's life! It's being a…pawn! It's destiny whether you like it or not. I know that seems crazy, but I've grown up hearing this story. It was as though my aunt Milly didn't have any choice in the matter."

"And your aunt Milly mailed you the dress?"

"Yes," Shelly wailed. "*Now* do you understand why I'm upset?"

"Frankly, no. Come on, Shelly, it's just an old dress. You're overreacting. You make it sound as if you're going to marry the next man you meet."

Shelly gasped audibly. "How'd you know?" she whispered.

"Know what?"

"That's *exactly* what happened to Aunt Milly. That's part of the legend. She tried to refuse the dress, but the seamstress wouldn't take it back, nor would she accept payment. When Aunt Milly left the dress shop, she had car problems and needed a mechanic. My uncle John was that mechanic. And Aunt Milly married him. She married *the first man she met,* just like the seamstress said."

Two

"Shelly, that doesn't mean *you're* going to marry the next man you meet," Jill stated calmly, far too calmly to suit Shelly.

Perhaps Jill didn't recognize a crisis when she came across one. They were talking about fate here. Predestination. Okay, maybe, just maybe, she was being a bit melodramatic, but after the ghastly day she'd had, who could blame her?

"Aunt Milly came right out and said I'm going to get married soon," Shelly said. "According to the family legend, the first man you meet when you get the dress is the man you'll marry."

"It's just coincidence," Jill reassured her. "Your aunt probably would've met her husband *without* the dress. It would've happened anyway. And don't forget, she's an old woman now," Jill continued soothingly. "I know this wonderful old lady who comes into the pharmacy every few weeks and she always insists *I'm* going to get married soon. I smile and nod and fill her prescription. She means well, and I'm sure your aunt Milly does, too. She just wants you to be happy, the way she was. But I think it's silly to take any of this prediction nonsense seriously."

Shelly exhaled sharply. Jill was right; Aunt Milly was a lovely woman who had Shelly's happiness at heart. She'd had a long, blissful marriage herself and wanted the same for her great-niece. But Shelly had plans and goals, none of which included meeting and marrying a stranger.

The story of Aunt Milly's wedding dress had been handed down through the family. Shelly had first heard it as a child and had loved it. She'd ranked the story of her aunt Milly and uncle John with her favorite fairy tales of Cinderella and Sleeping Beauty, barely able to distinguish truth from fantasy. However, she was an adult now. Her heart and her life weren't going to be ruled by something as whimsical as a "magic" wedding dress or a fanciful legend.

"You're absolutely right," Shelly announced emphatically. "The whole thing is ridiculous. Just because this wedding dress supposedly conjured up a husband for my aunt Milly sixty-plus years ago doesn't mean it's going to do the same thing for me, no matter what she claims."

"Well, thank goodness you're finally being sensible about this."

"No one bothered to ask me what I thought before shipping off a so-called magic wedding gown. I don't want to get married yet, so I certainly don't need the dress. It was a nice gesture, but unnecessary."

"Exactly," Jill agreed.

"I'm not interested in playing déjà voodoo." She paused to laugh at her own joke.

Jill chuckled, too. "I wouldn't be, either."

Shelly felt greatly relieved, and the tight muscles along the back of her neck began to relax. Jill was, as usual, full of practical advice. Aunt Milly was a wonderful old lady, and the legend was a delightful bit of family lore, but it would be laughable to take any of this seriously.

"How about meeting me for lunch tomorrow?" Jill suggested. "It's been ages since we got together."

"Sounds good to me," Shelly said. Although they'd been close friends since college, it took some effort on both their parts these days to make time in their hectic lives to see each other. "When and where?"

"How about the mall?" Jill asked. "That would be easiest for me since I'm scheduled to work tomorrow. I can get off a few minutes before twelve."

"Great. I'll see you at noon at Patrick's," Shelly promised. Meeting her friend for lunch was just the antidote she needed after her terrible day. But what did she expect on Friday, April thirteenth?

* * *

Shelly overslept, then got stuck in a traffic jam on her way to meet Jill the following morning. She detested being late, although she often was. Rather than fight for a convenient parking spot in the vast lot that surrounded the mall, she took the first available space and rushed over to the nearest entrance. Patrick's, a cozy, charming restaurant on the mall's upper level, was deservedly popular for business lunches. Shelly had eaten there often and especially enjoyed the spinach-and-shrimp salad.

A glance at her watch told her it was already after twelve, and not wanting to keep Jill waiting, she hurried toward the escalator, weaving her way through the crowd.

Her mind must have been on the salad she intended to order instead of the escalator because the moment she placed her foot on the first tread, she lost her balance.

"Oh…oh!" Swinging both arms out in a futile attempt to remain upright, she groped at thin air. She tried frantically to catch herself as she fell backward.

Landing in someone's arms shocked her as much as having lost her balance. Incredulous, she twisted around to thank her rescuer but this proved to be a mistake. Her action caught the man off guard, and before he could prevent it, they went crashing to the floor. Once again Shelly expected to experience pain. Instead, her waist was surrounded by arms that were surprisingly strong. His grip was firm but gentle, protective. As they fell, he maneuvered himself to take the brunt of the impact when they landed. Sprawled as she was above him, Shelly found herself staring down at the most attractive man she'd ever seen. Her heart thrummed. Her breath caught. Her body froze.

For a moment neither of them spoke. A crowd had gathered around them before Shelly managed to speak. When she did, her voice was weak and breathless. "Are you all right? I'm so sorry…"

"I'm fine. What about you?"

"Fine. I think."

She lay cushioned by his solid chest, their faces mere inches apart. Shelly's long hair fell forward, framing his face. He smelled of mint and some clean-scented soap. Her gaze wandered curiously over his features; at such close range she could see the tiny lines that fanned out from the edges of his sapphire-blue eyes, as well as the grooves that bracketed his mouth. His nose was classically straight, his mouth full and sensuous. At least his lower lip was. It didn't take her long to recognize that this man was uncompromisingly male. His eyes held hers reluctantly, as if he, too, was caught in the same powerful trance.

Neither of them moved, and although Shelly was convinced the breathless sensation she felt was a result of the fall, she couldn't seem to breathe properly even now.

"Miss, are you hurt?"

Reluctantly, Shelly looked up to find a security guard standing over her.

"Um… I don't think so."

"Sir?"

"I'm fine."

The arms that were holding hers securely began to loosen.

"If we could have you both sit over here for a moment," the guard instructed, pointing at a bench. "We have an ambulance on the way."

"An ambulance? But I told you I'm okay," she said.

The guard helped Shelly to her feet. Her legs were shaky and her breathing still uncertain, but otherwise she was unhurt.

"Officer, there's really no need," the man who'd fallen with her protested.

"Mall policy," the guard said. He hooked his thumbs into the wide leather belt and rocked back on his feet. "It's standard procedure to have all accident victims checked immediately."

"If you're worried about a lawsuit—"

"I don't make the rules," the guard interrupted her rescuer. "I just see that they're carried out. Now, if you'd sit over here, the medical team will arrive in a couple of minutes."

"I don't have time to wait," Shelly insisted. "I'm meeting someone." She glanced longingly at the upper level, wondering how she could get word of her delay to Jill. Needless to say, she'd forgotten her cell—could anything else go wrong? It didn't reassure her to notice the number of people clustered by the railing, staring down at her. Her little escapade had attracted quite a bit of attention.

"I've got an appointment, as well," the man said, looking pointedly at his watch.

The security guard ignored their protests. He removed a small notebook from his shirt pocket and flipped it open. "Your names, please."

"Shelly Hansen."

"Mark Brady."

He wrote down the information and a brief account of how they happened to fall.

"I won't have to go to the hospital, will I?" Shelly demanded.

"That depends," the guard answered.

This whole thing was ridiculous. She was perfectly fine. A little shaken, true, but uninjured. She suddenly realized that she hadn't thanked this man—Mark, was it?

"I'm terribly sorry about all this," she said. "I can't thank you enough for catching me."

"In the future, you might be more careful." Mark glanced at his watch a second time.

"I will be. But if it ever happens again, might I suggest you just let me fall?" This delay was inconvenient, but that wasn't any reason to be quick-tempered. She studied her rescuer and shook her head slightly, wondering why she'd been so impressed. He looked as if he'd stepped off Planet Nerd. Dark blue suit and tie, crisp white shirt, polished loafer-type shoes. This guy was as original as cooked oatmeal. About as personable, too.

If she was giving him the once-over, she discovered he was eyeing her, too. Apparently he was equally unimpressed. Her sweatshirt was a fluorescent orange and her jeans as tight as a second skin. Her ankle-high boots were black, her socks the same shade of orange as the sweatshirt. Her hair cascaded about her shoulders in a layer of dark frothy curls. Mark was scowling in obvious disapproval.

The wide glass doors at the mall entrance opened, and two paramedics hurried inside. Seconds later, when the ambulance arrived, two more medical people entered the building. Shelly was mortified that such a minor accident would result in all this scrutiny.

The first paramedic knelt in front of her while the second concentrated on Mark. Before she completely understood what was happening, her shoe was off and the man was examining her ankle. Mark, too, was being examined, a stethoscope pressed over his heart. He didn't seem to appreciate the procedures any more than she did.

It wasn't until he stood up that she realized how tall he was. Close to six-five, she guessed. A good match for her own five feet ten inches, she thought automatically.

It hit her then. Bull's-eye. Aunt Milly's letter had mentioned her standing beside a tall young man. Mark Brady was tall. Very tall. Taller than just about any man she'd ever met.

Aunt Milly's letter had also said something about Shelly's blue eyes. She'd ignored it at the time, but her eyes weren't blue. They were hazel. Mark had blue eyes, though. The kind of vivid blue eyes women generally found striking... Nor could she forget her initial reaction to him. She'd been attracted. Highly attracted. It'd been a long time since a man had interested her this much. Until he stood up, anyway. When she got a good look at him, she'd known immediately that they had nothing in common. She'd bet he didn't own a single article of clothing that wasn't blue, black or tan. Mark Brady was clearly a man without imagination or flair.

On a sudden thought, she glanced worriedly at his left hand. No wedding ring. Closing her eyes, she sagged against the back of the bench and groaned.

"Miss?" The paramedic was studying her closely.

"Excuse me," she said, straightening. She jerked impatiently on Mark's suit jacket. He was involved in a conversation with the ambulance attendant who was interviewing him and didn't turn around.

"Excuse me," she said again, louder this time.

"Yes?" Mark turned to face her, frowning impatiently.

Now that she had his attention, she wasn't sure she should continue. "This may seem like an odd question, but, uh...are you married?"

He frowned again. "No."

"Oh, no," Shelly moaned and slumped forward. "I was afraid of that."

"I beg your pardon?"

"Do you have a girlfriend? I mean, you're a good-looking guy. There's got to be someone important in your life. Anyone? Please, just think. Surely there's someone?" She knew she was beginning to sound desperate, but she couldn't help it. Aunt Milly's letter was echoing in her mind, and last night's logic had disappeared.

The four paramedics, as well as Mark, were staring at her. "Are you sure you don't want to come to the hospital and talk to a doctor?" one of them asked.

Shelly nodded. "I'm sure." Then before she could stop herself, she blurted out, "What do you do for a living?"

"I'm a CPA," he answered wearily.

"An accountant," she muttered. She should've guessed. He was obviously as staid and conventional as he looked. And as boring. The kind of man who'd probably never even heard of DVDs for entertaining bored house cats. He probably wouldn't be interested in purchasing one, either.

Her aunt Milly *couldn't* have seen Mark and Shelly together in her dream. Not Mark Brady. The two of them were completely ill-suited. A relationship wouldn't last five minutes! Abruptly she reminded herself that she wasn't supposed to be taking Milly's prediction seriously.

"May I go?" she asked the paramedic. "I'm not even bruised."

"Yes, but you'll need to sign here."

Shelly did so without bothering to read the statement.

Mark, however, seemed to peruse every sentence. He would, of course.

"Uh, Mark…" Shelly hesitated, and Mark glanced in her direction.

"Thank you," she said simply.

"You're welcome."

Still she delayed leaving.

"Is there anything else?"

She didn't know quite how to say this, but she felt the need too strongly to ignore it. "Don't take offense—I'm sure you're a really great guy—but I just want you to know I'm not interested in marriage right now."

Three

Jill was seated at the table, doodling on the paper place mat, when Shelly arrived. "What kept you?" she asked. "I've been here for almost half an hour."

"I—I fell off the escalator."

Jill's eyes widened in alarm. "My goodness, are you all right?"

Shelly nodded sheepishly. "I'm fine."

"Shouldn't you see a doctor?"

"I already have," she said, avoiding eye contact with her friend. "Well, sort of. The security guard called in the paramedics."

"No wonder you're late."

"I would've been, anyway," Shelly admitted as she reached for a menu, although she knew what she was going to order—the same thing she always did.

"This has really got you flustered, hasn't it?"

"It's more than the fall," Shelly explained, lowering the menu. "It's the man who caught me."

Jill arched her eyebrows jokingly. "Aha! I should have guessed there was a man involved."

"You might try to understand how I felt," Shelly said reproachfully. "Especially since I haven't recovered from receiving Aunt Milly's wedding dress yet."

"Don't tell me you're still worried about that first-man-you-meet nonsense."

"Of course not. That would be ridiculous. It's just… it's just I can't help feeling there might be *something* to that silly wedding dress."

"Then mail it back."

"I can't," Shelly said, slapping the menu down on the table. "Aunt Milly warned me not to. She didn't use exactly those words, mind you. She said I shouldn't ignore the dress. I mean, how can I? It's like an albatross around my neck."

"I still think you're overreacting."

"That's the crazy part. I *know* I am, but I can't seem to stop myself. I grew up hearing the legend of that wedding dress, and now it's in my possession. I've got a piece of family history hanging in the back of my closet. What if my mother hears about this?" She shuddered at the thought.

"So you hung the dress in your closet."

"I tried keeping it under my bed, but I couldn't sleep, so I finally got up and stuck it in the closet." She closed the menu and set it aside. "That bothered me, too. I tossed and turned half the night, then I remembered Aunt Milly had done the same thing when the seamstress gave her the dress."

"She put it under her bed?"

Shelly nodded slowly. "I seem to remember hearing that. She'd tried to refuse it, but the old woman insisted Aunt Milly take the gown home with her. By the time she got to her apartment she'd already met my uncle John, although she still didn't know she was going to marry him."

Jill raised a skeptical eyebrow. "Then what? After she put it under her bed and couldn't sleep, I mean?"

"Well, she did the same thing I did," Shelly said. "She shoved it in her closet." Shelly felt as if she was confessing to a crime. "I didn't want the thing staring me in the face so I hung it in the back."

"Naturally." Jill was trying, unsuccessfully, to disguise a smile. Shelly could see how someone else might find her situation humorous, but she personally didn't think any of this was too amusing. Not when it was her life, her future, being tossed around like…like some cosmic football. At this rate, she'd be married by nightfall!

"That's not the worst of it," Shelly added. She exhaled slowly, wondering why her heart was still beating so fiercely.

"You mean there's more?"

She nodded. The waitress arrived just then and took their orders, returning quickly with glasses of iced tea.

Shelly took a deep breath before she continued. "I literally fell into that man's—Mark Brady's—arms."

"How convenient."

"It's very nice of him to have broken my fall," she said sternly, "but I wish he hadn't."

"Shelly!"

"I mean it." She glanced around to make sure no one was listening, then whispered, "The man's an accountant."

Jill reacted in mock horror, covering her mouth with both hands. "No! An accountant?"

"Think about it. Could you honestly picture me married to an accountant?"

Jill mulled over the question for a moment. "Hmm, a CPA," she repeated slowly. "You still haven't memorized your multiplication tables, have you? You freeze up whenever you have to deal with numbers. No, I guess you're right, I can't see you with an accountant."

Shelly raised both hands, palms up, in a dramatic gesture. "I rest my case."

Jill reached for some bread, carefully selecting a whole-wheat roll. "Just because you fell into his arms doesn't mean you're going to marry him," she said in a matter-of-fact voice.

"I know that."

"Then what's the problem?"

"I can't make myself *believe* it," Shelly said. "I feel like one tiny pin fighting the force of a giant magnet."

"That's preposterous."

"I know," Shelly agreed readily. "I just wish I hadn't said anything to Mark."

Jill set the roll on her plate with exaggerated care. "You told him about your aunt Milly's wedding dress?"

"Of course not!" Shelly said. "I told him I couldn't marry him."

Jill's mouth dropped open. "You didn't! Did you?"

Shelly nodded. "I don't know what made me say anything so ludicrous. I can't imagine what he must think of me. Not that I plan on seeing him again, of course. Unless—"

"Unless what?"

Their lunches were served. Jill had ordered a hot spinach salad with slices of chicken. Shelly's spinach salad was piled high with shrimp, egg slices and black olives.

"Go on," Jill urged once the waitress had gone. "You don't plan on seeing Mark again unless—"

"Unless it's absolutely unavoidable."

"I take it this means your aunt Milly's first encounter with your uncle John wasn't her last." Jill giggled. "Silly me. Obviously it wasn't."

"No. Even though Aunt Milly didn't want to see him again. My uncle was a wonderful man, don't get me wrong, and he was perfect for Aunt Milly, as it turned out, but they were as different as night and day. Aunt Milly was a college graduate and Uncle John never completed high school."

Shelly sighed wistfully. At one time the story of their romance had been like her own personal fairy tale. But now she didn't find it nearly as enthralling. "He helped Milly fix her car the night it broke down. The very next day she was in court defending a client in a lawsuit—"

"Let me guess," Jill interrupted, "your uncle John was the man suing her client."

Shelly nodded. "Yes, and that was only the beginning. Every time they turned around they were bumping into each other."

"How soon after they met did they get married?"

This was the question Shelly had dreaded most. She closed her eyes and whispered, "Ten days."

"Ten days," Jill echoed with an incredulous look.

"I know. It seems that once they kissed, they both realized there wasn't any use fighting it."

"Did your aunt tell John about the seamstress and the wedding dress?"

Shelly shrugged. "I don't know, but my guess is she didn't…at least not at first." She hadn't touched her salad yet and paused to savor a forkful of her favorite seafood. Then she said abruptly, "They eloped without telling anyone."

"Children?" Jill wanted to know.

"Three boys. My mother's cousins."

"What about granddaughters? You'd think your aunt Milly would want to hand the dress down to one of them."

"All three of her sons had boys themselves. I guess you could say I'm the closest she's got to a granddaughter."

"Ten days," Jill repeated. "That's really something."

Forking up another succulent shrimp, Shelly continued her story. "That old Scottish woman knew about the wedding even before the family did. When Aunt Milly and Uncle John returned from their honeymoon, there was a wedding card from the seamstress waiting for them."

Jill propped her elbows on the table and gazed at Shelly. "Tell me what Mark Brady looks like."

Shelly frowned, trying to form her impressions of him into some kind of reasonably articulate description. He was compelling in ways she didn't quite understand. She sensed that he was principled and headstrong, but what made her so sure of that, Shelly couldn't explain. "He's tall," she began slowly. "And he was wearing a suit."

"How tall?"

"Basketball-player tall. He must be about six-five."

"Brown hair?"

Shelly nodded. "With blue eyes. *Really* blue eyes. I don't think I've ever met a man with eyes that precise color. They seemed to…" She hesitated, unsettled by the emotion that stirred within her when she thought about Mark. Although their encounter had been brief, Shelly was left feeling oddly certain that she could trust this man, trust him implicitly. It wasn't a sensation she could remember experiencing with any other man. She didn't like the feeling; it made her uncomfortable. Until Jill had started asking her about Mark, Shelly didn't realize she'd experienced *any* emotion toward him—except for embarrassment, of course.

"Why do you want to know?" she asked.

Jill gave her a knowing grin. "Because if he's as tall as you say, with dark brown hair and deep blue eyes, and he's wearing a suit, he just walked into this restaurant."

"What?" Shelly felt her stomach sink. "Mark's here? Mark Brady?"

"That's not so unusual, is it? This is, after all, the same shopping mall where you, uh, met—" Jill made a show of glancing at her watch "—thirty or so minutes ago."

"He's here." She reminded herself that Jill was right: Mark's choosing to have lunch at Patrick's was just a coincidence. Too bad she couldn't convince her racing heart to believe that.

"He's on the other side of the room," Jill whispered.

"Has he seen me yet?"

"I don't think so."

Without being obvious—or at least Shelly hoped she wasn't being obvious—she turned to look in his direction. At that same instant, Mark happened to look up. Their eyes met. Despite herself, she gasped. Her hands shook and she felt herself break out in a cold sweat.

Mark scowled and quickly looked away.

She couldn't blame him. He seemed surprised to see her there. Unpleasantly surprised.

"Well, is it him?" Jill demanded.

Shelly couldn't find her voice, so she answered with a nod.

"I thought it might be. What are you thinking?"

"That I've lost my appetite." Shelly doubted she'd be able to finish her lunch.

"You want my advice?" Jill asked, grinning broadly. "I don't have a lot of experience with magic wedding dresses, but I recently read a fascinating book on home remedies."

"Sure." At this point Shelly was feeling reckless enough to try just about anything.

"Garlic," Jill said solemnly. "Wear a garlic rope around your neck. Not only does it deter vampires and prevent colds, but it might ward off potential husbands conjured up by a magic wedding dress."

Four

Hard though she tried, Shelly had a difficult time ignoring Mark Brady. He sat there, stiff and unapproachable, at the other side of the small restaurant. Just as stiff and unapproachable as she was. Jill wanted to linger over her coffee before returning to her job at the Pay-Rite Pharmacy in the mall, but Shelly was eager to be on her way. The sooner she left, the sooner she could put this bothersome encounter behind her.

"Don't forget Morgan's baby shower on Tuesday night," Jill said as Shelly reached for her purse.

Shelly had completely forgotten about their friend's party, which was understandable given her present state of mind. Most of their college friends were married and several were now having babies. Rather than admit how absentminded she'd suddenly become, Shelly asked, "Do you want to drive over together?"

"Sure," Jill said. "I have to go directly from work so I'll stop off at your place and we can leave from there."

"I'll be ready." She tried to imagine their excitable classmate as a wife and mother. It was Morgan who'd gotten the entire dorm hooked on *Survivor*. Before anyone could figure out how it had occurred, all the girls were obsessed with the participants and their lives. It became as important as mealtimes to learn who'd been voted off and who'd won that week's challenges.

For no particular reason, Shelly thought of Aunt Milly's wedding dress—which seemed to have become her own private challenge. Sighing, she dropped her share of the bill and a tip on the table. "I'll see you Tuesday, then."

"Right. And, Shelly, don't look so worried. No enchanted wedding dress is going to interfere with your life—unless you allow it to."

Easy for Jill to say, since it wasn't *her* life and *her* great-aunt's wedding dress. Nevertheless, her advice was sound. Aunt Milly might have had some fanciful dream about Shelly's marrying a tall man with blue eyes, but that didn't mean it was going to happen, especially when Shelly was so determined that it wouldn't.

"You're absolutely right," she said emphatically. "I know I keep saying that, but…well, I seem to need reminding. So, thanks. Again." With a final wave, she wandered out of the restaurant, barely noticing the colorful shop windows as she passed them. As Jill had pointed out, Aunt Milly meant well, but the letter and the wedding dress shouldn't be taken too seriously.

Shelly knew exactly what kind of man she'd fall in love with, and he wouldn't bear any resemblance to Mark Brady. He'd be unconventional, and fervent about life, and as passionate as she was herself. Naturally, he'd appreciate her work and take pride in his own. He'd be a free spirit, like her. She'd prefer a man with gumption, too—someone who possessed initiative. It'd be nice if he was a little better at organizational skills than she was, but that wasn't a requirement.

With marriage so prominent in her mind, Shelly found herself standing in front of a jeweler's display window, studying a large assortment of wedding bands. She noticed one ring that stood out from the rest: three small rows of diamond chips, bracketed on each side by a thin band of gold. The ring was striking in its simplicity, its uncontrived beauty.

For the longest moment Shelly stared at the rings as she wove whimsical dreams around the happy bride and the tall groom. *Tall groom.* Her thoughts came to a skidding halt.

What on earth had come over her? She didn't know, but whatever it was, she didn't like it. Self-consciously she glanced around, fearful that someone was watching her. Well, a very specific someone, to be honest. Someone who definitely shouldn't see her gazing with open longing at a collection of absurdly high-priced wedding rings. Mark Brady.

With a sense of urgency, Shelly hurried toward the mall exit. It was all she could do to keep from breaking into a run. No matter how fast she walked, however, she couldn't shake the feeling that *he* was there, watching her. Twice she whirled around, convinced she'd see Mark Brady strolling behind her, sneering and making contemptuous remarks.

He wasn't there.

With profound relief, she arrived at the parking lot and located her car. She finally felt herself relax as she neared her apartment building. Once she'd parked her car, Shelly stopped in the lobby to collect her mail. As soon as she opened the small box, Mrs. Livingston's head poked out her door.

"Good afternoon, Shelly," she chirped, smiling at her expectantly.

It took Shelly a moment to realize that Mrs. L. must have been waiting to hear about the contents of her package.

"It's a lovely day," Shelly said conversationally, sorting through her mail. Two bills, a flyer and something from the Internal Revenue Service. The way her luck had been going, it was probably an audit notice. A quick inspection revealed exactly that. She closed her eyes and groaned inwardly.

"A lovely day indeed," Mrs. Livingston echoed cheerfully.

Muttering under her breath, Shelly stuffed the IRS notice back inside the envelope. When she looked up, she saw that the older woman was now standing in the hallway.

"I suppose you're wondering about the package," Shelly said resignedly, tucking her mail inside her purse. "It was a gift from my aunt Milly."

"Something from the past, I guess?" Mrs. Livingston asked.

"Why…yes. How'd you know?"

"I'd take whatever it is very, very seriously if I were you," Mrs. Livingston continued in a solemn voice. "Wizard wouldn't go anywhere near that box. Think what you want, but my cat's always had a sixth sense when it comes to this sort of thing."

"It's a dress, Mrs. L.," Shelly explained, hiding behind a false smile. "How am I supposed to take a dress seriously?" It was exactly what she'd vowed *not* to do.

Mrs. Livingston opened her apartment door and scooped the large black-and-white cat into her arms. "That I wouldn't know," she returned, her eyes narrowed. "All I can tell you is that Wizard felt skittish around that package. You don't suppose there's…magic in it, do you?"

Somehow Shelly managed a reply, although she felt certain it was unintelligible. Taking the stairs two at a time, she dashed into her apartment, leaning breathlessly against the door. Even Mrs. Livingston's cat knew there was something strange about Aunt Milly's wedding dress!

* * *

When Jill arrived late Tuesday afternoon, Shelly was ready and waiting for her, brightly wrapped baby gift in hand. She was eager to get out and socialize—eager to get out, period. Anything to escape another phone call from her mother, who'd recently heard from Aunt Milly. Now Faith Hansen was calling daily for updates on the romantic prospects in her daughter's life.

"Well?" Jill demanded as she entered the apartment. "Are you going to show it to me?"

"Show what to you?"

Jill gave her a look that seemed to question her intelligence. "The wedding dress, of course."

For several hours Shelly had succeeded in putting the dress out of her mind. "No," she said forcefully. "I want to forget about the whole thing."

"Met any tall blue-eyed men lately?" Jill couldn't resist asking.

"None," Shelly answered shortly. Checking her watch, she noted that they were early but suggested they leave, anyway. "Shall we go?"

"We've got lots of time," Jill countered, moving toward Shelly's bedroom. "Come on, it isn't going to hurt to let me look at the dress."

"Oh, all right," Shelly conceded ungraciously. Leading the way, she opened the closet door and reached into the back of the closet.

She brought out the lace-and-satin gown, holding it up for Jill's inspection. She'd hardly looked at the dress the day she'd received it, and now she was almost shocked by how beautiful it actually was.

The laughter drained from Jill's dark brown eyes as she stared at the gown. "Oh, Shelly, it's…lovely." She gently touched the Elizabethan sleeve and ran her finger along the delicate layer of pearls that decorated the cuff. The high neckline was also trimmed with an intricate design of pearls. "I don't know what I expected," Jill said in an awed whisper, "but certainly nothing as beautiful as this."

Shelly nodded wordlessly. The dress was far more exquisite than she'd realized. Her heart swelled with sudden emotion, and to her dismay, tears filled her eyes as she thought about the old Scottish woman who had so lovingly constructed the gown. Each pearl had been sewn into place by hand. She thought of her aunt Milly, as tall and statuesque as Shelly herself, wearing the dress. Then she recalled her uncle John, such a determined man, so wise and sensible. Shelly thought fondly of those two, who'd been so completely different, yet had loved each other so well….

For a moment neither she nor Jill spoke. "Have you tried it on?" Jill finally asked.

Shelly shook her head adamantly, not wanting her friend to know how emotional she'd become. "Heavens, no, but you can if you want."

"I don't think I could resist if I were you," Jill whispered, obviously affected by the dress, too. "Just seeing it…makes me wish I was a bride myself."

"There's always Ralph," Shelly teased. Jill had been dating Ralph, a computer programmer, for several months, but Shelly couldn't understand what her friend saw in him.

Jill threw her an irritated look. "The dress is for you, not me."

"But I don't want it," Shelly insisted, though she was no longer sure what she felt. Not since she'd really examined the dress and allowed herself to remember the wonder of John and Milly's romance.

"You're sure you don't mind?" Jill asked, slipping off her shoes. "I mean, if you'd rather I didn't try it on, I'll understand."

"No, feel free." Shelly strove for a flippant air. "As far as I'm concerned, the dress is nothing but bad luck. It arrived on Friday the thirteenth. The next day I had that minor accident on the mall escalator. Now I'm being audited by the IRS."

It was as if Jill didn't hear. "I doubt it'll fit," she said as she cautiously removed the gown from the padded hanger. "I'm a good five inches shorter than you and heavier on top."

"Maybe the dress was meant for you in the first place," Shelly ventured. Perhaps Aunt Milly had been confused and it was Jill she'd viewed in her dream. After all, Milly's eyes weren't what they used to be....

"Does your mother know?" Jill asked as she stepped into the dress. She raised it over her hips and turned around to let Shelly fasten the buttons that ran down the back.

"That's another thing," Shelly moaned. "Mom's been calling me every day since I got the dress, wanting to know if I've met anyone special yet."

"What did you tell her?" Jill asked, looking at Shelly over her shoulder.

"What's there to tell?" she asked irritably.

"Well, you might have mentioned Mark."

"Mark," Shelly repeated. She shrugged elaborately. "I haven't given him a thought in days." Not strictly true, but she'd been *trying* not to think about him. Even if he was interested in her—and he'd made very clear that he wasn't—she couldn't imagine two more ill-suited people. "I haven't seen him since Saturday and I doubt I'll ever see him again."

"You're sure of that?"

"Positive."

"Well, what do you think?" Jill asked next, pirouetting slowly in front of her. "My hair's a mess and I've got hardly any makeup on, but…"

Shelly studied her friend and sighed audibly. Never had she seen Jill look lovelier. It was as if the dress had been made for her. "Absolutely enchanting. It fits like a dream."

"I feel like I *am* dreaming," Jill admitted softly. "Here," she said, turning around, "undo me before I start longing for a husband and 2.5 children."

"Don't forget the house with the white picket fence," Shelly teased, unfastening the buttons.

Jill slipped out of the dress. "Your turn," she said as she laid it carefully across the bed. "If it fits me, then it can't possibly fit you. You've got the perfect excuse to send it back to your aunt Milly."

"I...don't know." Shelly bit her lip. She felt an inexplicable urge to keep the dress, and at the same time she would've willingly returned it to her aunt. Even while she hesitated, Shelly found herself undressing. She couldn't explain her sudden eagerness to try on the wedding gown any more than she could fathom its growing emotional appeal.

The dress slid easily over her hips. She turned around so Jill could secure the back, then glanced at the mirror, expecting to find the skirt miles too short. It would have to be in order to fit Jill as perfectly as it had.

"Shelly," Jill whispered, then cupped her hand over her mouth. "My goodness...you look beautiful...really beautiful."

That was what Shelly had felt the instant she'd seen her friend in the dress. "Something's wrong," she said once she found her voice. "Something's very wrong."

"No," Jill countered, "it's very right. It's as if the dress was made for you."

"Then answer me this," Shelly whispered. "How is it possible for the same dress to fit two women who wear totally different sizes?"

Five

Shelly struggled to open the door of the Internal Revenue office, her arms weighed down with a huge box stuffed full of receipts and records for the audit. By bracing the box against the wall with her knee, she freed one hand to open the door. For the first time ever, she'd completed her tax return early—all by herself, too—and *this* was her reward. She grumbled righteously and bit her lip, more in anxiety than annoyance.

She'd just managed to grasp the door handle, when the door unexpectedly opened and she staggered into the room, nearly colliding with an end table. She did a quick pirouette, convinced she'd ruined a new pair of panty hose. With a heartfelt sigh, she set her box of records on the floor and sank into the first available chair, neatly arranging her unaccustomed skirt around her knees. Only then did she bother to look around. There was one other person in the large reception area.

Shelly's heart did a nosedive, landing in the pit of her stomach. The man who'd opened the door for her, the man sitting in this very waiting room, was none other than Mark Brady—the man she'd hoped to avoid for the rest of her natural life. She gave an involuntary gasp.

Mark was leafing through the dog-eared pages of a magazine when he happened to glance her way. The automatic smile faded from his face, and his eyes narrowed as if he strongly suspected Shelly had purposely arranged this meeting.

"What are you doing here?" Shelly demanded.

"I might ask you the same thing."

"I didn't follow you here, if that's what you're implying!"

"Listen, Ms.….Hansen, I really couldn't care less." With that he returned to his magazine, but he raised his head again a moment later. "*You're* the person who blurted out to everyone within hearing distance that you weren't marrying me. As if I'd even asked! As if I even *knew* you!"

Shelly felt the heat rising up her neck and offered the first excuse she could think of. "I…was distraught."

"Obviously," he muttered from behind his magazine.

A few minutes of strained silence passed. Shelly shifted uncomfortably in her chair, checking her watch approximately every ten seconds. She was early for her appointment, but if this was where promptness got you, she'd prefer to be late.

"All right, I apologize," Shelly said when she couldn't tolerate the silence any longer. "What I said was ridiculous and…and out of turn—"

"Out of turn," Mark echoed, throwing the magazine down on the table. "I repeat—I don't even know you."

"I realize that."

He inhaled deeply, which drew her attention to his broad, muscular chest. She saw that he was as meticulously dressed as he'd been at their first encounter. His dark suit and silk tie, however conventional, added a touch of sophistication to his natural good looks.

"If there's anyone to blame for this it's Aunt Milly," Shelly said, more to herself than him.

"Aunt Milly?" Mark repeated, sounding unsure. He eyed her warily.

She'd said this much; she might as well launch into the whole ludicrous tale.

"Actually, it has more to do with the wedding dress than with my aunt Milly, although by now the two of them are inseparable in my mind. I don't usually dabble in this sort of thing, but I'm beginning to think there might be something supernatural about that silly dress, after all."

"Supernatural?"

"Magic, if you prefer."

"Magic in a wedding dress?" Mark gazed hopefully

at the door that led to the inner offices of Internal Revenue, as though he was anxious to be called away.

"It's unbelievable, but the dress fits both Jill and me, which is virtually impossible. You saw Jill—she's the friend I was having lunch with last Saturday. I know we were halfway across the room from you, but you couldn't help noticing how much shorter she is than I am. We're completely different sizes."

Mark hurriedly reached for the magazine as if he wanted to shut her out before she said anything else.

"I know it seems crazy. I don't like this any better than you do, but I'm afraid you're the one Aunt Milly mentioned in her letter." Well, it was only fair to tell him that.

Mark glanced in her direction again, blue eyes suspicious. "Your aunt Milly mentioned me in a letter?"

"Not by name—but she said she had a clear vision of me in the wedding dress and I was standing with a tall man. She also referred to blue eyes. You're tall and you have blue eyes and the legend says I'm going to marry the first man I meet after receiving the dress."

"And I just happened to be that man?"

"Yes," Shelly cried. "*Now* do you understand why I was so disturbed when we met?"

"Not entirely," Mark said after a moment.

Shelly sighed loudly. How obtuse could the man be? "You're tall, aren't you? And you have blue eyes."

He flipped intently through the magazine, not looking at her as he spoke. "I really don't care what the letter said, nor am I concerned about this wedding dress you keep bringing up."

"Of course you don't care," Shelly said indignantly. "Why should you? It must all seem quite absurd to you. And I'm aware that I'm overreacting, but I do have a tendency to get emotional. If it helps any, I want you to know I'm happy with my life just the way it is. I don't want to get married—to anyone." When she'd finished, she drew in a deep breath and began leafing idly through a magazine, doing her utmost to ignore him.

Silence returned. Silences had always bothered Shelly. It was as if she felt personally responsible for filling them. "If you want something to be grateful about, you can thank your lucky stars I didn't mention you to my mother."

"Your mother," Mark repeated. "Does she know about Aunt Milly sending you this…dress?"

"Of course she does," Shelly answered, closing the magazine. "She's phoned me every day since she heard, because she thinks I'm going to meet that special someone any minute."

"And you didn't say anything about me?"

"How could I? The instant I do that, she'll be calling the caterers."

"I see." The edges of his mouth lifted as though he was beginning to find the situation amusing. "She believes in the power of this dress, too?"

"Unfortunately, yes. You have to understand where

my mother stands on the issue of marriage," Shelly continued, undaunted.

"I'm not sure I want to," Mark muttered under his breath.

Shelly disregarded his comment. "By age twenty-eight—my age now, coincidentally—Mom had been married for eight years and already had three children. She's convinced I'm letting the best years of my life slip away. There's nothing I can say to make her believe differently."

"Then I'll add my gratitude that you didn't mention me."

Mollified, Shelly nodded, then glanced at her watch. Her meeting was in ten minutes and she was nervous, since this was the first time she'd done her own taxes. She should have known there'd be a problem.

"I take it you're here for an audit?" Mark asked.

She nodded again, studying her tax return, sure she'd be in jail by nightfall without even understanding what she'd done wrong.

"Relax."

"How can I?"

"Have you knowingly hidden something from the government? Lied about the income you received, or claimed expenditures you've never made?"

"Oh, no!"

"Then you don't have anything to worry about."

"I don't?" Shelly stared at him, envying his confidence. She'd been restless for days, worrying about this meeting. If it wasn't the wedding dress giving her nightmares, it was the audit.

"Don't volunteer any information unless they ask for it."

"All right."

"Did you prepare your own tax return?"

"Well, yes. It didn't seem that complicated, and well, this sounds silly but Jill bet me I couldn't do it. So I did. Back in February. You see, numbers tend to confuse me and I decided to accept the challenge, and…" She realized she was chattering, something she did when she was nervous. Forcing herself to stay quiet, she scanned her return for the hundredth time, wondering what she could have possibly done wrong.

"Do you want me to look it over for you?"

Shelly was surprised by his generosity. "If you wouldn't mind. Are you being audited yourself?"

Mark smiled and shook his head. "A client of mine is."

"Oh."

He crossed the room and sat next to her. When Shelly handed him her tax return, he quickly ran down the row of figures, then asked her several questions.

"I've got everything right here," she assured him, gesturing toward the carton she'd lugged in with her. "I really am careful about saving everything I should."

Mark gestured at the large cardboard box. "This is all for one year?"

"No," she admitted sheepishly. "I brought along everything I had for the past six years. I mean, it made sense at the time."

"That really wasn't necessary."

"I'd rather be safe than sorry," Shelly said with a shrug. She watched Mark as he scrutinized her return. At such close range, she saw that his eyes were even bluer than she'd thought. *Blue as the sky on a bright July afternoon...* Her heart felt heavy in her chest, and hard as she tried, she couldn't keep herself from staring.

Mark handed back her return. "Everything looks fine. I don't think you'll have a problem."

It was astonishing how relieved she felt at hearing that. No, at hearing that from *him*. Mark smiled at her and Shelly found herself responding readily with a smile of her own. The fluttery sensation returned to her stomach. She knew her eyes were wide and questioning and although she tried to look away, she couldn't do it.

Surprise mingled with gentleness on his face, as if he were seeing her for the first time, really seeing her. He liked what he saw—Shelly could read that in his eyes. Slowly his gaze traveled over her features, and she felt her pulse speed up. The letter she'd received from Aunt Milly flitted through her mind, but instead of dismissing the memory, she wondered, *Could there really be something to all this?*

Mark was the one to break eye contact. He stood abruptly and hurried back to his seat. "I don't think you have to worry."

"Yes, you told me."

"I mean about your aunt Milly's wedding dress."

"I don't have to worry?" Shelly repeated. She wasn't sure she understood.

"Not with me, at any rate."

"I don't quite follow…." If he was even half-aware of the way her heart was clamoring as they gazed into each other's eyes, he wouldn't be nearly as confident.

"I'm engaged."

"Engaged?" Shelly felt as though someone had slugged her in the stomach. Her first reaction was anger. "You couldn't have mentioned this sooner?" she snapped.

"It's not official yet. Janice hasn't picked out a diamond. Nor have we discussed our plans with her family."

The irritation faded, swallowed by an overwhelming sense of relief. "Engaged," she murmured, reminding herself that she really had no interest in marriage. And this proved there was no such thing as a "magic" wedding dress. If Mark was involved with Janice, he wouldn't be free to marry her. It was that simple. Shelly leaped to her feet and started to pace.

"Are you all right?" Mark asked. "You're looking pale."

She nodded and pressed her hands to her cheeks, which suddenly felt hot. "I'm so relieved," she whispered hoarsely. "You have no idea how relieved I am. You're engaged… My goodness, I feel like I've got a new lease on life."

"As I explained," Mark said, frowning, "it isn't official yet."

"That's okay. You're committed to someone else and that's all that matters. However—" she forced a smile "—you might have said something sooner and saved me all this anxiety."

"You did ask that day at the mall, but I was more concerned with avoiding a scene than revealing the personal details of my life."

"I'm sorry about that."

"No problem."

Shelly settled back in the chair and crossed her legs, hoping to strike a relaxed pose. She even managed to skim a couple of magazines, although she barely knew what she was reading.

Finally, the receptionist opened the door and called her name. Eager to get this over with, Shelly stood, picking up the large box she'd brought with her. She paused on her way out of the reception area and turned to Mark. "I wish you and Janice every happiness," she said formally.

"Thank you," he answered, then grinned. "Same to you and whatever, uh, lucky guy the wedding dress finds you."

Six

She should be happy, Shelly told herself early the following morning. Not only had she survived the audit—in fact she'd come away with an unexpected refund—but she'd learned that Mark was practically engaged.

Yes, she should be dancing in the streets, singing in the aisles… Instead she'd been struggling with a strange melancholy ever since their last encounter. She seemed to have lost her usual vitality, her sense of fun.

Now it was Saturday, and for once she had no looming deadlines, no appointments, no pressing errands. Remembering the exhilaration and solace she'd felt when she recorded an ocean storm sequence recently, Shelly decided to see if she could recapture some of those feelings. She headed over to Long Beach, a resort town on the Washington coastline. The sky was clear and almost cloudless; the sun was bright and pleasantly warm—a perfect spring day. Once she drove onto the freeway, the miles sped past and two hours later she was standing on the sandy beach with the breeze riffling her long hair.

She walked around for a while, enjoying the sights and sounds—the chirping of the sea gulls, the salty spray of the Pacific Ocean and the scent of wind and sea. She was satisfied with her beach DVD and started to work out plans for a whole series—the ocean in different seasons, different moods. That would be something special, she thought, something unique.

She wandered down the beach, kicking at the sand with the toes of her running shoes. Tucking her fingertips in the pockets of her jeans, she breathed in the vivid freshness around her. After an hour or so, she made her way back to the concession stands, where she bought a hot dog and a cold drink.

Then, just because it looked like fun, she rented a moped.

She sped along the shore, thrilled with the sensation of freedom, reveling in the solitude and the roar of pounding surf.

The wind tossed her hair about her face until it was a confusion of curls. Shelly laughed aloud and listened as the galloping breeze carried off the sound.

Her motorized bike rushed forward, spitting sand in its wake. She felt reckless with exhilaration, as though there was nothing she couldn't do. It was that kind of afternoon. That kind of day.

When she least expected it, someone else on a moped raced past her. Shelly hadn't encountered anyone during her ride and this person took her by surprise. She glanced quickly over her shoulder, astonished by how far she'd traveled. The only other person she could see was the one who'd passed her.

To her surprise, the rider did an abrupt turnaround and headed back in her direction. With the sun in her eyes and the wind pelting her, Shelly slowed to a crawl and shaded her eyes with one hand.

It wasn't until he was nearly beside her that Shelly recognized the other rider.

Mark Brady.

She was so shocked that she allowed the engine to die, her feet dropping to the sand to maintain her balance. Mark appeared equally shocked. He braked abruptly.

"Shelly?" He seemed not to believe it was her.

Shelly shook her head and blinked a couple of times just to make sure she wasn't fantasizing. She certainly hadn't expected to encounter Mark Brady on a beach two hours out of Seattle. Mr. Conservative riding a moped! This time, though, he wasn't wearing a dark suit. He didn't have his briefcase with him, either. And he looked even handsomer than usual in worn jeans and a University of Washington sweatshirt.

"Mark?" She couldn't prevent the astonishment from creeping into her voice.

"What are you doing here?"

She heard the hostility in his tone and answered him

coolly. "The same thing as you, apparently." She pushed the hair from her face, and the wind promptly blew it back.

Mark's blue eyes narrowed suspiciously. "You didn't happen to follow me, did you?"

"Follow you?" she repeated indignantly. She'd rarely been more insulted. "Follow you!" she said again, starting her moped and revving the engine. "May I remind you that I was on the beach first? If anyone was doing any following, it was *you* following me." She was breathless by the time she finished. "In fact, you're the last person I'd follow anywhere!"

Mark scowled at her. "The feeling's mutual. I'm not in the mood for another story about your aunt Martha's damn wedding dress, either."

Shelly felt an unexpected flash of pain. "I was having a perfectly wonderful afternoon until you arrived," she said stiffly.

"I was having a good time myself," he muttered.

"Then I suggest we go our separate ways and forget we ever met."

Mark looked as if he was about to say something else, but Shelly was in no frame of mind to listen. She twisted the accelerator on the handlebar of her moped and took off down the beach. Although she knew she was being unreasonable, she was furious. Furious at the surge of joy she'd felt when she recognized him. Furious at Mark, because he didn't seem even a little pleased to see her. She bit her lower lip, remembering the comment he'd made about not wanting to hear any more about her "damn wedding dress." Now, that was just rude, she told herself righteously. She could *never* be interested in a man who was not only conventional but rude.

Squinting, Shelly hunched her shoulders against the wind, in a hurry now to return to the boardwalk. She hadn't meant to go nearly this far.

The wet, compact sand made for smooth, fast riding and Shelly stayed close to the water's edge in an effort to outdistance Mark. Not that he was likely to chase her, but she wanted to avoid any possibility of another embarrassing encounter.

Then it happened.

A large wave came in, sneaking its way up the sand, creating a thin, glistening sheen. Shelly hardly noticed as her front tire ripped through the water, spraying it out on both sides. Then the moped's front wheel dipped precariously. One minute she was sailing down the beach at breakneck speed and the next she was cartwheeling over her handlebars.

She landed heavily in a patch of wet sand, too paralyzed with shock to know if she was hurt or not.

Before she could move, Mark was crouching at her side. "Shelly? Are you all right?"

"I…don't know." Carefully she flexed one arm and then the other. Sitting up, she tested each leg and didn't feel pain there, either. Apparently she'd survived the experience unscathed.

"You crazy fool!" he yelled, leaping to his feet. "What are you trying to do, kill yourself?"

"Ah…" It was painful to breathe, otherwise she would've answered him.

"Can you imagine what I thought when I saw you flying through the air like that?"

"Good riddance?" she suggested.

Mark closed his eyes and shook his head. "I'm in no mood for your jokes. Here, let me help you up." He moved behind her, sliding his arms around her waist and gently raising her.

"I'm fine," she protested the instant his arms surrounded her. The blood rushed to her head, but Shelly didn't know if that was because of her tumble or because Mark was holding her. Even when she was on her feet, he didn't release her.

"Are you sure you're not hurt?"

Shelly nodded, not trusting her voice. "I'm less confident about the moped, though." Her bike seemed to be in worse shape than she was.

"It doesn't look good to me, either," Mark said. He finally dropped his arms and retrieved the moped, which was lying on its side, the waves lapping over it. There were regular hissing sounds as the cold water splashed against the heated muffler. Steam rose from the engine.

Mark did his best to start the bike, but to no avail. "I'm afraid it's hopelessly wet. It won't start now until it's had a chance to dry. A mechanic should check it over to be sure nothing's wrong."

Shelly agreed. There was no help for it; she was going to have to walk the bike back to the rental shop. No small feat when she considered she was about three miles down the beach.

"Thank you very much for stopping," she said a bit primly. "But as you can see I'm not hurt…."

"What do you think you're doing?" Mark asked as she began pushing the moped. It made for slow progress; the bulky machine was far more difficult to transport under her own power than she'd expected. At this rate, she'd be lucky to return it by nightfall.

"I'm taking the bike back to the place where I rented it."

"That's ridiculous."

"Do you have any better ideas?" she asked in a reasonable tone of voice. "I don't understand what you're doing here in the first place," she said, sounding far calmer than she felt. "You should be with Janet."

"Who?" he demanded. He tried to take the moped away from her and push it himself, but she wouldn't let go.

"The woman you're going to marry. Remember?"

"Her name is Janice and as I said before, the engagement's unofficial."

"That doesn't answer my question. You should be with her on a beautiful spring day like this."

Mark frowned. "Janice couldn't get away. She had an important meeting with a client—she's a lawyer. Listen, quit being so stubborn, I'm stronger than you. Let me push the bike."

Shelly hesitated; his offer was tempting. She hadn't gone more than a few feet and already her side ached. She pressed one hand against her hip and straightened, her decision made. "Thanks, but no thanks," she answered flatly. "By the way, it's Aunt Milly who sent me the wedding dress, not Aunt Martha, so if we're going to get names straight, let's start there."

Mark rolled his eyes skyward, as though he'd reached the end of his limited patience. "Fine, I'll apologize for what I said back there. I didn't mean to insult you."

"I didn't follow you," she said.

"I know, but I didn't follow you, either."

Shelly nodded, deciding she believed him.

"Then how do you explain that we've inadvertently bumped into each other twice in the last week?" Mark asked. "The odds of that happening have got to be phenomenal."

"I know it sounds crazy, but... I'm afraid it's the dress," Shelly mumbled.

"The wedding dress?" Mark repeated.

"I'm really embarrassed about all this. I'm not sure I believe any of it myself. And I do apologize, especially since there's been an apparent mix-up...."

"Why's that?" Mark asked.

"Well...because you're involved with Janice. I'm sure the two of you are a perfect match and you'll have a marvelous life together."

"What makes you assume that?"

His question caught her off guard. "Well, because... didn't you just tell me you're about to become officially engaged?"

"Yes," he muttered.

Although she was reluctant to admit it, Shelly found pushing the moped extremely taxing, so she stopped to rest for a moment. "Listen," she said a little breathlessly, "there's no need for you to walk with me. Why don't you just go on ahead?"

"There most definitely is a need," Mark answered sharply. He didn't seem too pleased with her suggestion. "I'm not going to desert you now."

"Oh, Mark, honestly, you don't have to be such a gentleman."

"You don't like gentlemen?"

"Of course I do—but it's one of the reasons you and I would never get along for any length of time. You're very sweet, don't get me wrong, but I don't need anyone to rescue me."

"Forgive me for saying so, but you *do* appear to need rescuing." The look he gave her implied that he was referring to more than the moped.

"I was the one foolish enough to get the engine wet," she said brightly, ignoring his comment. "So I should be the one to deal with the consequences."

Mark waited a moment, as if debating whether to continue arguing. "Fine, if that's the way you feel," he said finally, straddling his moped and starting the engine, which roared to life with sickening ease. "I hope you don't tire out too quickly."

"I'll be okay," she said, hardly able to believe he was actually going to abandon her.

"I hope you're right about that," he said, revving the engine.

"You...you could let someone know," she ventured. Maybe the rental agency would send someone out with a truck to find her.

"I'll see what I can do," he agreed, then grinning broadly, took off at top speed down the beach.

Although she'd made the suggestion that he go on without her, Shelly had assumed he wouldn't take it seriously. She'd said it more for the sake of dignity, of preserving her pride. She'd been enjoying his company, enjoying the banter between them.

As he vanished into the distance, Shelly squared her shoulders, determined to manage on her own—particularly since she didn't have any choice. She'd been dragging her moped along for perhaps ten minutes when she noticed another moped racing toward her. It didn't take her long to identify the rider, with his lithe, muscular build, as Mark. She picked up her pace, unreasonably pleased that he'd decided to return. He slowed as he approached her.

"Still eager to be rid of me?"

"No," she admitted, smiling half in relief, half in pleasure. "Can't you tell when a woman means something and when she's just being polite?"

"I guess not." He smiled back, apparently in a jovial mood. "Rest," he said, parking his own moped and taking hers. "A truck will be along any minute."

Shelly sank gratefully down on the lush sand. Mark lowered himself onto the beach beside her. She plucked several blades of grass and began weaving them industriously together. That way, she wouldn't have to look at him.

"Are you always this stubborn?" he asked.

"Yes," she said quietly, giving him a shy smile. Shelly couldn't remember being shy in her life. But something about Mark made her feel shaky inside, and oddly weak. An unfamiliar sensation, but she dared not analyze it, dared not examine it too closely. She turned away from him and closed her eyes, trying to picture Janice, the woman he was going to marry. Despite her usually creative imagination, Shelly couldn't seem to visualize her.

"Shelly, what's wrong?"

"Wrong?"

"It's not like you to be so quiet."

She grinned. They were barely more than acquaintances, and he already knew her. "Nothing."

"I think there must be." His finger against the side of her face guided her eyes toward him. Their lips were so close. Shelly's breath seemed to be caught in her throat as she stared helplessly into the bluest eyes she'd ever seen....

His forehead touched hers, then he angled his face, brushing her cheek. Shelly knew she should break away, but she couldn't make herself do it. Gently, deliberately, he pressed his mouth to hers, his lips warm and moist.

Shelly moaned at the shock of sensation. Her eyes drifted shut as his mouth moved hungrily over hers, and soon their arms were wrapped tightly around each other, their bodies straining close.

The sound of the approaching truck intruded into their private world and broke them apart. Mark's eyes met hers, then he scowled and glanced away. But Shelly didn't know whether he was angry with her or with himself. Probably her.

Seven

"Hey," Shelly said reassuringly, "don't look so concerned. It was just an ordinary, run-of-the-mill kiss." She stood and brushed the wet sand from her jeans. "Besides, it didn't mean anything."

Mark's scowl darkened. "Didn't mean anything?" he echoed.

"Of course it didn't! I mean, we were both wondering what it would be like, don't you think? Good grief, we seem to be running into each other every other day and it's only logical that we'd want to, you know, experiment."

"In other words, you think the kiss was just a means of satisfying our mutual curiosity?"

"Sure. All this nonsense about the wedding dress overcame our common sense, and we succumbed to temptation." Thank goodness Mark seemed to understand her rambling. Shelly's knees were shaking. It was a wonder she could still stand upright. Although she'd tried to minimize the effects of his kiss, it left her feeling as though she'd never been kissed before. Her entire body had been overwhelmed by a feeling of *rightness*. Now all she felt was the crushing weight of confusion. She shouldn't be feeling any of these things for Mark. A CPA! An almost-engaged CPA, to boot.

"And was your curiosity satisfied?" he asked. His blue eyes probed.

"Uh…yes. And yours?"

"Yes," he muttered, but he was frowning again.

The kid from the rental agency leaped out of the truck and loaded Shelly's moped into the back. "You're not supposed to get the engine wet," he scolded. "It's in the rental agreement. You'll have to pay a fine."

Shelly nodded. She didn't have an excuse; she doubted the agency would accept her trying to escape Mark as a legitimate reason for damaging one of their vehicles.

Mark drove his moped, while Shelly got into the pickup's cab and rode silently down the long stretch of beach.

Shelly went to the office to deal with her fine and was surprised to find Mark waiting for her when she'd finished. "You hungry?" he asked in an offhand invitation.

"Uh…" She would've thought he'd be anxious to see the last of her.

"Good," he said immediately, not giving her a chance to reply. He grasped her elbow firmly as he led her to a nearby fish-and-chips stand. Shelly couldn't recall any other time a man had taken her elbow. Her first reaction was to object to what she considered an outdated gesture but she was surprised to find it oddly comforting, even pleasant.

They ordered their fish and chips, then carried the small baskets to a picnic table.

"I should've paid for my own," she said once they were seated, feeling vaguely guilty that he'd paid for both meals. Janice might be the jealous type, and Shelly didn't want her to hear about this.

His eyes met hers, steady and direct. "When I ask you to join me, I pick up the bill."

Any argument she had vanished before it reached her lips.

After that, Shelly concentrated on her fish and chips, which were fresh and absolutely delicious. Mark seemed equally preoccupied with his meal.

"What brought you to the beach today?" Shelly asked, finishing the last few French fries in her basket. Perhaps if they could determine what had brought them both to a lonely stretch of beach two hours from Seattle, they might be able to figure out how they'd happened upon each other once more.

"I have a beach house here. After tax time I generally try to get away for a few days. I like to come down here and relax."

"I had no idea." She found it inordinately important that he understand she hadn't somehow managed to stalk him across the state. Their meeting was pure coincidence…again.

"Don't worry about it, Shelly. You couldn't possibly have known about the beach house or that I intended to be here today. I didn't know it myself until this morning."

Shelly suddenly wished Mark hadn't kissed her. Everything was becoming far too complicated.

"You're very talented," he told her out of the blue. "I bought one of your DVDs the other day."

"How'd you know what I do?" Shelly felt flustered by his praise; she was at a complete loss to understand why it meant so much to her.

"I saw it on the income tax form and I was curious about your work."

"Curiosity seems to have gotten us both into trouble," she said.

Mark grinned, a shameless, irresistible grin. The kind of grin that makes a woman forget all sorts of things. Like the fact that he was practically engaged. And that he was a tall, blue-eyed stranger who, according to Aunt Milly's letter, would soon become her husband….

Shelly scrambled to her feet, hurrying toward the beach. Mark followed.

"You shouldn't look at me like that," she said, her voice soft and bewildered.

"You said it was just a kiss. Was it?"

"Yes," she lied boldly. "How could it be anything more?"

"You tell me."

Shelly had no answers to give him.

"While you're at it, explain why we keep bumping into each other or why I can't stop thinking about you."

"You can't?" She hadn't been able to stop thinking about him, either, but she wasn't ready to admit it.

"No." He stood behind her, his hands caressing her shoulders. Leisurely he stroked the length of her arms. His touch was so light that she thought she was imagining it, and she felt both excited and afraid.

He turned her around and gazed at her lips. "If that was just a run-of-the-mill kiss, then why do I feel the need to do it again?"

"I don't know."

His lips brushed hers. Briefly, with a whisper-soft touch, as though he was testing her response. Shelly closed her eyes and moaned. She didn't want to feel any of this. They were so far apart, such different people. Besides, *he* was involved with another woman and *she* was involved with her career.

When the kiss ended and he slowly released her, it was all Shelly could do to keep from sinking to the sand. "I have…to get back to Seattle," she managed to say, backing away from him. She turned and took four or five wobbly steps before she realized she was headed toward the Pacific Ocean.

"Shelly?"

"Yes?"

"Seattle is due north. If you continue going west, you'll eventually end up in Hawaii."

"Oh, yeah, right," she mumbled, reversing her direction, eager now to escape.

The first person Shelly called when she got home was Jill. "Can you come over?" she asked without preamble. She couldn't keep the panic out of her voice.

"Sure. What's wrong?"

"I saw Mark again."

"And?"

"Let me put it like this. We kissed and I haven't stopped trembling since."

Jill's romantic sigh came over the receiver. "This I've got to hear. I'll be there in ten minutes."

Actually it was closer to seven. Shelly had begun pacing the moment she got off the phone. She'd checked her watch repeatedly, waiting desperately for a dose of Jill's good sense.

"Shelly," Jill said, smiling as she breezed into the apartment, "what happened to your hair?"

Shelly smoothed down her curls. "I was at Long Beach."

"That's where you saw Mark? That's kind of a coincidence, isn't it?"

"I saw him earlier in the week, too.... Remember I told you I was being audited by the IRS? Lo and behold, guess who was in their waiting room when I arrived?"

"I don't need to be a rocket scientist to figure that one out. Mark Brady!"

"Right." Shelly rubbed her damp palms along her jeans in agitation. They, at least, had finally dried.

"And?"

Shelly groaned. "Can't you see what's happening? This is the third time we've been thrown together in the past few days. I'd never seen the man before, and all of a sudden he's around every corner. Then the wedding dress fit. It fit you…and it fits me."

"I agree that's all rather odd, but I wouldn't put too much stock in it, if I were you."

"Put too much stock in it… Listen, Jill, no man's ever made me feel the way Mark does—all weak inside and, I don't know, special somehow. To be perfectly honest, I don't like it." She closed her eyes, hoping to chase away the memory of his touch, but it did no good. "You want to know the real kicker?" she asked abruptly, turning to face her friend. "He's engaged."

"Engaged," Jill echoed, her voice as startled as her expression.

"He keeps insisting it's not official yet. Nevertheless he's involved with someone else."

"But it was you he kissed," Jill pointed out.

"Don't remind me." Shelly covered her eyes with both hands. "I don't mind telling you, I find this whole thing unnerving."

"Obviously. Here," Jill said, directing Shelly toward the kitchen. "Now sit down. I'll make us some tea, then we can try to reason this out. Honestly, Shell, I don't think I've ever seen you so upset."

"I'm not upset!" she cried. "I'm confused. There's a big difference. I'm… I'm trapped." Despite all logic to the contrary, she couldn't help fearing that the entire course of her life was about to change because her aunt Milly had fallen asleep watching *Dr. Phil* one day and had some nonsensical dream.

"Trapped?" Jill said. "Aren't you being a bit dramatic?"

"I don't know anymore." Shelly rested her elbows on the table, buried her face in her hands and breathed in deeply. She had a tendency to become emotional, especially over family issues; she realized that. But this was different. This was scary.

"Calm down," Jill advised. "Once you think it through in a rational manner, you'll realize there's a perfectly ordinary explanation for everything."

Jill's serenity lent Shelly some badly needed confidence. "All right, you explain it."

"I can't," Jill admitted matter-of-factly, pouring boiling water into Shelly's teapot. "I'm not even going to try. My advice to you—once again—is to quit taking all of this so seriously. If a relationship develops between you and Mark, just enjoy it—provided the other woman's out of the picture, of course! But forget about that dress."

"Easy for you to say."

"That's true," Jill agreed. "But you're going to have to do it for your own peace of mind."

Shelly knew good advice when she heard it. "You're right. I'm leaping into the deep end unnecessarily."

"A dress can't make you do anything you don't want to do."

Shelly always counted on her friend's levelheadedness. Although Jill had given her basically the same advice several days earlier, Shelly needed to hear it again.

Jill prepared two cups of tea and carried them to the table. "Are you going to be all right now?"

Shelly nodded. "Of course. I just needed a friend to remind me that I was overreacting." She took a sip of tea, surprised by how much it revived her. "You're still planning to see *Jersey Boys* with me tomorrow afternoon, aren't you?"

The recent Broadway hit was showing locally, and Shelly and Jill had purchased their tickets several weeks earlier.

"That's not tomorrow, is it?" Jill looked stricken, her teacup poised midway to her mouth.

"Jill…"

"I promised I'd work for Sharon Belmont. She's got some family thing she has to attend. She was desperate and I completely forgot about the play. Oh, dear, you'll have to go without me."

"You're sure you can't get out of it?" Shelly couldn't help feeling disappointed.

"I'm sure. I'm really sorry, Shell."

Although frustrated that Jill couldn't come with her, Shelly decided to go to the theater alone. She wasn't pleased about it and, given her proclivity for running into Mark Brady, she didn't feel entirely convinced that this wasn't another attempt by the fates to regulate their lives.

However, if she stayed home, she'd be missing a wonderful show. Not only that, she'd be giving in to a nebulous and irrational fear, something she refused to do.

The following afternoon, Shelly dressed carefully, in the type of conservative outfit her mother would have approved of. Mark, too, would approve of her rose-colored linen dress with its matching jacket…. The minute the thought flashed through her head, she rejected it.

She was on her way out the door when her phone rang. For a split second she toyed with the idea of not answering. More than likely it was her mother, checking in to see if Shelly had met a prospective husband yet. Her calls had become more frequent and more urgent since Aunt Milly's dress had arrived.

But years of habit prompted her to reach for the phone.

"Shelly." Mark's voice came over the line. "I was about to leave for the afternoon's performance of *Jersey Boys*. Since we seem to have this tendency to run into each other everywhere we go, I thought I should probably clear it with you. If you're going to be there, I'll go another time."

Eight

"Actually I was planning to see it this afternoon myself," Shelly admitted hesitantly. "Jill had to cancel at the last minute."

"It seems Janice can't attend, either."

Hearing the other woman's name, the woman Mark loved, had a curious and unexpected effect on Shelly. Her heart sank, and she felt a sharp pang of disappointment. She rebounded quickly, however, forcing a lightness into her voice, a blitheness she didn't feel. "Mark, there's no need for you to miss the show. I'll call the ticket office and see about an exchange."

"No, I will," Mark said.

"That's ridiculous. Jill really wanted to see this musical and—"

"Would it really be so terrible if we both attended the same performance?"

"Uh…" The question caught Shelly unprepared. Mark was the one who'd suggested they avoid each other.

"What could it possibly hurt? You have your ticket and I have mine. It'd be absurd to let them go to waste because we're afraid of seeing each other again, don't you think?"

Forming a single, coherent thought seemed beyond Shelly at that moment. After her conversation with Jill the day before, followed by the pep talk she'd given herself, she'd recovered a degree of composure. Now, all of a sudden, she wasn't sure of anything.

"I don't think it should matter," she said finally, although it *did* matter.

"Good. Enjoy the show."

"You, too."

The theater was within walking distance of her apartment building, and Shelly left as soon as she'd finished talking to Mark. He was right. Just because they each had tickets to the same play was no reason for either of them to be penalized.

So Mark was going to see *Jersey Boys*. It wasn't the sort of production she would've thought he'd enjoy. But the man was full of surprises. Riding mopeds on the beach, kissing so spectacularly, and now this…

Shelly's mind was full of Mark as she hurried down the steep hill on Cherry Street. The theater was only a block away when she saw him. Her pulse soared and she didn't know if she should smile and wave or simply ignore him.

She didn't need to do either. He stood on the sidewalk, waiting for her.

"You're late," he said, glancing at his watch. "But then you traditionally are." His grin was wide and welcoming. "I can't see any reason not to watch the play together," he went on. "What do you say?"

"You're sure?"

"Positive." He offered her his arm, and she reflected that it was the kind of old-fashioned courtesy she expected from Mark.

The usher seated them and smiled constantly as if to say they were a handsome couple. Shelly was tempted to explain that Mark was engaged to someone else; luckily she managed to hold her tongue. Minutes after they'd settled into their seats, the curtain rose.

The musical was as lively and as good as the reviews claimed, and Shelly enjoyed herself thoroughly. Throughout the performance, however, she was all too aware of Mark sitting next to her. She found herself wondering if he was equally aware of her. She also found herself wondering how long it would be before they "bumped" into each other again—and hoped it was soon.

By the end of the show, Shelly felt inspired and full of enthusiasm, eager to start a new project of her own. As she and Mark left the theater, she talked excitedly about her idea for the "ocean moods" series. He asked a few questions and even suggested some shots. Before she realized it, they were several blocks past the theater, headed in the opposite direction from her apartment. Shelly paused and glanced around.

"There's an excellent Chinese restaurant in this neighborhood," was all Mark said. Without giving her the opportunity to decline, he gently guided her toward the place he'd mentioned.

It was early for dinner, and they were seated immediately. Although they'd been talking comfortably during their walk, Shelly suddenly felt self-conscious. She played with her linen napkin, smoothing it across her lap.

"I'm not a big fan of musicals, so I hadn't expected to like the show as much as I did," he said after a while.

In that case, Shelly considered it a bit odd that he'd ordered tickets for this production, but perhaps he'd gotten them because Janice had wanted to see *Jersey Boys*.

"It's a little frightening the way we keep running across each other, isn't it?" she ventured.

"I can see how *you'd* find it disconcerting," Mark answered.

"You don't?"

Mark shrugged. "I haven't given it much thought."

"I'll admit all these…coincidences do throw me," she said, tracing the outline of a fire-breathing dragon on the menu cover. "But I'm learning to deal with it."

"So you feel you've been caught in something beyond your control?" Mark surprised her by asking.

Shelly lifted her gaze to his, struck by the intensity she read in his eyes. "No, not really. Well...a little, maybe. Do you?"

"It wasn't *my* aunt Milly who had the dream."

Shelly smiled and dropped her gaze. "No, but as my friend Jill reminded me recently, no sixty-year-old dress is going to dictate my life. Or yours," she felt obliged to add. Then she understood why he'd asked the question. "You must feel overwhelmed. All of a sudden I've been thrust into your life. There's no escaping me, is there?" she said wryly. "Every time you turn around, there I am."

"Are you going to stand up and tell everyone in the restaurant that you refuse to marry me?"

"No!" Shelly was shocked by his remark until she remembered she'd done exactly that the first time they met.

"If you can resist public declarations, then I think I can bear up under the pressure."

Shelly ignored his mild sarcasm. "I'm not interested in marriage yet," she told him solemnly—just in case he'd forgotten. "I'm satisfied with my life. And I'm too busy for a husband and family."

She hadn't noticed how forcefully she was speaking until she saw several people at other tables glancing in her direction. Instantly she lowered her voice. "Sorry, my views on marriage seem to be more fervent than I realized. But I'm not about to let either my mother or my aunt Milly determine when I decide to settle down and marry."

"Personally, I can't see you ever settling down," Mark said with a small grin. "You don't have to worry. When you're ready, you'll know it."

"Did you?" She hadn't meant to bring up Janice, but it seemed wise to remind him—and her—that there was someone else in his life.

Mark raised one shoulder casually. "More or less. I took a good, long look at my life and discovered I'd already achieved several of my professional goals. It was time to invest my energy in developing the personal aspects—marriage, children and the like."

Mark talked about marriage as if it were the next chapter in a book he was reading or part of a connect-the-dots picture. Shelly couldn't stop herself from frowning.

"You have a problem with that?"

"Not a problem, exactly. I happen to think of marriage a bit differently, that's all."

"In what way?"

He seemed genuinely interested, otherwise she would've kept her opinions to herself. "People should fall in love," she said slowly. "I don't think it's necessary or even possible to plan for that. Love can be unexpected—it can take a couple by surprise, knock them both off their feet."

"You make falling in love sound like an accident—like tripping on the stairs or something."

Shelly smiled. "In some ways, I think that's how it should be. Marriage is one of the most important decisions in anyone's life, so it should be a *deeply felt* decision. It should feel inevitable. It's the union of two lives, after all. So you can't simply check your watch and announce 'it's time.'" She was suddenly concerned that she'd spoken out of turn and might have offended him, but one quick glance assured her that wasn't the case.

Mark leaned forward. "I would never have guessed it," he said.

"Guessed what?" She was beginning to feel a little foolish now.

"That a woman who gives the impression of being a scatterbrain is really quite reflective. Beneath those glow-in-the-dark sweatshirts lies a very romantic heart."

"I seem to get emotional about certain things," she responded, studying the menu, eager to change the subject. "I really like hot-and-sour soup. Have you ever tried it?"

Their conversation over dinner remained light and amusing. Shelly noticed that Mark avoided any more discussion of a personal nature, as did she.

After they'd finished their dinner and Mark had paid the bill, they strolled leisurely back toward the theater. Mark offered to drive her home when they reached his parked car, but Shelly declined. Her apartment was only a couple of blocks north and she preferred to walk.

Walk and think. Their time together had given her plenty to think about.

"Thank you for dinner," she said as he unlocked the car.

"You're welcome," he answered. "Well, good night for now," he said, grinning. "I suspect I'll be seeing you soon."

She grinned back. "Probably within a day or two. Maybe we should synchronize our schedules," she teased.

"That wouldn't bother you, would it? If we ran into each other, I mean."

"Oh, no. What about you?" She hated the way her voice rose expectantly with the question. She certainly wasn't *bothered* by the prospect of seeing him again. In fact, she was downright eager to see what tricks fate would play on them next.

Mark's eyes found hers then, and he slowly pocketed his car keys. His look was so potent, so full of emotion, that Shelly took a step in retreat. "I had a wonderful afternoon, a wonderful evening. Thanks again," she said nervously.

Mark didn't say a word as he continued to gaze at her.

"The play was great, wasn't it? And dinner…fabulous." Shelly's throat seemed to close as Mark stepped onto the curb and walked toward her.

The whole world came to an abrupt halt when she realized he intended to kiss her. *Not again,* her mind shouted. *Please hurry,* her heart sang.

Her heart tripped wildly as Mark lowered his head, his mouth seeking hers. Despite the fierce battle inside her, Shelly had to admit how much she wanted this kiss.

If for no other reason, she told herself, than to prove that the first time had been a fluke.

Only it happened again. But this kiss was a hundred times more compelling than the first one they'd shared. A hundred times more exciting.

Shelly wanted to cry out at the unfairness of it all. If a man's kiss was going to affect her like this, why did it have to be Mark Brady's?

He broke away from her reluctantly, his warm breath fanning her cheek. His eyes were filled with questions, filled with surprise. Shelly wasn't sure what her own eyes were saying to him. She didn't even want to know.

"Take care," he whispered as he turned away.

Shelly stayed home from work on Monday. She wasn't sick, just puzzled and confused. Nothing about her relationship with Mark made sense. He was everything she *didn't* want in a man—and everything she did.

Shelly didn't realize how despondent she was until she found herself standing barefoot in front of her closet, carrying on a conversation with Aunt Milly's wedding dress.

"I'll have you know I had a perfectly good life until you got here," she muttered. "Now my whole world's been turned upside down." She slammed the door shut, then jerked it open. "No wonder Mrs. Livingston's cat wouldn't go near you. You're *dangerous*."

Nine

"The show was great," Shelly told Jill over coffee Wednesday afternoon. She'd stopped off at PayRite, hoping Jill could get away for lunch. "Even Mark—"

"Mark?" Jill's coffee cup hit the saucer with a clang. "He went to see *Jersey Boys?*"

Shelly nodded sheepishly. "I guess I forgot to mention I ran into him, didn't I? Actually he called me first and since we both had plans to attend the same performance, we decided to go together."

"Is there anything else you haven't told me?" Jill's eyes narrowed astutely.

Shelly tried to hide her uneasiness behind a relaxed shrug, but how well she succeeded in fooling Jill remained to be seen. "We had dinner afterward...as friends. It didn't mean anything. I did tell you he's engaged, didn't I?"

"*Unofficially* engaged." Jill was studying her closely and Shelly felt uneasy under her scrutiny.

"We've been friends for a long time," Jill reminded her. "I know you, and I know there's something troubling you."

Shelly nodded. There was no point in hiding the truth from Jill. Her need to confide in a sympathetic, understanding person was the very reason for her impromptu visit to Jill's workplace. Lunch had been a convenient excuse.

"You won't believe this," Shelly said, cradling the coffee cup in both hands and keeping her gaze lowered. "I can hardly believe it myself."

"You're falling in love with Mark."

Shelly's eyes shot upward. "It's that obvious?"

"No," Jill said softly. "But you look like you're about to break into tears."

"If I wasn't so darn irritated I would. Good grief, think about it. Can you imagine two people less suited to each other? Mark is so…so responsible…"

"So are you."

"Not in the same way," Shelly argued. "He's so sincere and—"

"Shelly, so are you."

"Perhaps, but I'm such a scatterbrain." She grimaced as she remembered that was the very word Mark had used. "I'm disorganized and always late and I like to do things my own way. You know that better than most."

"I prefer to think of you as creative."

Shelly sent Jill a smile of appreciation. "That's the reason you're my best friend. I don't mind telling you, Jill, I'm worried. Mark Brady may be the Rock of Gibraltar, but I doubt he's got an original thought in his head. Everything's done by the book or according to a schedule."

"You need someone like Mark in your life," Jill returned. "Don't look so shocked. It's true. The two of you balance each other. He needs you because you're fun and crazy and imaginative, and you need him because he knows his multiplication tables by heart and will remind you when it's time for meals."

"The problem is, Mark's the type of man who'd expect a woman to *cook* those meals."

Jill chuckled.

"If the fates are determined to match me up with a man," Shelly moaned, "couldn't it be with someone other than an accountant?"

"Apparently not."

"What really angers me is that I allowed it to happen. The first time he kissed me—"

"He *kissed* you?" Jill feigned a look of horror.

Shelly ignored it. "Yes. Twice. It's only natural—our being curious about each other, don't you think?"

"I suppose," Jill said quickly, no longer teasing. "So tell me what happened."

"Fireworks bigger than the Fourth of July. I've never experienced the feelings I do with Mark, and all because of a kiss." She paused. "Well, two kisses."

"And does Mark feel the same thing?"

"I—I can't speak for him, but I assume it's equally disturbing for him. He certainly looked as if he'd been taken by surprise."

"How do you get along with him otherwise?"

"Fine, I guess." Shelly took a sip of her coffee. "I'm sure I amuse him. But someone like Mark isn't looking for a woman to entertain him, any more than I'm looking for a man to handle my finances."

"His opinion of you has mellowed, hasn't it?" Jill asked, then answered her own question. "There was a time when he thought you were more than a little bizarre, remember?"

Shelly did, all too well. "At first I thought he was totally unexciting, but I've altered my opinion of him, too."

"So what's the problem?"

"I don't *want* to fall in love," Shelly said pointedly. "I've got bigger plans for my life than to tie myself down to a committed relationship right now."

"Then don't. It shouldn't be that difficult. Decide what you want and disregard everything else. There's no law that says you have to fall in love this minute. For that matter, no one can regulate when and who you marry, either. Not even your aunt Milly."

Jill was saying everything Shelly wanted to hear. Ev-

erything she *needed* to hear. But it didn't make any difference; her heart was already involved. If she could
forget she'd ever met Mark, she would. But it was too
late. She was in love with him. With Mark, who was
in love with someone else. Mark, who saw love and
marriage as goals to be achieved within a certain time
frame. He'd probably never done anything impulsive
in his life.

A relationship between them would never last. If he
wasn't smart enough to figure that out, she was. Something had to be done and soon, and Shelly knew it would
be up to her to do it.

Shelly didn't have long to wait before she saw Mark
again. They met at the main branch of the Seattle Public Library on Wednesday evening. She was returning
ten overdue books. Six months overdue. The library had
sent her three warnings, each progressively less friendly.

She was half-afraid the buzzer inside the library entrance would go off the moment she walked through
the hallowed doors, and armed officers would haul her
away.

"I wondered when we'd find each other again," Mark
said, strolling up to her at the counter. She'd seen him
almost immediately and tried to pretend she hadn't.

Shelly acknowledged him with a quick nod and ordered her heart to be still. She managed a slight smile.
"Hello again," she said, drawing a checkbook out of
her purse. At least she'd come prepared. The fine for

the books was sure to be monstrous; in fact, it might be cheaper to buy them.

Mark set the two volumes he was borrowing on the counter. Shelly noted the titles—*Tools for Time Management* and *The State of the Language,* and groaned inwardly. To someone like her accountant friend, these books were probably easy reading. Her own tastes leaned more toward mystery and romance, with a little nonfiction thrown in.

"Have you got time for a cup of coffee?" Mark asked as she wrote out the check to pay her fine.

She was gladdened by the invitation, but knew she had to refuse it. Before he could say or do anything to change her mind, she shook her head. "Not tonight, thanks."

His smile faded as though her refusal had startled him. "You're busy?"

She nodded, smiling at the librarian as she handed over her check. The librarian smiled back. It had been a civilized exchange, Shelly thought, and her library card had't been confiscated, despite her transgressions.

"You've got a date waiting for you?"

It took Shelly a second to understand that Mark was referring to her refusal to join him for coffee.

"Not exactly." She turned away from the counter and headed toward the exit. To her surprise Mark followed her outside.

"Something's wrong," he said, standing at the top of the steps.

She stopped her descent and stood below him, looking up. Pretense had never suited Shelly; she was too innately honest to hide her feelings. "Mark, I think you're a very nice man—"

"But you don't want to marry me," he concluded for her. "I've heard that line before, remember? Actually, half the mall heard it, too."

"I've already apologized for that. It's just that…all right, if you must know, I'm beginning to like you…really like you, and frankly that terrifies me."

Her candid response seemed to unnerve him. He frowned and rubbed the side of his jaw. "I know what you mean. I'm beginning to like you, too."

"See!" she cried, raising both hands. "If we don't take care of this now, heaven only knows what could happen. It has the potential of ruining both our lives. We're mature adults, aren't we?" At the moment, though, she felt singularly lacking in maturity.

All her senses were clamoring, telling her to enjoy their brief time together, despite the consequences. It was what her heart wanted, but she couldn't allow her life to be ruled by her heart. Not when it came to Mark.

"Liking each other doesn't have to be a federal crime," he said, advancing one step toward her.

"You're right, of course, but I know myself too well. I could easily fall in love with you, Mark." She didn't dare admit she already had. "Before we knew it, we'd be spending more and more time with each other. We might even become seriously involved."

He remained suspiciously silent.

"You're a wonderful man. If my mother were to meet you she'd be shouting from the rooftops, she'd be so thrilled. For a while I might convince myself that we could really make something of this relationship. I might even consider taking cooking classes because you're the kind of man who'd expect a woman to know how to make a roast and mashed potatoes."

"It'd probably come in handy someday," he said.

"That's what I thought," she murmured, disheartened. "I'm not a traditional woman. I never will be. The only time I ever baked a pie I ended up throwing it in the garbage disposal—and it broke the disposal."

"A pie ruined your garbage disposal?" Mark repeated, then shook his head. "Never mind, don't bother explaining. It seems to me you're getting ahead of yourself here. You're talking as though coffee together means a lifetime commitment."

Shelly wasn't listening. "What about Janice?" she demanded. "*She's* the one you should be inviting to coffee, not me."

"What's Janice got to do with this?" he asked impatiently.

"Janice," Shelly snapped, her own temper short. "The woman you've decided to marry. Remember her? The love of your life? The woman you're unofficially engaged to marry."

"It's not unofficial anymore," Mark explained evenly.

"Oh, great, you're taking me out to dinner, kissing

me and at the same time picking out engagement rings with another woman." She had to admit he'd never lied to her about his relationship with the faceless Janice. He'd been forthright about it from the beginning. But it hurt, really hurt, to learn that he was going ahead with his plans to marry Janice.

He was about to speak, but she forestalled him, struggling to force some enthusiasm into her voice. "Congratulations are in order. I wish you both the very best." With that she turned and bounded down the stairs, taking them recklessly fast.

"Shelly!"

She could hear Mark calling after her, but she ignored him, desperate to get away before the lump in her throat made it impossible to breathe. Tears had formed in her eyes and she cursed herself for being so ridiculous, for caring so much. Her vision blurred and she wiped a hand across her face, furious at her lack of control. This marriage was what she'd hoped would happen. What she wanted for Mark. *Wasn't it?*

"Shelly, for heaven's sake, will you wait?"

When she reached the bottom of the steps, Shelly moved into a side street, hoping to disappear in the crowd, praying Mark wouldn't pursue her.

She thought she'd escaped until a hand on her shoulder whirled her around.

"Shelly, please listen," Mark pleaded breathlessly,

Ten

"You broke off your engagement with Janice?" Shelly demanded furiously. Something inside, some reservoir of emotion, had burst wide-open. "You fool," she shouted. "You idiot!" Her eyes brimmed with tears, and deep in her heart she felt the stirrings of glad excitement. "That was the worst thing you could've done!"

"No," he said. "It was the smartest."

"How can you say that?" she wailed.

"Shelly?"

He reached for her as though to offer comfort, but Shelly jerked away and stepped back, freeing herself from his grasp. "Janice was perfect for you," she lamented.

"How do you know that?" he asked calmly and much too reasonably to suit Shelly. "You never met her."

"I didn't need to. I know she was right for you. You'd never have asked her to marry you if she wasn't."

"Janice is a wonderful woman and she'll make some man a good wife, but it won't be me."

"You're crazy to break off your engagement. Crazy!"

"No, I'm not," Mark returned confidently. "I'm absolutely certain I did the right thing. Do you know why?"

Shelly could only shake her head, wiping away the tears with the back of her hand. She was ecstatic—and yet she was so frightened. She loved him; she was sure of it. Then why had everything become so difficult and confused?

"What you said about love the other day changed my mind."

"You *listened* to me?" she cried in real horror. "Do I look like an expert on love? I've never been in love in my life!" Not counting what she felt for him, of course. She'd always thought love would clarify her life, not make it more complicated.

Mark paid no attention to her outburst. "You helped me understand that I was marrying Janice for the wrong reasons. I'd decided it was time to settle down. Janice had come to the same conclusion. She's thirty and figured if she was going to marry and have a family, the time was now. It wasn't a love match, and we both knew it."

"This is none of my business," Shelly said, frantically shaking her head as if to chase the words away. "I don't want to hear it."

"You *are* going to hear it," Mark insisted, clasping her elbows and gently drawing her closer. "You claimed people shouldn't plan love. It should take them by surprise, you said, and you were right. Janice and I are fond of each other, but—"

"There's nothing wrong with fond!"

His eyes widened. "No, there isn't," he agreed, "but Janice isn't a zany producer. I like spending time with you. I've come to realize there's a certain thrill in expecting the unexpected. Every minute with you is an adventure."

"A relationship between us would never last," Shelly insisted, drawing on the most sensible argument. "It would be fine for a while, but then we'd drift apart. We'd have to. In case you haven't noticed, we're nothing alike."

"Why wouldn't a relationship last?" Mark asked patiently.

"For all the reasons I listed before!" Mark was so endearing, and he was saying all the words she'd secretly longed to hear, but nothing could change the fundamental differences between them.

"So you aren't as adept in the kitchen as some women. I'm a fair cook."

"It's more than that."

"Of course it is," he concurred. "But there's nothing we can't overcome if we're willing to work together."

"You know what I think it is?" she said desperately, running her splayed fingers through her hair. "You're beginning to believe there's magic in Aunt Milly's wedding dress."

"Don't you?"

"No," she cried. "Not anymore. I did when I was a little girl… I loved the story of how Aunt Milly met Uncle John, but I'm not a child anymore, and what seemed so romantic then just seems unrealistic now."

"Shelly," Mark said in exasperation. "We don't need to do anything right away. All I'm suggesting is we give this thing between us a chance."

"There's nothing between us," she denied vehemently.

Mark's eyes narrowed. "You don't honestly believe that, do you?"

"Yes," she lied. "You're a nice guy, but—"

"If I hear any more of this nice-guy stuff I'm going to kiss you and we both know what'll happen then."

His gaze lowered to her mouth and she unconsciously moistened her lips with anticipation.

"I just might, anyway."

"No." The threat was real enough to make her retreat a couple of steps. If Mark kissed her, Shelly knew she'd be listening to her heart and not her head. And then *he'd* know… "That's what I thought." His grin was downright boyish.

"I think we should both forget we ever met," she suggested next, aware even as she said it how ludicrous she sounded. Mark Brady had indelibly marked her life and no matter how much she denied it, she'd never forget him.

"Don't you remember that you threw yourself into my arms? *You* can conveniently choose to overlook the obvious, but unfortunately that won't work for me. I'm falling in love with you, Shelly."

She opened her mouth to argue that he couldn't possibly love her—not yet, not on such short acquaintance—but he pressed his finger to her lips, silencing her.

"At first I wasn't keen on the idea," he admitted, "but it's sort of grown on me since. I can see us ten years in the future and you know what? It's a pleasant picture. We're going to be very happy together."

"I need to think!" She placed her hands on either side of her head. Everything was happening much too quickly; she actually felt dizzy. "We'll leave it to fate... how does that sound?" she offered excitedly. It seemed like the perfect solution. "The next time we bump into each other, I'll have more of a grasp on my feelings. I'll know what we should do." She might also hibernate inside her apartment for a month, but she wasn't mentioning that.

"Nope." Mark slowly shook his head. "That won't work."

"Why not?" she asked. "We bump into each other practically every day."

"No, we don't."

He wasn't making any sense.

"*Jersey Boys* was a setup," he informed her. "I made sure we bumped into each other there."

"How? When?"

"The day at the beach I saw the ticket sticking out of your purse. Our meeting at the theater wasn't any accident."

Mark couldn't have shocked her more if he'd announced he was an alien from outer space. For the first time in recent memory, she was left speechless. "Tonight?" she asked when she could get the words out. "The library?"

"I'd decided to stop off at your apartment. I was prepared to make up some story about the wedding dress luring me into your building, but when I drove past, I saw you coming down the front steps loaded down with library books. It wasn't hard to figure out where you were headed. I found a parking space and waited for you inside."

"What about…the IRS office and the beach?" She didn't know how he'd managed *those* meetings.

Mark shook his head again and grinned. "Coincidence, unless you had anything to do with them. You didn't, did you?"

"Absolutely not," she replied indignantly.

Still grinning, he said, "I didn't really think you had."

Shelly started walking, her destination unclear. She felt too restless to continue standing there; unfortunately the one action that truly appealed to her was leaping into his arms.

Mark matched his own steps to hers.

"It's Aunt Milly's wedding dress, I know it is," Shelly mumbled under her breath. She'd tried to bring up the subject, but Mark had refused to listen. "You broke off an engagement because you believe fate's somehow thrown us together."

"No, Shelly, the dress doesn't have anything to do with how I feel," Mark said calmly.

"But you'd already decided to marry someone else!"

"I'm choosing my own destiny, which is to spend the rest of my life with you."

"You might have consulted me first. I have no intention of getting married…not for years and years."

"I'll wait."

"You can't do that," she cried. He didn't understand because he was too respectable and adorable and too much of a gentleman. The only thing that would work would be to heartlessly send him away.

She faced Mark, careful to wear just the right expression of remorse and regret. "This is all very flattering, but I don't love you. I'm sorry, Mark. You're the last person in the world I want to hurt."

For a moment Mark said nothing, then he shrugged and looked away. "You can't be any more direct than that, can you? There's no chance you'll ever fall in love with me?"

"None." Her breath fell harshly, painfully, from her lips. It shouldn't hurt this much to do the right thing. It shouldn't hurt to be noble. "You're very nice, but…"

"So you've said before."

Falteringly, as though the movement caused him pain,

he lifted his hand to her face, his fingers caressing the curve of her jaw.

Until that moment, Shelly hadn't understood how fiercely proud Mark was. He could have dealt with every argument, calmed every doubt, answered every question, but there was nothing he could say when she denied all feeling for him.

"You mean it, don't you?" he asked huskily. He was standing so close that his breath warmed her face.

Shelly had schooled her features to reveal none of her clamoring emotions. His touch, so light, so potent, seemed to clog her throat with anguish, and she couldn't speak.

"If that's what you want—" he dropped his hand abruptly "—I won't trouble you again." With those words, he turned and walked away. Before she fully realized what he intended, Mark had disappeared around a corner.

"You let him go, you idiot!" she whispered to herself. A tear escaped and she smeared it across her cheek.

Mark meant what he'd said about not bothering her. He was a man of his word. He'd never try to see her again—and if they did happen upon each other, he'd pretend he didn't know her.

He might eventually decide to marry Janice. Hadn't he admitted he was fond of the other woman?

Shelly's heart clutched painfully inside her chest. Before she could stop herself, before she could question the wisdom of her actions, she ran after Mark.

She turned the corner and was halfway down the block when she realized he wasn't anywhere to be seen. She came to a skidding halt, then whirled around, wondering how he could possibly have gotten so far in such a short time.

Mark stepped out from the side of a building, hands on his hips, a cocky, jubilant smile on his face. "What took you so long?" he asked, holding out his arms.

Shelly didn't need a second invitation to throw herself into his embrace. His mouth feasted on hers, his kiss hungry and demanding, filled with enough emotion to last a lifetime.

Shelly slid her arms around his neck and stood on her tiptoes, giving herself completely to his kiss, to his love. All that mattered was being in his arms—exactly where she was supposed to be.

"I take it this means you love me, too?" he whispered close to her ear. His voice was rough with emotion.

Shelly nodded. "I'm so afraid."

"Don't be. I'm confident enough for both of us."

"This is crazy," she said, but she couldn't have moved out of his arms for the world. Breathing deeply, she buried her face in his chest.

"But it's a good kind of crazy."

"Aunt Milly saw us together in her dream. She wrote to me about a tall, blue-eyed man."

"Who knows if it was me or not?" Mark whispered into her hair and brushed his lips over her temple. "Who cares? If fate had anything to do with me finding you or if your aunt Milly's wedding dress is responsible, I can't say. Personally, I couldn't care less. I love you, Shelly, and I believe you love me, too."

She glanced up at this man who had altered the course of her life and smiled, her heart too full for words. "I do love you," she said when she could. "An accountant! In a suit! Hardly the husband I imagined for myself."

Mark chuckled. "I would never have guessed I'd fall head over heels in love with a woman who wears the type of clothes you do—but I did."

"I love you, too," Shelly said and closed her eyes.

The morning of her wedding day, Shelly couldn't sit still. Her mother was even worse, pacing in front of her, dabbing her eyes and sniffling.

"I can't believe my baby's getting married."

Shelly had to restrain herself from reminding her dear mother that less than a month before, she'd been desperate to marry her daughter off. Thank goodness Jill was there. Without her best friend to reassure her, Shelly didn't know what she would've done. While her mother fussed with the caterers, complained to the florists and fretted about who had a key to the kitchen in the reception hall, Jill led Shelly upstairs to her childhood bedroom and helped her dress. When Shelly was finished, Jill stood back to examine her.

"Well?" Shelly asked, smoothing her hand down the antique dress, loving the feel of the satin and lace against her fingers. It was probably her imagination but now that she was wearing the dress, really wearing it, she could almost feel its magic.

Tears gathered in Jill's eyes as she stared at her friend. "That bad?" Shelly teased.

Jill pressed her fingers to her lips. "You're beautiful," she whispered. "Mark isn't going to believe his eyes when he sees you."

"Do you really think so?" Shelly hated sounding so insecure, but she wanted everything to be perfect today. She was crazy in love—and crazy enough to give her mother free rein planning her wedding. Crazy enough to go through with a formal wedding in the first place. If it'd been up to her, they would've eloped weeks ago. But Mark had wanted a proper wedding and her mother certainly wasn't going to be cheated out of this moment. So Shelly had gone along with it.

Mark and her mother had defeated most of her ideas. She'd wanted to hire clowns to entertain at the reception, but her mother didn't seem to think that was a good idea.

Shelly had never been that fond of white wedding cake, either. She'd suggested Cherries Jubilee instead, but Mark was afraid something might catch on fire and so in the interests of safety, Shelly had agreed to a traditional cake, decorated with pink roses.

A knock sounded on her bedroom door and Jill opened it. In walked Aunt Milly, looking absolutely delighted with herself.

She introduced herself to Jill, then turned to gaze lovingly at Shelly. "So I see the dress worked."

"It worked," Shelly agreed.

"You love him?"

Shelly nodded. "Enough to eat white wedding cake."

Milly laughed softly and sat on the edge of the bed. Her hair was gray and her face wrinkled, but her eyes were still blue and clear. It was difficult to tell that she was a woman well into her eighties. She clasped both of Shelly's hands in her own.

"Nervous?"

Shelly nodded again.

"I was, too, although I knew to the bottom of my heart that I'd made the right decision in marrying John."

"I feel the same way about Mark."

Aunt Milly hugged her tightly. "You're going to be very happy, my dear."

An hour later Shelly and Mark stood at the front of a packed church with Pastor Johnson, who'd known her most of her life. He smiled warmly as he spoke a few words, then asked Shelly to repeat her vows.

Linking hands with Mark, she raised her eyes to his. Everyone else faded away. Aunt Milly. Jill. Her mother. Her long-suffering dad. Her brothers and their wives. There were only the two of them. She felt a jolt of pure joy at the love that radiated from Mark's eyes. He stood tall and proud, his gaze holding hers, the love shining through without question, shining through for her to read. Shelly knew her eyes told him the same thing.

Later, Shelly couldn't remember speaking her vows,

although she was sure she did. The words came directly from her heart. Directly from Mark's.

They'd been drawn to this place and this time by forces neither fully understood. Shelly wasn't entirely sure she believed Aunt Milly's wedding dress was responsible, but as Mark had said, it didn't matter. They were there out of love. She didn't know exactly when it had happened. Perhaps that day on the beach, when Mark first kissed her. Something had happened then, something that touched them both.

The love that began as a small spark had grown and flared to life until they'd been brought here, to stand before God and family, pledging their lives to each other.

To love. To cherish. All the days of their lives.

* * * * *

ONE PLACE. MANY STORIES

Bold, innovative and
empowering publishing.

FOLLOW US ON:

@HQStories